BOOKS IN THE "BECK" SUSPENSE/THRILLER SERIES

The 19th Element
The Missing Element
The Covert Element
The Exiled Element

Published by
John L. Betcher
Red Wing, Minnesota
www.johnbetcher.com
2012

Copyright 2012 by John L. Betcher
All rights reserved. This book, or parts thereof,
may not be reproduced in any form
without permission from John L. Betcher.

This is a work of fiction. Any similarities to real
persons or situations are coincidental.

Cover design by Clay Rivers

ISBN-13: 978-1475180589
ISBN-10: 1475180586

THE EXILED ELEMENT

A James Becker Thriller

by

John L. Betcher

www.johnbetcher.com

For Lynn, Anne, and Kate.

PROLOGUE

Two years ago, mid-July, somewhere in the Nevada desert.

Army Colonel Colin Jackson commanded this slice of desert pie known to outsiders variously as "Groom Lake," "Paradise Ranch," "Watertown Strip," "Dreamland," "Home Base," "Homey Airport," and most commonly, by its official Atomic Energy Commission designation – "Area 51."

A remote detachment of Edwards Air Force Base, the bulk of which stood in the Mojave Desert nearly two hundred miles to the Southwest, Area 51 was home to the darkest of the nation's "black projects" – undertakings that only a handful of select personnel had any inkling existed.

Area 51's facilities included nearly a hundred buildings of varying shapes and sizes, from 10 x 10 foot storage buildings, to expansive metal structures that were almost certainly hangars for aircraft of some sort. There were also a scattering of landing strips running in seemingly haphazard directions. Two were topped with asphalt. The remainder ran through the salt flats, using the smooth, hardened crystals as their base. One of the runways stretched an unheard of 23,200 feet from end to end – more than four times the length of a typical runway at a commercial airport.

While all activities at Area 51 were highly classified, rumors had the military base as home to: the captured Roswell aliens and their spaceships, clandestinely procured Russian military weaponry, time travel technology, weather control equipment, and all manner of UFO-related meetings and activities – including actual conferences with extra-terrestrial beings.

Colonel Jackson wasn't chatting with any aliens today. But his official duties did included introducing United States Senator

Elbert Grossman, Chairman of the Senate Armed Services Committee, to one of his country's best kept military secrets. A project that bore the designation "Aurora" and had garnered enough of the U.S. military budget in recent years to draw the Senator's attention.

* * *

After landing at Las Vegas International, the Senator's limo dropped him at Crystal Springs, Nevada, where he boarded a specially designed "security bus." Small skylights provided his only windows on the world. Opaque panels surrounding all but the bus driver's compartment occluded views of the roadway and exterior terrain.

The Senator found the trip from Crystal Springs to the secret base – about twenty minutes via a dirt lane known as Groom Lake Road – to be less than comfortable. The air conditioning in this vehicle was inadequate, and the seating area clearly had not been designed to accommodate a person with his ample frame.

Upon arriving inside the Area 51 compound, the bus driver issued him a pair of refractive goggles, which he would need to wear whenever he walked outside the base's buildings. The goggles were really more in the nature of blinders than anything else. While the Senator could see well enough directly ahead to allow him to walk safely, black slats blocked his peripheral vision, and thick, concave lenses distorted any forward images more than thirty feet distant.

The Senator had to concede the simplicity and effectiveness of the blackout bus and the security goggles in maintaining the secrecy of whatever sensitive activities happened to be underway at the base. But being impressed by the security measures didn't keep him from being annoyed at the inconvenience . . . and the damn heat.

"Welcome to nowhere, Mr. Senator." The voice was Colonel Jackson's. It accompanied his offer of a handshake. The Colonel loathed escorting Congressional dignitaries around his base, but knew how important such visits were to maintaining funding for his projects.

"Good day, Colonel." The Senator pumped the Base Commander's hand vigorously. "Quite a nice facility you've got here . . . at least what I can see of it. Helluva cooker today, though."

The Senator dabbed a handkerchief at his brow.

The temperature this day had peaked at 115 degrees Fahrenheit in the shade. Jackson showed no effects of the heat, but the Senator, fifty-two years old with a build that begged for a coronary infarction, melted like butter in a saucepan.

"Yes . . . well. I assume you understand the need for our security measures, Mr. Senator. I apologize if they have caused you any discomfort."

"Of course. Of course. No need for apologies, Colonel." The Senator was a politician and knew very well that one could snag more flies with honey than vinegar – frankly, manure might be even better.

Perceiving the Senator's discomfort, Colonel Jackson promptly escorted the Senator to the air conditioned comfort of the Colonel's office.

After removing his goggles, the Senator took up a position directly in front of the air conditioning vent and mopped his face once more. Colonel Jackson stood beside his desk, waiting for the Senator to recover from the heat.

"Now that I'm here," the Senator said, finally, "where shall we begin?"

The Colonel motioned him to one of the military-issue vinyl/metal side chairs arranged beside the Colonel's metal desk. Senator Grossman couldn't help but notice the austerity of this office compared to his senatorial chambers on Capitol Hill.

The Senator took a seat, as did Colonel Jackson.

Pushing his chair back slightly from the desk, Jackson withdrew a clipboard and pen from a side drawer. On the clipboard were several sheets of letter-size white paper. Swivelling the board 180 degrees to face the Senator, Jackson slid the documents across the desktop until they came to rest directly in front of Grossman.

"Standard 'read in' documents, Senator." He held the pen toward Grossman. "Please let me know if you have any questions."

The documents acknowledged that the Senator was aware of the sensitivity of the information he was about to receive and spelled out his responsibilities for maintaining absolute confidentiality "in all matters pertaining thereto."

"Thank you," Grossman said, accepting the pen and beginning to review the top document. The Colonel waited patiently as the Senator read each page in turn. When he had finished, Grossman returned to the top sheet and began initialing pages, finally signing his full name at the bottom of the last.

"Very good, Senator. Now . . . there are a few things I need to tell you before we head off to Hangar 16."

* * *

Several months later, in Washington, DC.

The time was 8:45 p.m. on a cool fall day and Senator Grossman was headed for his usual Tuesday evening dalliance. Depositing his black Lincoln in a remote area of the local shopping mall, which was about ready to close for the night, he turned up the collar on his trench coat. Pulling the brim of his dark grey fedora lower over his brow, he huffed and puffed the fifty-or-so yards to the entrance to the Rockville Metro Rail station.

The Rockville Metro platform was elevated and exposed to the elements. It was also visible to prying eyes, if one's eyes should be so inclined. But the Senator wasn't worried about spies or gawkers. If some newspaper reporter had been following him, the Senator would have certainly noticed the tail in the open parking lot. Grossman was hiding his face from the station's ever-present security cameras.

This was not a part of town where one might expect to find a sitting U.S. Senator boarding the Metro. In fact, such a sighting would be unusual anywhere in D.C. Members of Congress employed chauffeurs to deliver them directly to the private entrances beneath the buildings on Capitol Hill. But even for the Metro, Rockville Station was particularly remote – the second to last stop on the outbound Red Line and a good half hour ride from Metro Center and the Federal Triangle.

No one would even *think* to look for him riding a train, especially boarding at this suburban, middle class stop.

When the Red Line train to downtown arrived, Grossman was one of only four passengers to embark upon it. He selected his usual seat in the rear of the deserted car, opened his briefcase, and began to scan the *New York Times*. Perhaps there would be another article about the new defense funding bill of which he was co-author. He enjoyed reading about his accomplishments in the papers.

Some twenty-five minutes later, the train pulled into the station at Dupont Circle. This hub for protesters, foreign college students, and tourists was elegantly anonymous by virtue of its constant activity. There was always a distraction. An impromptu saxophonist hoping for pocket-change donations, his reedy wailings echoing through the underground concrete cavern. A fund raising student on the street above, soliciting money to save the starving children. A guitarist noodling on a park bench bordering the Circle, his instrument case seeded with bills and open for further contributions. Flamboyant gay men dancing in a conga line in the street between Starbucks and Krispy Kreme.

Of course, Dupont Circle had its mainstream museums, art galleries, and various other cultural attractions. Nevertheless, Grossman considered the area to be the two-bit circus of the beltway. He found the varied cultural displays a source of humor and a target for his derision. He would never come here at all if it weren't for the lovely young woman in the second floor brownstone apartment awaiting his arrival just two blocks from the park.

Grossman never realized what an anomaly he was in this place, with his briefcase, trench coat, and fedora, trudging among the early evening buzz of the neighborhood. He was not as anonymous as he believed.

It was at the periphery of Dupont Park where the Arab man had first spotted the Senator one Tuesday evening months ago. Thinking that Grossman reeked of power and influence, the Arab had taken Grossman's picture and discovered the Senator's identity.

After that, the Arab had staked out the Dupont Circle rail station for a week before he saw Grossman again. This time he followed Grossman to the brownstone, noted its address, and waited the short hour until his departure.

The next Tuesday, the Arab had been able to see which door bell the Senator had pushed to obtain access to the building, and observed the Senator's shadowy bulk behind the sheers in the second floor front flat. The filmy silhouette of a curvaceous woman embraced the Senator in a way that the Arab was quite confident Grossman's wife would not approve of.

The man realized the value of this knowledge concerning Grossman – Chairman of the Senate Armed Services Committee – and his weekly visits to Dupont Circle. It was only a matter of time until he would find a buyer.

CHAPTER 1

No woman expects her mugger to be wearing a metal codpiece. But that is precisely what Beth Becker found when she landed a well-placed pump in her attacker's groin, felt the steel through the top of her soft leather shoe, and heard a "clank" echo through the concrete parking ramp.

The evening had started out normally enough. Certainly there were no indications that a thug would endanger Beth's life mere hours later.

She had just come from an evening fund-raiser for the Minneapolis Art Institute, one of Beth's most favored Twin Cities museums of classic art. The affair had been held in the commons of a luxurious downtown Minneapolis hotel.

She'd departed the hotel through the skyway and entered the empty ramp elevator, depressing the button for Level 7, where her silver Mitsubishi rag top convertible awaited her.

Just as the doors were closing a man's voice had called to her. "Hold the elevator, please."

Instinctively, Beth reached for the "Open" button, but then decided that personal safety outweighed good elevator manners when an unchaperoned woman was alone and isolated in a big city. She allowed the doors to continue closing.

A split second before the stainless doors would have been shut tight, a black-gloved hand, followed by a black leather jacket sleeve, slipped between them into the elevator car, causing the doors to open again.

Beth's instincts had her on alert. This was probably just another arts patron headed for his car. But preparedness is next to godliness in certain situations. This was one of her husband's oft-repeated axioms. She clenched her key fob in her right fist, with the longest key protruding menacingly from between the second and third fingers. The key was a subtle weapon, but one that could inflict a vicious face wound on a would-be assailant, if need be.

The doors opened to reveal a tall, broad-shouldered, red-headed man of perhaps twenty-five years and two hundred pounds. Much larger than Beth. The leather coat, denim jeans, and work boots made him an unlikely attendee at the gala that evening.

"Sorry," Beth said.

"No problem. I still made it." He smiled, but his smile offered no assurances. The dilated pupils of his blue eyes revealed what Beth recognized as an unbalanced, and likely drug-impaired, psyche within. She should distance herself from him as soon as possible.

The doors were already closed. So Beth depressed the button for Level 3, hoping to make a quick exit. When the car stopped on the ramp's third floor, the man moved to block her exit. His pale and whiskered face now wore a maniacal grin.

"Let's go up a little further. Okay?"

That was when Beth had found out about the codpiece.

Her kick to his groin had evoked only a broader grin on the man's face. The doors closed as she lashed at him with her keys. But he caught her arm in a strong hand and twisted it behind her.

At this point, Beth knew she was going to get hurt. That much was unavoidable. She would suffer any pain necessary to survive. Her instincts took over. From here on she would execute her training, no matter what it took. Survival was all that mattered.

The man held Beth pinned against the rear wall of the elevator until the bell rang and the doors opened on Floor 7.

"Now, let's go get your car. I'm not gonna to hurt you. We're just gonna take a ride. Okay?" His voice was falsely sweet.

Beth knew better than to allow him to take her to a place of his choosing. But she played docile.

"Okay. Just don't hurt me. Please!"

The doors began to close. While retaining his grip on Beth, he punched the "Hold" button.

"Okay let's go."

Still holding her right arm in a painful twist, he spun her around and pushed her through the doors into the deserted ramp.

"You're hurting my arm. You said you wouldn't hurt me. I'll go with you. Just please stop hurting me."

Apparently, the mugger didn't consider Beth a flight risk in her medium-heeled pumps. And he was plenty big to control her while they walked together. He released her arm from his grasp.

Beth rubbed her sore shoulder, then turned to him and said, "Thank you."

He started to say "You're wel . . ." when Beth launched forward, drilling her keys into his solar plexus. She'd succeeded in slowing him up, but his surprise and lack of air wouldn't last long.

He was too big for her to muscle into a control hold, so she elected a key jab to the face. Since there was no point pulling punches, she drove the key straight into his left eye. He yowled in pain, his hands clutching at the bleeding socket. But he must have had enough drugs onboard to keep him moving.

He staggered toward Beth, reaching out with both hands for her shoulders. "You bitch!"

Beth ducked low, loading her powerful thighs for what she hoped would be a final blow. Dropping the keys and leading with the heel of her right hand, she launched upward, sending the full force of her leg and back muscles into the man's nose, forcing it toward his forehead, smashing cartilage, and driving nose bone fragments into his brain.

He recoiled from the strike, staggering in an attempt to regain balance. He let out a beastly yell as he took a last step toward Beth, his one eye dead and black, and his nose gushing red. Beth retreated, finding herself up against the trunk of a parked vehicle, with no time or room to escape to the side.

An eerie smile crossed the man's mangled face as he crashed to the concrete at Beth's feet.

Beth stepped over the prostrate body, distancing herself from the attacker. Seeing no movement from the man, she retrieved a cell phone from her jacket pocket and punched in "911." Her breathing was heavy and her pulse raced as she reported, "There's been an assault on Level 7 of the Radisson Ramp downtown. One injured and one probably dead. Send police and ambulance."

* * *

When the Minneapolis Police patrol officers arrived a few minutes later with guns drawn, the scene hadn't changed. Of course, Beth had already confirmed that her assailant was, indeed, dead. But she was still near him, leaning against the trunk of a black Mercedes, her legs weak and hands shaking.

The officers appraised the trembling woman, and then the hulking frame of the man splayed out on the concrete floor.

The female officer spoke first.

"What the hell happened here?"

Beth's nerves were fried.

"He mugged me," she said, and then collapsed to the floor.

* * *

When Beth awoke, she was in a hospital bed with her husband seated at her side, holding her hand. Beth reached for his face, but was stopped by the IV attached to her arm. She was groggy from the sedative the doctors had prescribed.

"What happened to me?"

"How do you feel, Beth? Does anything hurt?"

Beth mechanically inventoried her members. "My right shoulder's sore, and my right foot hurts. Otherwise, I think I'm fine."

As her eyes began to clear, she focused on her husband.

"There was a man in the parking garage," she said.

"Yeah. He tried to mug you. Do you remember?" Her husband leaned over and kissed Beth's forehead.

"Yeah. I do . . . sort of. I think I kicked his ass."

She searched her memory for further details, then propped herself up on her elbows.

"Did I kill him?"

"Beth. He's dead. And you're alive. And that's the only way this deal could come out right."

Despite her decades of work at the CIA, Beth had never killed anyone before. She struggled to absorb the thought.

"Am I in trouble?" She searched his eyes.

"No. In fact, you did the City of Minneapolis a big favor. The guy who attacked you had raped and killed three other women over the last year. The cops matched tissue and finger prints from one of the other crime scenes. They know what happened and we're all overjoyed you're here and in one piece.

She flopped down on her back.

"I need to sleep, Babe."

"You close your eyes. I'll be here when you wake up."

CHAPTER 2

Two weeks later.

An exhausted Beth Becker made her way down the vacant institutional hallways of CIA Headquarters in McLean, Virginia. The trauma of the mugging had, for the most part, passed. Her shoulder and foot were fine, though the psychological turmoil of killing a man with her bare hands lingered on . . . and might do so forever.

This evening CIA had summoned Beth from her home in Red Wing, Minnesota to its headquarters for a last minute "extremely urgent" assignment.

It had been 5:30 a.m. when the Delta red eye deposited her and her "go bag" at Ronald Reagan International. Dulles would have been closer to Langley, but Delta was the only major airline with a Minneapolis hub, and they flew to Reagan.

There she'd been met by a silent, black-suited chauffeur, standing at attention beside a gleaming black Lincoln. Washington higher-ups were never subtle about flaunting power through the vehicle fleets they controlled.

Beth laughed under her breath at the sign he held with military precision – "Elizabeth Weston." She hadn't gone by that name in nearly a decade. The Agency had assigned it to her when she first began working in Classified CIA operations. The name protected her identity from unwanted intrusions into her life after service . . . at least that was the theory. Now the CIA itself was violating the quietude of her retirement – on a Sunday, no less.

Following a short limo ride, she'd arrived at CIA headquarters. The electronic entrance pass awaiting her at Langley's front gates allowed her unrestricted access to the administrative offices. The fact that Beth was permitted to move about Langley without an escort would have been unheard of for most visitors to CIA HQ. But Beth's part-time job doing CIA decryption work from her home in Red Wing, Minnesota required her to annually renew her Top Secret security clearance. To the CIA, Beth was "one of us."

Nearing the end of the terrazzo-floored fifth level hallway, Beth turned to open the translucent glass-paneled door labeled "Deputy Director Simon Connor." She was mildly surprised to find the Deputy Director's bright and cheery administrative assistant on duty behind her burled walnut desk. Beth supposed if the Deputy Director's reason for this meeting had been urgent enough to collect her on short notice from Minnesota, it had also warranted dragging his underpaid and overworked secretary out of bed on a Sunday morning.

"Good morning, Ms. Weston. I trust you had a pleasant trip?" The woman's bubbly tone *had* to be manufactured. But Beth had to admit it was convincing.

"Highlight of my day so far." Beth winked at the young woman, who showed no indication of comprehending the irony in Beth's statement.

"May I offer you a cup of coffee? We have espresso, French press, latte, Arabic . . . almost anything. Your choice."

"Thank you. I'll have a good old Café Americano, black, please."

Beth deposited her bag on one of four walnut chairs in the assistant's office.

"I'll be happy to safeguard that for you, Ms. Weston, if you'd like. I can take it behind my desk."

"Thanks, but I'd like to keep it with me. My gun's in there and I might have to shoot the Deputy Director for disturbing a pleasant weekend with my adoring husband." This time Beth didn't wink.

Clearly not accustomed to flip comments about visitors shooting her boss, the young woman recoiled a bit, but managed to keep the coffee in the cup.

"Very well, Ms. Weston. Here's your Americano, black. Please let me know if it is unsatisfactory in any way." After extending the white ceramic mug to Beth, the woman slipped back behind her desk, all the while keeping a eye on this unusual visitor.

Beth remained standing while a moment of silence ensued.

"So . . ." she said after a few seconds. "Is the boss ready to see me?"

"I'm afraid he's still en route, Ms. Weston. Please make yourself comfortable here and let me know if there is anything further you will require . . . anything at all." She motioned to one of the side chairs.

Placing her cup on an end table for the time being, Beth removed her coat (which the assistant scrambled to hang up for her) and took a seat next to her luggage.

Beth was not disturbed at her boss's late arrival. In fact, she would have been shocked if he'd been there waiting for her. In D.C., it was SOP for a superior to arrive late to a meeting, simply to establish a position of power early on. This was a tactic Beth had employed herself on frequent occasions, in a lifetime long past.

She sipped her coffee. Probably a Starbucks dark roast. No Mr. Coffee swill for this bureaucrat's guests. Nothing but the best. Even the coffee was a power play. She supposed that, so close to the D.C. beltway, everyone needed to keep up appearances. After all, without appearances, what did a bureaucrat have to distinguish himself? High buck coffee was merely one new power tactic the Agency had added since her time in the service.

After a suitably intimidating period, the Deputy Director strode through the outer office door. He turned to Beth, who noted his entrance, but remained seated.

"Ah, Beth Becker. Good to see you again. So sorry to keep you waiting." The man spoke with a noticeable British accent. "Early meeting with Homeland Security. There's no end to the free assistance those chaps require."

He moved closer to Beth and extended a hand.

She rose and returned a firm shake.

"May we go into your office now, Simon? I'm bursting at the seams to hear your plans for me." Beth offered a fake smile.

"Yes, of course."

"Becky," he said to the receptionist, "I'll have my usual."

"Right away, Sir."

Connor opened the heavy wooden door to his inner office and bade Beth to follow him inside. The door closed behind them with a click.

Simon removed his trench coat, placing it on a hanger inside a closet. He wore a navy power suit, red tie, and shoes that had been buffed to the verge of causing blindness.

Beth didn't wait for Connor to sit. She selected a richly appointed leather and walnut side chair, turned it at a forty-five degree angle to the desk, sat down, and crossed her legs at the knees.

In contrast to Connor's outfit, Beth wore a finely tailored black cashmere jacket over a short-sleeved black cashmere top. Buttery tan leather pants and medium-heeled black and tan St. John's pumps completed her ensemble. Beth's soft, sandy-blonde hair was pulled up in a French twist, while a modest gold chain adorned her neck.

Before Connor even had a chance to speak, Becky appeared with his coffee delivery. Picking up the coffee mug, Connor took his place behind the massive wooden desk and surveyed his subject.

"Well, Beth. I see you've forgotten how to dress for business meetings. I hope your other skills haven't suffered similar decay."

Beth leaned forward, her hands on the desk top.

"First of all, you know damn well my name is Elizabeth Weston. Where the hell do you get off using the name 'Becker' in front of your secretary!"

Connor reclined in his high-backed leather chair, a smarmy grin on his face.

"Now, now, Beth. Becky has all the necessary clearances. No need to get all worked up . . ."

"The hell there isn't! What happened to 'need-to-know'? Did the CIA change that policy while I was gone? And who read her in on my private life anyway. For God's sake, Simon!"

Connor sat up straight in his chair.

"I've been patient with you, Becker, because you've been out of the loop for a while. But protocol requires you to address me as

Deputy Director, *not* by my first name."

"I'll tell you what, Simon, when you stop using that fake English accent, and quit addressing me as 'Becker.' I'll call you the freaking Prince of Hearts if you like."

Connor's face flashed red for a moment, then returned to its normal incandescent pallor.

Their eyes held equal contempt, one for the other.

Finally, Connor sat back and crossed his hands over his soft belly.

"Alright, *Ms. Weston*. It seems we've gotten off to a poor start this morning. Let's begin again, shall we?"

His voice still carried the accent. Beth imagined he'd used it for so long, he couldn't remember how to speak any other way. His tone remained disrespectful, but at least his words offered a fresh beginning. She'd do her best.

Beth reclined in her chair once again. Connor couldn't help staring as she crossed her long legs in the tight-fitting leather.

"Well, Deputy Director, you called this meeting. What's up?"

"They've assassinated the Egyptian President." He said it without emotion or further explanation.

"You mean the new guy who just took office last week? What was his name? Mahmoud Shalaby?"

"At least you still keep up on world events. Yes. That's the gentleman."

"So when you say 'they've assassinated Shalaby,' who do you mean by 'they' exactly?"

Connor pondered the question as though it was entirely unexpected.

"We're assuming it was Islamic Terrorists, of course," he finally spat out. "Shalaby was a conservative Muslim, to be sure, but who can be conservative enough for these bloody extremists? Some Muslim group likely took him out to destabilize the country and give the Salafis another crack at the presidency."

Beth lamented how little the Washington machine had learned about geopolitics during her absence.

"So . . . my role? I'm guessing the SigInt folks need some

assistance with increased message volume in the Middle East? And that's why you wanted me here?" Signal Intelligence, derived from wire-tappings, radio intercepts, and internet traffic, always spiked during geopolitical crises.

"SigInt is, indeed, pressed, but we are interested in assistance of a different sort."

"We?" Beth asked. "Who besides you wants my help?"

"Actually . . . the Director wants to tap your experience concerning the Egyptians."

Beth knew and respected CIA Director Holford. If he had asked specifically for her help, he probably had a reason. She'd still like to hear it from Simon.

"You're kidding, right? The Agency must have two dozen people in Cairo who've got more current intel than mine. What's my connection, beyond a short stint at the Embassy more than twenty years ago?"

Connor remained silent.

"Okay," Beth said, "you want my expertise on Middle East power dynamics?"

"Yes. That is partly your connection. Yes."

"Alright, here's what I think. Of course, Islamic Extremists are one possibility for the assassination. But there are at least half a dozen others."

Connor eyed the ceiling. "So whom do you surmise might be behind this act of villainy?"

Beth ignored the Deputy Director's expression, and his British speech affectation, and continued.

"How about the Supreme Council of the Armed Forces? The SCAF has been running Egypt behind the scenes at least since Nasser, and they've openly claimed power since the Egyptians ousted Mubarak in 2011. Maybe the SCAF doesn't relish relinquishing their control.

"Then there are the more liberal Egyptians . . . they may feel disenfranchised. After all, the old guard *has* co-opted *their* revolution. Young liberals fought and died in those protests at Tahrir Square. There's certainly enough emotion in that movement to fuel an assassination attempt.

"And of course, our good friends in Israel aren't above removing an Egyptian leader if they feel threatened by the new regime."

Connor interrupted.

"Israel? They're our best ally in the region. You don't seriously believe they would assassinate a foreign head of state without consulting with the U.S. first."

"Maybe they *did* consult us, Simon, and we gave them the okay. Even you can't be naive enough to believe our hands are clean when it comes to Middle East politics!"

"Not Israel. I don't see it. You're just Jew-bashing with that allegation."

Beth remembered all too well how the slightest questioning of military aid to Israel, or cooperation with its government, called forth shouts of antisemitism inside the beltway. Israel had always possessed a lobbying strength in U.S. politics that was disproportionate to its strategic position in the region. Criticizing Israel in any way could easily lose a government employee their job. Fortunately for Beth, she didn't have a Washington job to lose. She was merely a consultant, and one the Agency needed more than she needed it – at least, so it seemed at the moment.

"Don't give me that anti-Jew BS, Simon! If you'll recall, Israel invaded Egypt and Jordan in 1967 without approval from LBJ. They bombed the hell out of Gaza on their own initiative. And when the U.S. asks Israel for something as small as ending construction of new settlements in the occupied territories, they blow us off. In fact, I believe they recently suggested the U.S. should return to our national boundaries prior to the Mexican cession of 1848, giving California and three other states 'back' to Mexico. They're our good buds all right."

Beth raised an eyebrow at Simon.

"And don't tell me the Mossad isn't capable of executing foreign civilians. Who do you think's been killing the Iranian scientists lately? It's either Israel, or us, or both."

Connor's face grew redder by the minute.

"So now you're accusing the U.S. Government of assassinating a foreign president? You know that's against the law."

Beth found Simon's adherence to the party line both ridiculous and aggravating.

"Like the CIA would never act outside the law?"

Connor gave no response. Beth assumed he knew better.

"Would you like me to continue?" Connor correctly interpreted the dare for what it was.

"No. I think you've made your point . . . not that I care."

Beth's struggled to control her aggravation.

"If you don't want my opinions, stale as they may be, then why'd you drag me to Langley in the first place?"

"As I said, I didn't. It was the Director's idea. He seems to think you possess some unique qualification for this assignment."

"What assignment is that? I thought I'd be on the next plane back home as soon as our little meeting was over."

"We . . . the CIA, that is . . . want you to go undercover at the U.S. Embassy in Egypt – sort of pick up where you left off there twenty-five years ago."

Beth stood.

"No, thank you. I'm outta here."

She turned toward the door.

Connor leaned back in his chair and put his feet on the desk.

"Before you depart in a huff, don't you want to know *why* the Director wants you, and only you, for this assignment? Why you are uniquely qualified for this assignment in one respect?"

Beth looked back over her shoulder at Connor.

"And what respect is that?"

"Someone at the Egyptian General Intelligence Directorate asked to meet with you specifically. She claims to know you from your past time in Cairo and doesn't trust anyone else with certain information she deems 'critical' to Egyptian – U.S. relations."

Beth turned to face him.

"This has got to be some sort of ruse, Simon."

Connor tried not to flinch at the repeated use of his given name.

"Exactly who wants to meet with me?"

"Rasha Metwally."

Beth returned to her chair.

"Rasha Metwally." Beth's eyes drifted upward as she scoured her memory. "You know, I do remember her. She was a messenger for Egyptian Foreign Affairs when I worked the 'back office' in Cairo. She'd deliver diplomatic pouches to us and wait in the Embassy foyer for our responses."

"Well, apparently, she has more than a pouch for you now. So will you accept the assignment? Or are you going to deprive your country of this woman's invaluable tidbit?"

Beth neither liked nor trusted Connor. Yet, this was an intriguing opportunity . . . if what Simon had said was remotely true.

"Simon, you'll have to pardon my skepticism, but if you expect me to take your proposition seriously, I'll need to speak with Director Holford."

"I anticipated you might say that. And while I am personally wounded at your lack of confidence in me, I have arranged for the Director to be available to meet with you this evening. Becky will relay the details.

Simon stood.

"I believe our meeting is now concluded, *Ms. Becker*. Please show yourself out."

CHAPTER 3

Eighteen months ago, Egypt.

Inside a classified underground laboratory twenty-five miles northeast of Cairo, three white-coated Egyptian scientists labored over the small pile of aluminum castings on the table before them. They were building a model airplane. But it wasn't just any airplane . . . it was Aurora.

They had manufactured the parts in 1/30th scale with the highest possible precision based on digitized plans provided to the engineers by the United States of America. Well . . . the plans were definitely of U.S. origin, but perhaps the word "provided" wasn't entirely accurate. An operative of the Egyptian General Intelligence Directorate (GIS) – Egypt's version of the CIA – had procured the plans from the Americans. A certain U.S. Senator with an immense assortment of scandalous baggage had facilitated the delivery.

After acquiring the Top Secret information, GIS had had sought out these three scientists – considered Egypt's finest minds in aeronautical engineering. What was their opinion? Could they turn these technical drawings and specifications into a tangible product – into the fastest air-breathing plane on the planet?

Upon initial review of the Aurora designs, the scientists were excited to take advantage of this opportunity to accelerate their own technological knowledge. They had worked on experimental military aircraft for the SCAF before. They even had experience with one component of Aurora's advanced propulsion system – its pulse jet engines. While it was true that some of Aurora's other technologies were revolutionary, and different from other projects the scientists had worked on, they saw no reason, with detailed drawings and specifications in hand, why they could not duplicate the American achievement in building this aircraft.

Once the scientists had expressed optimism to the GIS Director, he had wasted no time in conscripting them to lead Aurora's construction team. At that time, the Director had made it clear that the incentives for their success were considerable. Or more precisely, the disincentives for their failure were unacceptable – at least to the scientists and their immediate families.

Given the Director's response to their optimism, the scientists may have regretted their original confident appraisal of the project's feasibility. But it was too late to turn back now. They would need to make good on their predictions.

CHAPTER 4

At CIA Headquarters. McLean, Virginia.

Beth had more than a few hours to kill before her meeting with Director Holford. Since she hadn't planned on spending the night, she hadn't booked a hotel room. Accordingly, there was no comfy bed to offer her a much needed nap. She decided the next best option was more caffeine in the SES lounge.

SES was the Senior Executive Service, mainly a government "pay grade" designation that allowed the big wigs to make more money than the normal GS (Government Service) pay system allowed. But of course, employees classified as SES also lorded the acronym over the mere GS folks whenever possible. One of the SES perquisites was a deluxe private lounge which Beth now intended to occupy . . . by force if necessary.

Upon arrival at the lounge, she found it unlocked and deserted. Perfect. Dropping her bag in one corner, she shed her top coat and cashmere jacket, hanging them in the coat closet. She found the complimentary cappuccino machine and punched up a double espresso. Café Americano wouldn't touch the headache she had coming on. A Power Bar from the vending machine would provide lunch later.

With coffee in hand, and reclining on one of the leather sofas that squeezed government budgets still seemed able to fund for the bureaucratically privileged, she punched up her husband on her encrypted cell. Even though the call was theoretically "secure," Beth and her husband, James "Beck" Becker, wouldn't be discussing anything Classified, just to be safe.

"Hi, Beth. Jefferson Avenue is a lonely place in your absence. How's Virginia treatin' you?"

"Ha ha. It was dark when I last saw the outside world. It's pretty crappy inside though."

Beth settled into a corner of the sofa and tucked her shapely legs beneath her.

"Well . . . Minnesota hasn't been all peaches either. My laptop had some glitch this morning and it took me two hours to figure out I needed to shut the darned thing off."

Beth smiled. She'd told him more times than she could count that the first fix for computer problems was to reboot the machine. Despite his skills with military technology of every variety, he couldn't seem to master a simple PC – or more likely, he didn't *want* to.

"I hear ya, Babe. Those computer glitches can be bitches."

"Ah . . . some poetry for the morning. But I don't sense any sympathy in there."

Beth laughed.

"At least your senses still work."

"So besides missing me to death, how've your conferences with the potentates gone? Famously, I hope."

"Not so much. You do remember that my meeting was with that pinhead, Simon, right?"

"Not your favorite guy?"

"I think you know the answer to that one. He hasn't changed a bit since I left D.C. Oh, except he picked up a British accent on a London assignment and hasn't been willing to part with it. Now he's so bloody brilliant one might think him to be worldly."

"We *are* both talking about the same Simon right . . . from the deep south? Mr. 'Hey all, y'all. Where's them chitterlings and grits?"

"Yup. Only I guess he's decided the British persona is more upwardly mobile than the drawl. Sadly, he's probably right. Appearances are everything in this vortex of mediocrity."

"Okay . . . enough chit chat," Beck said through the phone. "I got dishes to wash, windows to clean, carpets to vacuum. Did I say dishes to wash?"

"Nice try. I've only been gone," Beth glanced at her Tag Heuer, "nine hours. And the place was spotless when I left. Either you had an early morning kegger, or there's somewhere else you wanna get to."

"Okay, Ms. Smartypants. I've got a meeting with Gunner coming up yet this morning. He can wait for a while though. I'm truly dying to know what computer gobbledygook they want you to resolve now. Please, please, please."

"Here's your only warning. I'm tired and cranky and your snide level is off the charts. So cut me a break from your humor right now. Okay?"

"Absolutely. Sorry. I love you, and you know I want to hear all about whatever got you hauled off to Virginia. So please, proceed."

Beth took a deep breath.

"I'm sorry, too, Babe. I'm just in a bad mood, that's all."

"No worries. Carry on."

"So here's the deal . . . at least as much as we can discuss right now." Beth relayed the substance of her meeting with Simon and that she had another meeting with "his boss" that evening.

"So it looks like they may want me to take a trip . . . duration undetermined. I don't know whether I'm up for it. It'd be a chance to make a difference . . . maybe a big difference. But I'm not exactly psyched for re-upping at this point in our lives. I'd rather spend time with you and the girls, at least when they're available."

"I understand."

Beth laughed. "I'm so glad you've finally learned to say that after all these years of marriage, but right now I'd really like your advice."

"Thanks for appreciating my husbandly efforts. Here's what I would do. Listen to the guy tonight. You'll know a lot more after you talk to someone you trust. Then . . . and this is the important part . . . tell him you'll think about it and get back to him when you can. Don't commit to anything when your brain is awash in melatonin."

"I don't know, Babe," Beth said. "I expect this whole deal is pretty time sensitive and there'll be a serious push for a quick decision, followed by immediate action."

"Look at it this way. They can't make you go. There don't seem to be any qualified substitutes. Let 'em wait for a few hours. They're not going anywhere."

Beth sighed deeply, then sipped the espresso.

"I know you're right, James. In fact, I suppose I knew that before I asked you. Guess the neurons aren't hitting on all cylinders right now."

"How could they be? Now, you need to get a nap someplace. Check into a hotel or something."

"Actually, other than the presence of an espresso machine, this lounge I'm in will probably work out just fine. In fact, my eyes are already closing. I'd better hang up and catch a few winks."

"Nothing like a conversation with the old ball and chain to bore you into oblivion. I should get a commission from the sandman."

Beck chuckled.

"Now get some sleep."

There was a long pause.

"Beth? You still there?"

"G'night, Babe."

CHAPTER 5

At Red Wing, Minnesota.

I had just told Beth that I'd be meeting with Gunner. Since she'd apparently hit the snooze button on our phone call, I decided now was as good a time as any.

Gunner, aka Doug Gunderson, was Ottawa County's Chief Deputy Sheriff. He was also one of only a few people in Ottawa County who knew anything about my rather special government background and related skills.

I had never planned to let him in on my secrets, especially because if word got to the wrong people, my entire family would be in mortal danger. But I had known Gunner since we were both kids, and he'd pinned me down one night, demanding to know where I had really been for twenty years of my life.

He can be an assiduous investigator and he managed to get me to cough up a rough sketch of my life story as a military intelligence operative. He'd promised that my secret was safe with him. To date, that was a promise he had faithfully kept.

Anyway, Gunner knows I have some background that can be useful to law enforcement in certain situations. And he knows that I often take a different tack in my investigational approach than the one provided in the Sheriff's Manual.

But he also knows we're both pulling the rope in the same direction and have the same goals. So for the most part, we're able to resolve our differing styles in the interest of catching the bad guys.

Gunner had asked me to stop down to his office at the Law Enforcement Center (LEC) to "chat." Gunner never just wanted to "chat." In fact, he usually was just fine not seeing or hearing from me for days or even weeks at a time. So when the invitation presented, I took him up on it.

Arriving at the LEC, I muscled open the stiff outside doors, crossed the lobby, and offered myself up to the uniformed receptionist/dispatcher.

"Attorney James Becker. Chief Deputy Gunderson is expecting me," I said.

It was sort of refreshing to speak that phrase when it was actually true. I have to admit that, on occasion, I have intruded at Gunner's office without invitation, generally introducing myself in the same manner.

After punching up Gunner's extension and announcing my arrival, the receptionist hung up the phone.

"Chief Deputy Gunderson will be with you shortly. Please have a seat."

She gestured toward the molded yellow plastic lobby chairs that resembled something out of a Jetsons' cartoon. I'd tried sitting in one once. It wasn't worth the effort. The chairs didn't require an eject button . . . it was designed into them.

I decided to examine the picture array of "Past Sheriffs of Ottawa County" hanging on one wall. I noted that black and white pics remained the standard for Ottawa County Sheriff photographs. Kodachrome hadn't yet arrived in law enforcement memorabilia.

Presently, the metal door to the detectives' inner offices opened and Gunner stuck his head out.

"C'mon in, Becker. I've been waiting for you. What's the hold up?"

"Damsel in distress," I said, as I slid past him into the hallway.

"That figures."

We reached Gunner's office and he took his seat in the metal and vinyl swivel chair behind the desk, while I was left, as usual, to clear files from a side chair before I could sit.

"Wanna cuppa Joe?" Gunner offered. He was pretty chipper this morning.

"That'd be great."

I waited.

"You know where the coffee is. I'm not your flunky. Get your own."

I was familiar with Gunner's style of entertaining and didn't take offense. I filled my cup with the dregs of the 7:00 a.m. brewing, including a nice scum of coffee grounds that had made it through the reused filter, then took my seat again.

"Here's to Midwestern hospitality," I said, raising the ceramic mug as a toast in Gunner's direction.

"Yeah, well, this ain't the frickin' Ritz, you know. Now, you got any other bitches before we talk?"

I considered a list of possibilities, but thought better of it.

"Nope. I'm all yours." I sipped the coffee, straining the grounds with my teeth.

"Okay. Well, here's the deal. I've just been advised by the Sheriff that Ottawa County is going to be hosting a 'significant dignitary' later this month, and I'm in charge of coordinating local security with the Staties, the FBI, and everybody else."

Gunner eyeballed me, waiting, I presumed, for some ooing and ahhing.

"That's darn impressive, Gunner. Sounds like a huge responsibility. And you're just the guy to pull it off."

"I should think so. And yet, I'm a touch light on experience in that specific area."

We don't get tons of celebrities visiting us in Ottawa County.

"So what can I do to help?"

Gunner leaned back in his chair, taking care to limit his recline within the aging contraption's tolerances.

"You been around Washington, right? You've prob'ly seen how this stuff works – who does what and when and stuff. Maybe you could give me a little prep session so I'm ahead of the game. You know, so I make a good impression on the 'dignitary' and his guys."

Actually, I *did* have experience guarding dignitaries on occasion in my past life. My role had always been to do my darndest to make sure nobody got killed. My unique training and expertise allowed me to choose how I did that. Other than making sure none of the other security folks shot me, I hadn't needed to do any coordinating with them.

But I had definitely been close enough to the rest of the security folks to see how this "assignment" was going to go down for Gunner.

He'd be allowed to scope out routes and venues ahead of time – a task which would be duplicated by the FBI and private security. Once the "dignitary" was in the vicinity, either the FBI or private security was probably going to shove everybody else in a corner and tell them to keep the coffee and donuts coming.

Gunner's a good cop and I don't want you to think that, just because he lacks experience working a security detail, he's not a top notch law enforcement officer. Other than his insistence that everything be done "by the book," I've found him to be one of the best investigative cops I've encountered . . . and I've encountered quite a few. Now was probably not a good time to give Gunner the bad news.

"Gunner. I'd be more than happy to give you a hand, but I need to know more about this 'dignitary' before I can offer anything useful. Do you know anything at all about him, or her, yet?"

"Nope. So far, 'dignitary' is all I've got. It's damn odd this person is keeping everything so tight lipped. Maybe he's a famous gangster and the mob is still after him."

Gunner smiled.

"Yeah. Some Cosa Nostra Don is coming to Red Wing to give your deputies a seminar on receiving bribes for fun and profit."

Gunner chuckled.

"Now wouldn't that be interesting! But seriously . . . when the time comes, are you free to lend a hand?"

"Usual pay scale?"

"Yup. Free." Gunner smiled.

"Hey. No problem, Gunner. Just ring me up when you get more deets and I'll get my butt right down here to help you out. Deal?"

"I s'pose there isn't much else to be done about it for now. So . . . deal."

We shook on it.

CHAPTER 6

In Washington, D.C.

Beth's meeting with Director Holford was to be a dinner at 1789, a long-established, upscale restaurant on 36th Street Northwest in Georgetown. Before catching a cab, she freshened up in the women's lavatory and decided that her present attire – her only attire – would suffice for this session with the Director.

Upon arrival at 1789 a few minutes before 7:00, the appointed time for her to rendezvous with the Director, she was moderately surprised to find that he had already been seated.

The maitre d' bid her follow him to the Director's table. Given the early hour, her stroll through the restaurant went mainly unnoticed by the few other patrons, most of whom leaned in closed conversations across dark wooden tables and deep booths.

The Director had reserved a table in a secluded alcove near the rear of the establishment – no doubt a location that had served him often for confidential chats. He held a lowball glass of brown liquid in one hand while his bespectacled eyes perused the contents of a thin manila file on the table top.

When he notice her approaching, he closed the file, removed his readers, and rose to greet her.

"Good evening, Elizabeth. I'm so pleased you could spare me the time for this visit while you're in town." He slipped out from behind the table and extended his hand.

Beth noted the warm tone in his voice as she gave his hand a firm shake.

"Good evening, Director."

"Elizabeth. There is no need for formality this evening. Please call me Joseph." He stepped a bit closer to her and turned the handshake into a friendly hug, which Beth returned without trepidation. Then, backing away from the embrace, Beth spoke.

"Certainly, Joseph. I wasn't sure how meticulous D.C. had become about protocol in my absence. I'm glad to see that you, at least, haven't changed."

He pulled out a chair for her, pushing it in as she sat.

"Ha! Forty pounds and a head like the capitol dome. I'm afraid I have changed a great deal in a decade since we last met in person. But passage of time doesn't require me to be rude to my good friends."

"Thank you, Joseph," Beth said, as the Director retook his seat.

"So tell me, Elizabeth, has life treated you well since your retirement? You are still a stunning dresser, I see."

Beth glanced down to see how well her clothing had survived the flight, limo, nap, and taxi ride.

"I'm holding up." She smiled.

"And your life, Elizabeth? All's well I hope?"

"My life's good, Joseph, just as always. My husband keeps me worrying, but it's simply not realistic to think he's going to sink into an easy chair and thumb a remote all day. He's good for me – keeps me young, you know. My consulting provides a nice diversion from less intellectual pursuits and allows me to keep my technical skills sharp. And there's no job like being a mother to our great kids."

"How's your family, Joseph? Well I hope?"

"Linda died of cancer two years ago."

"Oh, Joseph. I'm so sorry." Beth reached across the table and covered his hand with hers.

"Her pancreas went bad and the whole thing was over in three months." He paused in momentary reflection. "But the boys are doing great. Followed the old man into the Civil Service. I'm afraid I can't discuss the details. But then, I don't need to explain that to you, do I Elizabeth?"

She withdrew her hand and nodded.

The waiter arrived in a black bow tie and pleated white shirt with a glass of water for Beth and asked if further drinks were required.

"Yes, please. Another bourbon for me, neat with a twist. And for you Elizabeth?"

"I'll have a cognac, please. Whatever brand you're pouring will be fine."

"Nonsense, Elizabeth. This is on my tab." Turning to the waiter he said, "Louis the Fourteenth for the lady."

"Very fine choice, Sir." The waiter backed away to retrieve the drinks.

"I'd have thought with the government's budgetary fiasco, the cocktails might've taken a hit," Beth said with a smile.

"Nonsense. In the scheme of things, with a billion spent here and a billion spent there, what's a nice cognac for a valued public servant every twenty years or so . . . ."

"I'm not one to argue, Joseph."

After a few minutes, the waiter returned with their fresh drinks.

"Would you like a moment before ordering, Sir?"

"Yes, please. Keep your eyes peeled and I'll let you know when we're ready. In the meantime, we'd prefer not to be disturbed."

"Very well, Sir." The waiter again departed with a bow.

"I bet the mac and cheese in this place is to die for," Beth said, swirling the cognac in its glass.

The Director laughed.

"Elizabeth, you have always cracked me up. Brains, beauty, and a sense of humor . . . it's no wonder you gave up government work."

Beth inhaled the cognac's aroma, then took a slight sip.

"That's very kind of you, Joseph. But I think I could get used to the pampering if $5000 a bottle cognac is typical of what Uncle Sam is serving in the higher echelons these days."

"Call the epicurean delights my one indulgence. The rest of the time, work is just as it's always been . . . and will, no doubt, always be. Hard choices with little support from those who need to give it. That part hasn't changed, Elizabeth. Few are willing to stick their necks out to do what's right, at least not if it might be politically unpopular. That shall never change, I'm afraid."

He took a swallow of the new bourbon.

Beth swirled the cognac, enjoying its heady fragrance.

"Well, Elizabeth. I suppose it's time to get down to business. You've had a long day already. And I can imagine your conference with Simon the Brit may have been less than pleasant."

"Is that what people call him now?" Beth laughed.

"That's what I call him, at least. Hell. He's puts up such a façade, I don't know how anyone could take him seriously."

"So why make him Deputy Director?"

"Hells bells, Elizabeth. You know in the government world we can't just fire someone for being a dweeb. We're stuck with him unless he decides to run naked through the streets. Might as well put him in an office and get him out of people's way. Anyway, he's not a complete idiot. He has capabilities and insights in there somewhere, that is of course, if one is willing to dig deep enough."

"Now I'm remembering why I left government employ."

Beth smiled and took another tiny sip of the ancient french brandy.

"Enough about Simon. We could enjoy the entire evening at his expense. But that's not why I've brought you here under such urgent circumstances."

"Yes," Beth said. "Simon mentioned something about a special request . . . that someone in Egypt wanted to speak with me personally."

"Indeed. And we believe this person may provide a unique opportunity for us to see inside an organization where politics have prevented us, thus far, from treading. When you knew her, she held a position of little consequence."

The Director leaned in and Beth did likewise.

"But times have changed, Elizabeth, and this woman now works at GIS."

The Director leaned back and enjoyed another healthy swallow of the bourbon.

Beth pondered the new information.

"Do you think this contact has something to do with the assassination?"

"It's certainly possible, but I hate to assume. It could as easily be a hundred other things. U.S. relations with Egypt are at a nadir since Mubarak's ouster. If this woman has info about the assassination, great. But we'll take what we can get right now. The Egyptians have devoted plenty of their own resources to solving the assassination, I'm sure."

There was silence as the Director watched Beth swirl, then sip, her cognac.

"Listen, Joseph," Beth said finally, "you know I trust you. I wouldn't even consider an assignment of this nature on the word of Simon Connor. Be straight with me, Joseph. How important is my involvement in this matter to the U.S.? And does it have to be *me* and not one of your current employees? You know I'll be stepping on toes if you pull me into this with any authority to act."

"Elizabeth, I give you my solemn word. As God is my witness . . ." He crossed himself. "You are the only person for this assignment. If you decline, of course we will still pursue this opportunity the best we are able. But in my opinion, only with your direct involvement do we have a reasonable chance of success."

Beth considered the Director's words and sipped the cognac once more.

"Do you have a file for me to review, Joseph?"

The Director pushed the manila folder across the table toward Beth.

"Classified. Top Secret. The 'read in' is on top, that is, if you're willing to consider this assignment further."

Beth looked at the top page describing the sort of Top Secret information contained in the folder and her obligations to keep the information solely to herself and to disclose it only to others who had been "read in" to the assignment.

"Joseph. I need twenty-four hours. Will you read me in and allow me to consider the contents before I decide?"

"With your signature, you may consider it done."

Beth autographed the "read in" sheet and passed it back to the Director.

"Thank you, Elizabeth. You know how to reach me tomorrow. Now . . . shall we order? I'm famished."

Beth suddenly became aware that she hadn't eaten anything

since the vending machine in the Langley Lounge. Beth slid the manila folder into an outside pocket of her purse.
　"Yes, let's."

CHAPTER 7

One year ago, at the Egyptian underground facility.

"Gentlemen. You have been nearly six months building your toy airplane. It baffles my superiors why this task consumes such great time and expense."

The three scientists and their khaki-tan-uniformed Commander stood under bright fluorescents around a stainless steel lab table in the windowless room.

One of the scientists, a grey-haired Arab named Hamadi, dared to speak.

"Commander. Sir. Please allow me to assure you the model inside this enclosure is no toy. It is crafted from parts made by Egypt's best foundry workers, engineers, and scientists. It has been no mean undertaking to create from the computerized plan the aircraft we are about to show you."

"Yes. I'm sure this toy made very hard work for you all. Let us see this thing on which you have wasted so much of Egypt's time and resources."

The two other scientists . . . one, a tall younger man with olive skin, strong hands, and thick black hair, and the other a shorter, bearded version of Hamadi . . . leaned over the table, carefully removing the wooden casting box that covered the airplane.

The plane claimed more than a meter of the table's length, its triangular-shaped, delta-wing form measuring more than half that distance across. Most anyone who looked upon the elegance and precision of the craft's steely presence would have been impressed.

As the scientists made way, the Commander paced the table's perimeter, inspecting the model from every angle.

"So this is Aurora?"

Hamadi stepped forward to answer.

"Yes, Commander, although the actual airplane will be thirty times larger – over thirty meters in length and nearly twenty from wing tip to wing tip. And of course, the model is made from common steel, not the rare metals the designs require. It would have taken us even longer to build the model had we cast these parts in the other materials."

The Commander reached out and attempted to manipulate the plane's control surfaces.

"These flaps don't even move. Is this the best you can do? Perhaps my superiors will need to rethink the choice of experts to oversee this responsibility." The word "experts" came with spit.

"But Commander, Sir. The actual control surfaces will move so very little that we were not able to incorporate their movement into the model. At speeds many times that of sound, control surfaces must operate very subtly or they will tear free from the craft. I assure you, this model is as accurate as can be made anywhere in the world."

Hamadi and the other scientists all knew that statement wasn't true. But they had little choice in the matter. Their very lives depended on keeping this project moving forward.

"Yes, yes, yes. You have excuses. I hear them. I will take this toy model to my superiors and they will decide how we shall proceed. But before I depart, I shall allow you one opportunity to sway my judgment. Tell me again when a real airplane will come of your work? One that will fly? One that we can sell to the Russians or the Chinese?"

"One year," Hamadi promised. "No longer. Our facility is now prepared and we have already begun making patterns for full size parts. One year will suffice."

The commander knew that this construction project had to succeed. The digital plans could not simply be turned over to Russia or China for them to build the airplane. If the plans were sold without proof that the design would work as promised, there would be no payment until proof of their viability could be produced. All of that process would be in foreign control, with no way for Egypt to dispel claims that the plans were faulty and the designs, useless.

No. Even though Egypt had no use for such a long range and expensive aircraft, the plane must be built first in Egypt, to preserve its value – which was likely in the tens of billions of dollars US.

The Commander also knew that the scientists and engineers assembled in this facility were the very best available in Egypt. His superiors had hand picked them for this project. He could threaten them, try to make them work harder, but in the end, he was stuck with them.

"I will send my men to take the toy to the powers that be, and I will relay your time line. They shall decide whether it will be mercy or justice for you all."

CHAPTER 8

Location unknown.

The day after the President's death, an encrypted email arrived at the organization's headquarters. Only the man in charge had the decryption code to open it. He did so at the computer in his private office.

My Friend,

As you have seen, the assignment is complete. The President is dead. Wire remaining funds to the designated account immediately. Perhaps we can do business again one day.
Out.

R

The man behind the desk chuckled. "Complete, indeed," he said to himself, deleting the email from his hard drive.
He called his assistant on the intercom. "I have a job for you, my dear."
She appeared at the door, ready to serve.
"Please take care of this for me right away, won't you?"
He handed her an official slip of paper, signed by him, and containing account and routing numbers. The document instructed the organization's banker to transfer $1,000,000 US to a certain bank account in the Cayman Islands. The Memo at the bottom of the paper read, "Military Supplies – Security."
The assistant took the paper, perusing it briefly.
"It will be my pleasure, Sir." With that, she departed, closing the

office door behind her.

The man rose and crossed to the expansive windows that filled one wall of his office. He stood, observing the cityscape below and the hazy horizon beyond.

They think they know what they're doing – what is happening around them, he thought. *Yet they are ignorant of everything that matters. It will always be so. I and a select few others will forever hold their destinies in our hands.*

Their kings will fall. Their potentates will crumble, and not one of them can foresee nor alter his own fate.

He returned to his desk and fired a fat Cuban cigar. Bluish-white smoke swirled around and before him.

We are smoke. None can grasp us nor control our paths.

CHAPTER 9

Back in Red Wing.

By the time Beth arrived back home on Jefferson Avenue, it was past 2:00 a.m. I had been asleep since 11:00, but I'm easily awakened – a habit I developed during years working where such things meant life or death.

I waited until she'd entered the upstairs bath and I heard the shower flowing. When she emerged, I was standing in the doorway in my pajama bottoms.

Beth had begun toweling off in the shower without seeing me.

"Hey," I said.

She looked up.

"Oh, hey, Babe. Sorry I woke you."

"Pretty much unavoidable," I said. "Not your fault. Can you come to bed? Or are you pulling an all-nighter?"

Beth had finished drying herself. I watched as her naked body brushed past me and on into our bedroom. I followed.

"I'm completely fried and crashing from caffeine buzz," she said, slipping into her cotton jammies. "I'll tell you all about my trip in the morning."

She fell into bed and managed to drag some covers over her legs and torso. I tucked her in properly.

"It's good to have you home, Beth. Sleep well."

She was out as soon as her head hit the pillow. I could tell it'd been a trying day. I crawled into my side of the bed and lay on my back, staring at the dark ceiling.

"I love you," I whispered. "Goodnight."

* * *

It was a little after 9:00 a.m. when Beth came downstairs, still wearing her PJs. I had brewed a pot of fresh coffee in the machine and was working on my second cup when she joined me at the granite kitchen table.

I could see she was still waking up. So I allowed her to gain her wits before trying to start a conversation.

After three or four sips of coffee, and a full-body stretch, she turned toward me.

"Good morning, Babe. You're looking a lot more chipper than I feel."

I laughed.

"The long hours get harder with age I'm afraid."

She raised an eyebrow at me.

"Not that you're getting old or anything . . . just not any younger."

This time I got a head tilt and thought I'd better change my tack.

"I can't say how chipper you feel, but you're looking fantastic. How *do* you do it?"

Now it was Beth's turn to laugh.

"You're such a loser . . . and I'm unbelievably lucky I married you."

"True," I said, returning to my coffee. "Who could argue with that."

I could see that Beth's cup was emptying, so I freshened it from the pot.

"Thanks, Babe."

"Least I could do after you've just put in a hard day's night."

"About that . . . I've got about ten hours to make a decision that has potential to upset our retirement routines considerably. I want your input, but I've gotta read through the file first. I think I'll get at that right now, if you'll excuse me."

"Certainly. Hope it's a good read."

"Oh, they always are." There was more than a touch of sarcasm in her voice.

Beth headed out of the kitchen leaving me to read the newspaper and wonder what the next ten hours would hold.

* * *

As noon approached, I decided I'd arrange for a nice lunch. We'd only had coffee for breakfast, and I was sure Beth could benefit from something healthy to eat.

While she continued to mull over the contents of the manila file on our livingroom's red leather couch, I ducked out to Smokey Row and picked up two salads and a loaf of freshly baked bread. Smokey Row is equal parts bakery and coffee shop. I can't say one part is better than the other. But both together make for a heavenly breakfast or brunch.

I managed to escape the aroma of fresh-baked goodies without picking up caramel rolls, or cheese Danish, or anything of the other treats that had beckoned me through the display case glass, and made it out the door with our salads and bread.

Arriving back at 1011 Jefferson Avenue, I parked the Pilot in front and entered through the columned screen porch that spanned the width of our Georgian Colonial.

I looked in on Beth.

"Time for a lunch break. It'll help you focus those stunning eyes and sharpen your already incisive neurons."

Beth looked up. "You didn't try to cook, did you?"

"Not to fear. I picked this up from the professionals at Smokey Row." I rattled the bag containing our lunch.

"Sounds great. Shall we eat on the porch? Might be one of our last chances before cold weather."

"I aim to please. You sit tight and I'll get us set up."

A few minutes later, I had the front porch wicker and glass table looking quite presentable. The ice water had been poured. The salads were in their bowls. And the bread was sliced in a cloth-lined basket, with butter at the ready.

Beth took a seat at the table. I remained standing.

"Today we are serving your choice of a simple chicken salad with apple and grape slices on a bed of romaine, or cranberry spinach salad, with toasted almonds, dressed with a sweet and tangy vinegar and oil dressing, and chocked full of sesame and poppy seeds."

"Hmm. I think I'll go with the chicken and fruit. Always a personal favorite."

"Chicken it is," I said, delivering the salad bowl onto her dinner plate, then joining her at the table with the spinach and cranberries.

We said a brief table grace and dug in.

I'm sure Beth was famished, but she ate with patience and dignity . . . at least as much dignity as one can have when one is still dressed in one's pajamas at lunchtime.

After allowing a few moments for each of us to begin our meals, I couldn't wait any longer.

"So, Beth. Have you gleaned enough juicy details from that bestseller in there to know whether I can help with anything?"

"Hmm. Now that's always a dangerous question. Do you think you can exercise appropriate restraint and maybe just help me talk through it?"

"Well . . . that won't be easy. But I promise to endeavor to succeed." I smiled.

"That doesn't comfort me. But we need to discuss this anyway."

"Okay," I said, dabbing my mouth with a cloth napkin. "Fire away."

"To start out with, I can't share all the details with you. It's Top Secret and you haven't been read in on this mission. So I'll share what I can."

I understood Beth's limitations concerning the info. Although I, too, had a Top Secret clearance, her info was need-to-know, and I didn't have the appropriate permissions to gain access.

"Understood."

"As I'm sure you've heard by now, someone assassinated the new President of Egypt the day before yesterday."

"Yeah, I saw that on CNN."

"The Agency wants me to spend some time at our Embassy in Cairo on an assignment that may or may not relate to the presidential assassination."

"Need to know?"

"Actually, nobody's sure exactly what information I might find once I get to Egypt."

"I'm assuming they want your code-breaking skills. Isn't it possible for you to do that stuff from home?"

"That's a reasonable question, but I can't answer it. If I accept this assignment, I *have* to go to Cairo, probably for weeks . . . maybe months. The timing depends on what I find when I get there."

This was a much bigger deal for the Becker family than I had anticipated.

"You know, Cairo isn't the greatest place for Americans right now. Since the Egyptians found out that U.S. support for Mubarak wasn't their only problem, they've been flailing around looking for somebody to blame for their persecution."

Beth gave me a motherly look.

"I'm sure you'll recall that I spent a number of years in Cairo. I'm up to speed on the Middle East and its . . . idiosyncracies. I'd be stationed at the Embassy. I know there's still a risk. But do you think any group in Egypt is really stupid enough to assault our Embassy? Arresting a few American pro-democracy advocates is one thing . . . but attacking the Embassy would be declaring war on the United States.

"Under the Camp David Accords, the U.S. basically bribed Egypt, Israel, and Jordan to make peace. We pay all of them billions every year as our part of that deal. If the SCAF allowed anyone to attack the U.S. Embassy, they'd be risking eighty percent of their military budget in the process. I'm pretty sure it's in their best interests to keep me safe while I'm there."

"I don't doubt you're right, Beth. But I seem to recall the SCAF just standing by while rioters overthrew the Israeli Embassy in Giza last year."

Beth took a deep breath.

"Babe, you are a wise man, and so skilled at many things, but trust me, you *do not* understand Middle East politics."

Beth waited for me to react. Eventually, I rocked my head back and forth in tacit acknowledgment that she might be right about my relative ignorance in this area.

"In Egypt, *everybody* hates Israel," she continued. "And *everybody* wishes Israel would go away. But no sensible Egyptian wants war with Israel, and no sensible Israeli wants war with Egypt. Everybody's got too much too lose. The SCAF knew Israel wouldn't respond with force in that Embassy assault. They were just letting Egyptians blow off steam. A lot of young Egyptians are mad as hell at their situation and the SCAF didn't want that hostility directed at them.

"Of course, one could debate the wisdom of their strategy, since almost all Egyptians seem to have realized by now that Mubarak wasn't their problem, it was the army and the SCAF all along. Mubarak was just the front man."

"Okay," I said. "It seems you've got a good grasp on the risks of this assignment. How 'bout the benefits?"

"Sorry. I can't go into details with you. But U.S. interests in the region are already in jeopardy. I *might* be able to do something meaningful to . . . repair . . . some of that mess."

"Do your bosses know how the President was killed?"

"It doesn't seem so. Reports are conflicting. Or maybe they're just not sharing."

"Ahh . . . well, during your absence, I've been scanning the internet for clues. Lots of folks have . . . er . . . insights into the matter. Wanna hear some likely causes of death according to the World Wide Web?"

Beth folded her hands in her lap. "I can hardly wait."

"I made a list." Reaching into my shirt pocket, I produced a sheet of yellow-striped note paper containing my written recollections.

"Let's see . . . for methods of execution we have – sniper bullet, earphone bomb, backstabbing by someone on the platform, time-delayed poisoning, cosmic radiation, a bolt from a cross-bow, and 'struck down by God.'"

"Had you considered all of those?"

"Hmm. The crossbow thing is creative. If God is involved, I'm not sure what I can do to help restore order. And I'm going to have to throw out cosmic radiation."

"Yeah. I thought you might."

"But I'll keep the others in mind. Is that it?"

"No. Not even close. I've got likely suspects, too."

"Can't wait to hear these. I s'pose God's on this list as well?"

"Natch. Goes without saying."

I referred to my paper again.

"Okay . . . for the possible baddies, in no particular order, we've got the Israeli Mossad, Egyptian Muslims – both right and left wing – an as yet unidentified militant faction of Egypt's Coptic Christian minority . . ." I checked to make sure Beth was still listening. She was doing her best.

" . . . the CIA, al Qaeda, Hamas, Syria's President Assad, and Kim Jong Il."

I looked up again.

"You mean the North Korean President, Kim Jong Il?" Beth said.

"Yup."

"He's dead."

"Uh huh. But you can't just discard these thing out of hand."

I smiled. Beth smiled back.

"And you've got more brilliant insights to share, I'm sure."

"Naturally. You want to know the motives, right?"

Beth sighed.

"Okay. Hit me."

"Other than the obvious – to wit, the CIA, the Mossad, God, and I suppose, Kim Jong Il – the Muslims either wanted strict Sharia law, or someone more liberal and democratic. Assad needed to draw attention away from domestic slaughter in his own country. Al Qaeda was just trying to get its good terrorist name back – they've been in decline since bin Laden's demise. Hamas, who you might think would be entirely supportive of their only meaningful ally in the region, feared continuation of the peace treaty with Israel."

"Is that it?" Beth pleaded.

"No. There's more."

"Okay. Not today. I think I've got the gist of world opinion. I'll bulk up my background data through more traditional channels."

"Right. It's a lot to take in all at once, what with God and dead people and all. I'll just leave the rest of the list with you for later reference."

I passed the yellow page across to Beth.

"Bless you!" She looked truly thankful.

"Other than more forensics concerning the assassination, do you have further thoughts to offer?"

I considered all that I'd heard and all that I'd read.

"I have just one question for you. What have you decided? Are you headed for Egypt or not?"

I wet my parched lips with a sip of water. I guessed I'd been talking longer than I'd realized.

Beth allowed herself a moment for reflection. No doubt I'd overwhelmed her with my copious insights.

"I think I'd like to take a stab at this assignment. There's a good reason why I should be the one to go to Cairo, though I can't tell you what it is. And I just might be able to accomplish some small bit of something that would be good for all players in the region – not just the U.S. – unless, of course, I get hit by a gamma ray blast, or God takes me out. I'm honestly not worried about the dead guy."

I leaned back in my chair, hands on its arms.

"Then I think you should do it. Accept the assignment."

Beth looked surprised at my reaction.

"What will you do about your longings for me while I'm gone?" Beth purred, then followed with a smiled.

"Hey, you know me. Gunner and I'll keep each other entertained. In fact, he's got some dignitary coming to town and wants my security advice. It won't be easy, but I'll keep my 'longings' in check. You know, I even heard somewhere that absence makes the heart grow fonder."

"Yeah. My intel has it that the guy who said that didn't have a choice in the matter. He was just looking on the bright side. In fact, I think his gal pal ditched him in the end."

Beth smiled again.

Did I mention that I love her smile?

"I shan't worry on that score. You've established your fidelity by tolerating my escapades for these past many years. It's only the bad guys who might threaten you that give me pause."

"Hey. I'm not so bad at protecting myself, you may recall. Besides, I'm pretty sure there must be *someone* else in all of Egypt who can protect me for you."

We both smiled.

"Then it's decided. When do you leave?"

"I'll find out more details when I get back to Holford with my decision. I'm guessing they'll want me there yesterday."

"Ah, yesterday. All my troubles seemed so far away."

Beth flicked water from her glass in my direction.

"Okay, McCartney. I've gotta finish the briefing and then call Holford. I shall beckon you when I'm free."

"I'll just clean up these dishes and remain available. Get back to work. Shoo." I waggled my hand at her.

Beth returned to her labors, and my mind began rolling through the list of all the horrible things that could happen to her while she was gone. Force of habit, I suppose.

CHAPTER 10

One year ago at the Egyptian General Intelligence Directorate (GIS). Cairo.

"So this is the Aurora aircraft."
The voice belonged to GIS Director, Murad Muwafi. A stern, white-haired man, with a long history in both foreign and domestic intelligence activities, he wore his trademark black suit and navy tie. Muwafi had assumed the Directorship from Omar Suleiman, President Mubarak's last-minute appointee as Vice President shortly before Mubarak's fall from power.
When the SCAF took over governance, they hadn't seen fit to include Suleiman among their number, choosing instead to paint the former administration with a broad brush and eliminate as many stale reminders of its existence as possible. It seemed Suleiman had hitched his cart to the wrong horse, and as a result, had never been seen in public again.
Muwafi could not help but be mindful of the manner in which his newly acquired position had become vacant. His sole mission was to please whomever would be in power the longest. Right now, that was the SCAF. But he was mindful, too, that democracy might be on the horizon for Egypt. As a result, those who knew him best saw him for the fence sitter that he was – unable to take a decision without first weighing its political effects on his own career. If he could pull off a huge financial win with the Aurora project, his job would be secure regardless of who ran the country.
"Yes, Director," the Commander answered.
Muwafi strolled around the glass display case in the GIS high security wing.
"It is impressive, no?" the Director said.

"Mr. Director, it will indeed be impressive, if and when the plans are realized in full scale. Right now, it is six months of not very much."

The Director turned to Commander Saed.

"Do you have concerns that this project will not come to fruition, Saed?"

The Commander spoke freely.

"I have always said as much. Even with the stolen plans, this plane is beyond the abilities of our scientists and manufacturers to build, let alone of our fighter pilots to fly."

"I take your advice to heart, as I always have, Saed, but this plane cannot remain half-pregnant forever. I only told the Supreme Council that we possessed these plans. It was their choice to build the prototype rather than risk losing this valuable assets to our trading partners. Do you say we should stop now? Report utter failure?"

"Mr. Director. That is, of course, your decision, not mine."

"That may be true, Saed. But if we choose to report failure at this juncture, I will require your presence to explain why this significant matter, which I have tasked to *your* command, has come to nothing. Is that what you want me to do?"

The Commander was a soldier. He took orders and carried them out to the best of his ability. Yet he understood the implication in the Director's tone.

"If you insist on my opinion, Mr. Director, then I would choose to continue the project for now." The Commander cringed. "The benefits to Egypt could be great. I must place the greater good above my own self-interests in this matter."

He hung his head.

"I thought that might be your recommendation, Saed. Now . . . is there anything further you will need to complete this glorious and patriotic task? You know the full resources of GIS are at your disposal."

The Commander paused.

"Have we additional scientists or engineers who may have greater knowledge or skill than those already assigned to my duty?"

"Saed, my friend. You know that you already have the best minds in all of Egypt. Surely you are not saying that Egyptian education and expertise is somehow . . . second rate?"

"Certainly not, Mr. Director. I only wished to be confident . . . to guarantee this project's success."

"Very well then, Saed. Be about your business. I shall expect your regular reports, with a final completion date of one year from today. You are dismissed."

The Commander saluted the older man, who half-heartedly returned the gesture. Commander Saed departed the Directorate with the knowledge that his only hope of avoiding prison, or worse, was success of the Aurora project. He would have to make it so.

CHAPTER 11

Two days after the President's Assassination.

The sniper had received the remaining monies due him for the Egyptian job and presently lay enjoying a professional massage beneath a beach palapa at an exclusive Dominican resort.

The dark-skinned young woman in the white masseuse uniform rested her hands quietly upon his wiry but well-muscled shoulders for nearly a minute.

"Terminado, Señor. ¿Quedó usted satisfecho?"

He remained motionless on the massage table's white cotton sheets.

" Si, Señorita. Muy bien. Your hands are a miracle for this tired horse." His Spanish was merely passable and carried a South Texas accent.

"Lo siento, Señor. No habla Ingles." She gave a shy smile.

"That's no problemo, Señorita. La cuenta, por favor?"

She produced the hotel charge book from her apron and offered it to him with a nod.

After signing and including an ample gratuity, he returned the book to the woman.

"Mañana, Señor? Al misno tiempo?"

"Si. Same time tomorrow. Gracias."

The masseuse covered the sniper's back and Speedo with a white terrycloth towel before departing.

As he lay in the palapa's shade, on the edge of sleep, he pondered his career choice. Not the moral implications, certainly . . . but how wise he had been to accept that first offer after departing Special Forces.

Life is good, Amigo. Life is good.

CHAPTER 12

At Cairo International Airport.

Beth had, indeed, been pressed into service the next day after arriving home. She'd boarded a Lufthansa flight at Humphrey International in the Twin Cities last night around 11:00 p.m. local time, transferred to another Star Alliance carrier, EgyptAir, at Frankfurt, and had just arrived here in Cairo at 6:00 p.m. today.

She'd heard that the Cairo airport had been remodeled since her last visit, but she was still amazed at the shining steel escalators, the smoothly functioning people mover, and the gleaming glass domes lofting above common areas and walkways. All of this had been accomplished since 2000.

The airport represented a magnificent transformation from "the old days." Beth began to wonder how much the Embassy had changed and whether she could, in fact make the adjustment to 21st Century Cairo.

Upon collecting her baggage at the carousel, she followed the English language signs that brought her to Customs and Immigration Services. Finding no specific area for diplomatic entries into Egypt, she waited in line for one of the Customs agents to become available.

When she presented her diplomatic passport and Visa to the agent, he compared her face to the photo in his hand. Apparently satisfied with the resemblance, he waved her through without any attempt to question her or search her luggage. After she'd left the customs area, the agent placed a telephone call to advise security to monitor the American diplomat.

Outside the terminal, the air was still and warm. The smell of auto exhaust mixed with diesel fumes permeated the sheltered passenger pickup area. This could be any major airport in any major city. Beth found nothing familiar from her previous time here.

Locating the black limousine with twin American flags flying above its front quarter panels was hardly a challenge. Beth waved at the driver and he pulled up beside her.

After a perfunctory welcome and a further checking of her papers, he opened a rear door for her while he loaded her bags.

Before turning herself over to an unknown chauffeur in an unauthenticated vehicle, Beth called the Embassy and to request a description of the driver and the car. When she had confirmed all was copacetic, she followed the driver's direction and sat in the back, enjoying a brief stretch of both arms and legs in the ample rear of the limo while awaiting the driver's return.

The trip to the Embassy proved uneventful. The driver didn't care to chat, which was fine with Beth, who'd planned to rest her eyes, but immediately dropped off to sleep. She awakened as the limo rocked over the speed bump at the entrance to the Embassy's underground garage.

By this time it was after 7:00 in the evening and most Embassy employees had departed for their homes in the Cairo suburbs. A young, professionally attired, and cheerful American woman wearing a brunette bob met Beth's car on its arrival and escorted Beth and her baggage handler to the Embassy apartment that would serve as Beth's home for the next . . . well . . . no one knew how long. The young woman's name was Tara.

Beth surveyed the fourth floor premises. The room smelled faintly of pine cleaner and fresh paint . . . or perhaps it was the new carpeting. The decorating was standard government issue. There were framed prints on the walls – most likely the same ones that hung in each apartment on this floor.

Tara gave Beth the apartment keys and a hi-tech, electronic Embassy Employee Pass while the handler placed her luggage in the room.

"I hope these accommodations will be adequate, Ms. Weston."

"Yes, Tara. These will be fine. Please call me Elizabeth."

"Certainly, Elizabeth. Will there be anything else I might provide for you this evening?"

Beth remembered the days long ago when she had been the page who'd met seasoned diplomats upon arrival in Egypt. Had she been this staunch and formal? Probably.

"Actually, Tara, you can tell me how can I get on the internet from my room. If possible, I'd like an encrypted connection from here. Otherwise, normal web access will do for now."

Tara produced what appeared to be a business card from her suit breast pocket. "The internet access procedure is on this card. It's not encrypted though. And we don't use wireless networks here." She caught herself, realizing who she was speaking to. "But then, I'm sure you knew that. Will you need an ethernet cable?"

"No, thanks. I've got one in my bag. Are you able to request an encrypted link for me here? Or is that something I need to do myself tomorrow?"

"I'll be happy to make the request for you, Ms. West . . . ah . . . Elizabeth. Someone may contact you to validate your request. But I'm sure that, for *you* there won't be a problem.

"Is there anything else?"

Beth swept her eyes around the room once more.

"Yes, actually. I assume that my bags and I passed through a bug detector or two on the way in here, but could you arrange for a more thorough sweep of all my things as soon as possible. I wouldn't want to be bringing in any unwanted ears. And this is probably standard procedure, but I'd really appreciate a double-check of the room as well, including a search for optical and sonic detectors that might be listening from outside. I need this room to be 100% bug-free from the get go.

"Can you get the ball rolling on those things as well, Tara?"

Beth smiled at the young woman.

"I believe I can make those arrangements through my supervisor in the morning. Will that be soon enough? Otherwise, I can contact her this evening."

Beth knew Tara didn't want to bother her boss after work hours. And her boss probably didn't want to have her dinner interrupted either.

"Tomorrow will do fine. Now I think I'm all set. So perhaps you're done for the day?"

"Just about. It was nice to meet you Elizabeth. I'm sure you'll be seeing me around. I kind of run all over."

Beth smiled. Tara exhaled and returned the smile.

"About a hundred years ago I wore your shoes, Tara. I haven't forgotten what it's like. Let me know if I cause you too much trouble, okay?"

"Thank you, Elizabeth. I hope you enjoy your first evening in Cairo."

Beth laughed.

"If the bed works, I'll be in heaven. Thanks again. You enjoy your evening, too."

Tara prepared to close the apartment door. "Goodnight, Elizabeth. Sleep well."

"Thanks again, Tara. I'll see ya around."

Tara nodded formally, then backed out into the hall, softly closing the wooden door behind her.

Beth unbuttoned her jacket and hung it in the closet. The bed beckoned, but she needed a shower before a restful night's sleep. That horizontal dream date would have to wait just a few more minutes.

Her thoughts drifted back to Red Wing and the husband she'd left behind. She hoped she'd made the right decision coming to Cairo.

CHAPTER 13

Nine months ago at the Egyptian underground facility.

The three Egyptian scientists had made great strides toward constructing a full scale prototype of Aurora. The composite casting process had proven daunting. The plans called for many components to be made from titanium and magnesium alloys. Titanium alloyed with aluminum was easy enough to work with. But the magnesium and zinc alloy, required for many of the larger parts, posed significant challenges.

For one thing, magnesium was stable enough in its solid state, but when heated to its melting point, reacted explosively in air. This meant that all magnesium alloy parts had to be cast entirely within chambers filled with argon gas. The casting process was identical to that used for simple parts made of aluminum or steel, but meeting the tight tolerances of intricate fuel channels and wiring conduit within the castings became almost impossibly cumbersome inside an argon chamber, where workers standing outside the enclosure, had to melt, mix, and pour the alloys into the molds using extendable rubber gloves or robotic arms.

And if pouring the magnesium wasn't complex enough, the scientists also needed to tightly control the cooling and contraction of the alloy inside the sand mold. Within the molds themselves, they had incorporated reservoirs to hold the necessary additional metal to fill the areas where cooling had contracted the hot metal – the metal that had originally completely filled the mold.

But cooling the reservoir itself – a relatively large mass of molten metal – at a rate that would allow it to meld with the faster-cooling, thin fuel channels and conduit, while still assuring that the entire alloy casting would develop the optimal crystalline structure for strength and stability – now that was a process the scientists had never before pressed to these extremely tight tolerances.

As the project had progressed, the scientists' original confidence had begun to wane. The casting process for the exotic metals was proving beyond the capabilities of their metallurgists and foundry personnel to carry out with the necessary precision.

"Is there any hope this thing will fly when we are through?" one scientist asked his companions.

"There is still hope," another said.

Hamadi's assessment was less optimistic.

"We shall require a miracle for this to work. Let us all pray that someone else makes bigger mistakes than we. Or I fear we shall soon meet Allah face to face."

With dread and misgivings, the scientists moved ever closer to the day when Aurora would be expected to fly.

CHAPTER 14

Back in Red Wing.

It'd been a few days and I hadn't heard anything more about Gunner's "dignitary." A call was in order.

Gunner's phone rang twice.

"Gunderson."

"Good morning, Chief Deputy. Just checking in to see what's new on the security detail."

"You know, Beck, I often wonder what you do with yourself when your not riding my tail. Do you do *any* lawyer work at all anymore?"

I laughed.

" 'Course I do, Gunner. But I've got that office running like a finely oiled machine. I don't have to actually *be* there all that much."

"You realize that if you don't improve your pretend lawyer persona, somebody might just start asking questions about what the heck it is that you *do* do."

"Do do?"

"Yeah."

"Well, let 'em ask. As long as you don't tell, I won't. Maybe I've got a lot of important big shot clients from the Cities, so I'm not around here all that much. Or maybe the County Attorney has got me on retainer to keep the Sheriff's Department out of its own do do."

"Do do?"

"Yeah."

"Well . . . I don't think so."

"What don't you think?"

"That I want you telling my citizens that you're looking after me. So don't."

He'd had enough of my sparkling repartee for the day.

"Maybe it's you who's looking after me? How 'bout that?"

There was a pause.

"What? Look, can we just get back to the security thing?"

"Glad you mentioned it. What's new? Do you know yet who you're protecting?"

I flinched as Gunner obviously dropped his phone. Then in the background I thought I heard him say something like "Sonofabitch."

I stifled a laugh.

"Gunner? Gunner? You okay?"

He came back on the line.

"Just spilled frickin' hot coffee all over my uniform. Shit!"

I could visualize the scene in Gunner's office perfectly. I'd been there before when there'd been a coffee incident. He had too many files on his desk and often set his coffee mug on top of them. Java upheaval was bound to happen at periodic intervals. Again, I tried not to laugh.

"Look," I said, "you let me know when you're ready to talk business. I'll wait for your call."

I heard Gunner's phone hit the floor again.

"Goddammit!"

And I disconnected the call. Best to let Gunner regain his composure.

A few minutes later my cell rang. It was Gunner.

"Hi, Gunner. Everything okay?"

"Hell, yeah. I just gotta get a new filing system around here. Anyway... Sheriff says our dignitary is a member of Congress, but he can't say who. You got any idea why that might be? Those politicos usually advertise all over hell when they're planning a visit. Why the cloak and dagger stuff?"

"They advertise when they're campaigning, but it's an off year – no election this fall. Maybe it's a private visit."

I waited for Gunner to respond.

"Yeah. That makes sense, I guess. But if he's keeping his travel schedule on the down low, doesn't seem too bright for him to tell me, and every other cop in the southern half of Minnesota, that he's coming. D'ya think?"

Gunner had a point.

"And don't those Congress guys have plenty of Secret Service and stuff? Why would they need my little old kick-the-shit-off-our-boots Department to help?"

"I know a little about Congressional security, Gunner. They don't get the same kind of protection that a President does. In fact, they don't get any. I suppose the government figures killing one Congress member out of 535 isn't going to motivate too many potential killers to take the risk."

The line was silent for a moment.

"So you mean those guys . . ."

"Or gals," I reminded.

". . . or gals," Gunner squeezed through an obviously tightened jaw. "So they don't have any security at all?"

"Lots of them hire private security, Gunner. It's just the government doesn't provide it. It's on their own dime."

"Well, that at least makes some sense. So do you s'pose this guy . . . or gal . . . is extra security conscious and has some private muscle?"

"That *would* make sense, given that somebody wants to coordinate with Ottawa County for security."

Gunner paused again.

"So why is this particular . . . politician . . . so afraid of getting whacked? Why're they so jumpy?"

"Who knows, Gunner. Maybe somebody gave 'em a scare at another public outing. Maybe there's marital infidelity involved. The point is, something's got them spooked, and unless you're told what, you're probably never going to know."

"So we're back to ground zero on this security thing then, huh."

"Square one."

"What?"

"Ground zero is where something blows up. Square one is where you start."

I could hear Gunner roll his eyes through the phone.

"If you knew I meant 'square one,' then why the hell didn't you just shut up and let me move on?"

"Hmm . . . force of habit, I guess."

"Well, get over it. Take a ten step program or something."

"Twelve step."

"Becker, you make me want to spit!"

"I suppose."

I'll get back in touch when I know more and we can get off 'square one.' *Don't* call me before I call you!"

I paused to see if there was more. Nothing.

"Got it," I said. "You do have my number, right?"

Click.

Gunner's not as surly as he might seem. He just doesn't appreciate witty banter.

I would await his call.

CHAPTER 15

At the U.S. Embassy. Cairo.

Egyptian cultural traditions dictated that Beth's wardrobe for this assignment assume a more conservative tenor than her typical Western style. She needed to cover her arms and legs whenever she was outside the Embassy or meeting with Egyptian or other Arab men. Fitted clothing would cause unwanted attention to body parts other than her brain.

Beth had selected two distinct, but equally acceptable "looks" for Cairo dress.

For more casual encounters, or for walking Cairo's crowded streets, she had packed a selection of "Diane Sawyer" outfits. These consisted of loose-fitting, tan khaki pants, with a colorful variety of long-sleeved, crew-neck, cotton tunics, to be worn with or without a drapey cotton sweater or tunic jacket.

For those times when she needed to project a more empowered presence, Beth reserved a selection of cotton "power suits" – mainly navy, dark grey, or black with mid-calf length skirts, long jackets, and white or cream blouses, buttoned up to the neck.

She would not be wearing any jewelry in Egypt, other than her plain gold wedding band.

Today would be a Diane Sawyer day. She preferred to get acquainted with the Embassy staff without coming off as a stuffed shirt from D.C. A casual Beth would be more approachable.

As she entered the lower level Embassy cafeteria, Beth saw the object of her breakfast meeting – Deputy Ambassador, Thomas Hitchens – already seated at a table for two. He either didn't notice her arrival, or didn't know what she looked like.

Beth chose fresh fruit and vanilla yogurt from the food counter, then approached Deputy Ambassador Hitchens. He looked up from his *Wall Street Journal* and stood to greet her.

"Elizabeth Weston, I presume?"

"The same," Beth said, placing her plastic tray on the table.

"My pleasure to meet you, Deputy Ambassador Hitchens."

They exchanged a firm handshake.

"Okay. We're going to need to shorten that title up a bit. Please call me Tom or 'Hitch,' as you prefer."

"My pleasure, 'Hitch.' Please call me Elizabeth."

"Well, Elizabeth, let's have a seat and get acquainted, shall we?"

"We shall."

Elizabeth took her seat as Hitch returned to his. It was apparent from the condition of his tray that his breakfast had been a full meal of fried eggs, sausage, and hash browns. This diet, Beth imagined, accounted for Hitch's portly composition.

Covering his roundish exterior, Hitch wore a too-small blue cotton blazer, a white cotton short-sleeved dress shirt (as revealed by his bare wrist bones) with a green and blue striped tie, and a pair of tan chinos that could well have come from his clothes hamper. A suede pair of Birkenstock sandals over bare feet completed the eclectic ensemble.

Beth knew better than to judge a man by his attire, but Hitch had compiled a memorable look.

"Do you mind if I continue with breakfast while we visit?" Beth asked. "I'm famished."

"No, no. Not at all. I've got my coffee to keep me busy."

Beth decided to ask a question, giving Hitch the chance to talk while she peeled a banana. Beth knew Hitch had been read in on this mission. No one else was within earshot.

"I'm given to understand that I've attracted the attention of an Egyptian woman with some information we'd like to obtain. Rasha Metwally?"

This was business as usual for Hitch. He dabbed his napkin at a coffee stain on his belly.

"Yes. That's the woman. I've memorized her file. We first took notice of her when she was a page for the Egyptian government back when you were here, in the late '80s, I believe."

Beth swallowed a bite of banana.

"Yes. That's my recollection. She delivered Classified documents for the Ambassador's attention."

"Indeed. That would be her. Do you recall anything else about her from that time?"

Beth rubbed her forehead.

"Not much, really. My cover job at the Embassy while I was code-cracking in the back room, was as a page and document clerk. Frequently, Rasha would hand off her documents on my signature. She seemed polite, smiled a lot, and was patient while she awaited a response. I may have fetched her water or a snack when she had a long wait. I was pretty diligent at the time about making a good impression for the U.S. in Egypt. I may have done a few little things for Rasha, but mainly I kept to my own business."

"Yes, well, others with greater influence might have benefitted from following your example. By that time, we'd managed passable relations with President Mubarak, who was favorably inclined to the money coming from the U.S. owing to Egypt's official recognition of Israel at Camp David. Recognizing Israel was a disaster in Egypt, not only for President Sadat, who met up with an assassin shortly afterward, but for the Egyptian people, who believed their government had betrayed them to their greatest enemy. The U.S. role in brokering that deal, and subsequent support for Israel, chilled popular Egyptian sentiment toward us considerably. In fact, for several years after Camp David, it was unsafe for Embassy personnel to walk the streets of Cairo without Egyptian escort.

"But I'm sure you don't require a history lesson."

Beth was well acquainted with the history of Egyptian-Israeli-U.S. relations since Camp David. Egypt, Israel, and even Jordan had made out handsomely with what amounted to a U.S. "peace-bribe." But in Egypt, Mubarak and the military were the primary beneficiaries. Egyptian citizens saw no "trickle down" effect of those billions in U.S.-Egyptian "aid." Since Mubarak had gotten what he wanted, Egypt's government applied little effort, and even less financial support, to growing the domestic economy, the result of which was that Egypt's people languished in relative squalor, with government apathy sapping all hope of bettering their lot in life.

"No. I think I've got a pretty good understanding of where relations are now and how they got there. Please go on about Rasha."

"Yes. I apologize. I talk far too much. Must be the diplomat in me." He chuckled.

"Anyway . . . getting back to Rasha and your assignment . . . whatever relationship you and she developed those many years ago, she either values it today, and has trust in you, or – pardon the implication – she sees you as an opportunity to plant disinformation within the U.S. intelligence community."

Beth savored a bite of an Egyptian-grown strawberry while considering the possibilities.

"Who did Rasha contact when she asked for me?"

"Good question. Her present employ is with GIS, the Egyptian intelligence folks . . ."

"Yes, I'm familiar."

"Ah. Of course, you would be. My apologies. I am remiss in neglecting your affiliations. In any case, according to our sources, Ms. Metwally holds an administrative assistant position in the GIS. We're not sure who her bosses are or whether her job is relevant, though the latter certainly seems likely."

"Agreed. And . . . the manner of her contact with us?" Beth found Hitch pleasant enough, but the man took forever to get to the point.

"Yes. She . . . or at least, *allegedly* Rasha . . . authored an encrypted communication dispensed from GIS HQ and directed to one 'Silver Star.' The message contained several verses from the Quran, and the following note, all in Arabic, of course:"

He recited from memory:

I must speak with Elizabeth Weston concerning a matter of urgency to our countries.

"The encryption was one used commonly by GIS, and of course, we decrypted it."

Beth pondered a for moment.

"Do we know who Silver Star is?"

"Not a clue. And we were not able to confirm receipt of the message at any location, which is exceedingly odd. But there I go, preaching to the choir again."

It was odd that the message appeared to have no recipient . . . as if Rasha had just put it "out there" for someone to find. Then again, since she didn't know an appropriate recipient, perhaps this delivery method was eminently sensible.

"She didn't say how we should respond?"

"No. But that didn't keep us from trying, of course. We attempted to contact her by phone using anonymous Blackberrys. We posted a message for Silver Star to contact one of our blind FaceBook identities. We even tried a newspaper personal ad seeking 'Silver Star' in several Cairo newspapers, in Arabic of course."

That pretty much covered the basics.

"Have you back-fed a message to the original message source yet?"

"No. Of course, we considered doing so. But with such an approach comes a risk of discovery, which we elected to delay until we knew whether you were available."

Beth thought postponing this communication tactic had been a wise decision. Incoming electronic traffic would be monitored by the GIS.

"Okay," Beth said. "Please cease all other attempts to contact Rasha and I will initiate the connection. Is that acceptable?"

"Of course. But how do you plan to do it?"

"I'm not exactly sure just yet. But I'll figure it out."

"You come highly recommended for this mission, Elizabeth. I shall pursue a totally alien path for a bureaucrat and allow you to proceed as you see fit. You may contact me once you have engaged the subject."

Beth was more than a little surprised to have been given free rein to make the contact.

"Thank you, Hitch."

"My pleasure. Make me proud." He smiled broadly.

"I'll do my best toward that end. Now . . . may I ask how I go about getting hi-level encrypted communications in my room, and a thorough bug sweep as well?"

"Both are in process, my dear. I may talk a lot, but I am also a man of action." He postured with hands on hips and shoulders back.

Beth laughed.

"I bet you've got super hero tights on under the disheveled diplomat outfit."

Hitch let out the air he'd been holding in with a "Ha!"

"So you spotted my disguise. But of course you would, wouldn't you. You *are* good, Ms. Weston, very good. I shall have to keep an eye on you. Perhaps I can learn something."

Both arose from the table.

"I'm already learning from you, Hitch. And my sincerest thank you for the quick work on my room."

"Nothing you wouldn't have done in my place. Do have a pleasant stay in Cairo, and I shall see you when I see you."

A quick handshake and Hitch was gone.

Beth reminded herself how many spooks work in diplomatic missions around the world. There may yet be more layers to the seemingly obvious Mr. Hitchens. He was almost certainly with the CIA, after all.

CHAPTER 16

At the GIS office building. Cairo. Three months ago.

GIS Director, Murad Muwafi wanted an update on the Aurora project. It had been nine months since Commander Saed had promised completion within one year. Of course, he had seen the progress reports. But they were written by the scientists, and he knew their content might be optimistic. So he had called Saed back to his office for a first hand update.

There was a knock on the Director's door.

"Come in, Commander. I have been expecting you."

The door opened and Saed entered, closing it behind him.

"Good Day, Mr. Director."

The GIS Director remained behind his large wooden desk, but did not offer the Commander a chair. The Commander remained standing, not at attention, but hardly at rest either.

"The Aurora reports look promising, Saed. But you and I both know that these scientists have a propensity to exaggerate progress on an assignment of this nature. You are in charge of Aurora. What is your assessment? Will Aurora fly in three months' time?"

The Commander felt the weight of the Director's words. This was *his* project. If it failed, he would be the scapegoat. But if somehow the scientists could make Aurora fly, the accolades would fall to the Director. His own name would not earn so much as a footnote on the report to the SCAF.

"As you have said, Mr. Director, that is what the scientists tell me. I can see the frame of the aircraft, and it is impressive, indeed. But I have no independent means to assess progress of interior components, electronics, hydraulics, or other technical aspects of the construction. I must rely upon the engineers and scientists for that information."

The Director frowned.

"And you deem such reliance prudent, Saed? If I were you . . ." The Director's voice deepened. ". . . I would find a way to *verify* this data."

"Yes, of course, Mr. Director. May I engage a separate team of scientists to examine the work of those already included in Aurora's secrecy?"

"Saed. We have discussed this subject before. As you well know, more eyes mean more mouths. I will not risk compromising the integrity of the project by introducing additional opportunities for exposure of our prize. The last thing we need is the Americans to learn of our undertaking. One cruise missile from the Mediterranean and our plan has come to naught.

"No Saed. I will not authorize the risk. You must verify with your current personnel."

The Commander had anticipated the Director's response, but knew he'd had to make the request . . . for his own records.

"Then I shall make due with the resources allowed, Mr. Director."

Saed prepared to leave.

"We have a new matter to be discussed, Saed. A matter of utmost importance and urgency."

"How may I be of service, Director?"

"The Senator who provided us with the Aurora plans has gotten himself into trouble of late. According to our sources, in the part month, the Senator has suffered no less than two attempts on his life. His security thwarted both assailants and the American press does not seem to have picked up on the stories. So it appears he has been successful in covering them up . . . at least for now. But his erratic behavior concerns me, Saed."

"I understand, Director. If his behaviors are exposed in public, he may lose his seat of power and then have little reason to keep the existence of our project to himself."

"Precisely, Saed. He poses a grave danger to Aurora . . . a danger we must address with all diligence. He must de silenced, Saed. Do you understand?"

"Do you not fear that an assassination of a United States Senator might draw unfavorable attention to Egypt and the Intelligence Directorate?"

"That is why we shall employ an independent contractor to perform this service. I have had rare occasion to use such talent before. Although I have not been in touch with the man for several years, I believe with some diligence, you can locate him for me."

"If that is your wish, Director, then that is my command. I shall locate this assassin. Will you provide me information from past contacts?"

"I shall provide what you need to begin your search. The man calls himself, The Raptor. The name is dramatic, but no more so than his results. You will find him for me and then I will eliminate Senator Grossman."

"Yes, Director."

"You have your assignments. You are dismissed, Commander." The Director opened a manila file on his desk and began reading.

"Yes, Director. Good day, Sir." The Director shooed Saed away without looking up. The Commander spun 180 degrees on his boot heel, and left.

* * *

"I'm tired of your blanket assurances," the Commander said to the three scientists. "Show me which parts of this aircraft are presently operable."

The three men in white lab coats exchanged long looks between themselves.

Finally, Hamadi, the eldest and most experienced, responded to the Commander's request.

"Please follow me to the hangar floor, Commander. I will show you what I am able. But I caution you that your expectations of visible progress should not be too high. Most aircraft components will be made operational when the electronics have been installed, and that will not be for several weeks, at least."

The Commander was unimpressed with excuses.

"Just show me something, Hamadi. I want to see tangible progress. Now."

"Yes, Commander. Please follow."

The foursome made their way past computer clean rooms, and electronics testing laboratories, down the long, steel-grid staircase to the hangar floor.

The Commander could not help being impressed by the scale of this aircraft – 30 meters from nose to tail, and at least 20 meters across the rear edge of the elegantly aerodynamic delta wing. Aurora hung suspended by cables from the hangar ceiling with the help of three, powerful overhead cranes.

As they walked beneath the wing, the Commander was again awed by the size of Aurora's rectangular engine cavities, but dismayed when he climbed a ladder and saw no engines inside.

"Are there not even engines, Hamadi! Only these shells?"

"The engines are complete, Commander. The combustion chambers contain no moving parts."

The Commander appeared doubtful.

"Explain it to me. How is this possible?"

Hamadi realized for the first time how advanced this technology was beyond anything the Commander had experienced with fighter jets and bombers.

"Sir. If the engines had moving parts, the airflow at Mach 20 would rip them from the fuselage. At hypersonic speeds – those in excess of Mach 5, that is, five times the speed of sound – the compression of the air as it enters the front of the engine cavity, and constricts to the slightly smaller rear, creates enough heat by itself to burn the fuel."

Hamadi could tell that the Commander had not understood.

"Sir. It is like a diesel engine. You know how these work, yes?"

"Of course, but I am no fool. This is nothing like a diesel engine."

"Please allow me to explain, Sir."

The Commander nodded his assent. His expression remained

skeptical.

"In a diesel engine, air and fuel enter a chamber where a piston compresses the gas mixture until it becomes so hot the oxygen and diesel fuel combine to cause an explosion. Yes?"

He waited to be sure the Commander still followed his train of thought.

"It is the same with Aurora. The fuel flows into the combustion chambers – the engine cavities. But because the airspeed is so great at incredibly high speed, the compression as it passes through the narrowing engine cavity causes the plane's methane fuel to ignite." He paused again to search for comprehension in the Commander's eyes.

The Commander held his hand to his chin.

"Proceed."

"But this combustion is different than a diesel engine because it does not require repeated compression and explosion. The compression, and therefore, the combustion, are constant. The engine burns its fuel in a single, continuing explosion . . . an explosion that propels the craft forward at incredible speeds, far faster than any normal jet aircraft could withstand.

"Do you now see, Commander?"

"You are saying that Aurora's propulsion will only operate at unimaginable air speeds. How do you plan to accelerate Aurora sufficiently to run these unique engines?"

"Commander. Sir. Acceleration is a two stage process. Solid rocket boosters will aid the takeoff. These will be attached beneath the wings and will be released when they have done their work.

"The rockets will accelerate Aurora to a speed in excess of Mach 1, at which time the pilot will engage the pulse jet propulsion system. The pulse jets are also located within the hollow engine cavities. Unlike the scramjets which will operate only at speeds in excess of Mach 5, the pulse jets can become functional at Mach 1, or even slightly slower speeds."

"And where are these so called pulse jets? As I have seen, the engines are empty. Do you think me a fool?"

Hamadi's frustration at the Commander's lack of

comprehension was building, though he would not let his irritation show.

"Sir. The pulse engines operate like gasoline motors within the engine cavities. Pumps inside the wings inject fuel into the combustion chambers where spark generators embedded in the engine walls ignite the fuel/air mixture. The ignition cycle is very rapid – many explosions per second. The aerodynamics of the engine cavity at Mach 1 force the fuel explosions out the rear of the engines, providing forward thrust to the aircraft. The pulse jets will bring Aurora to the Mach 5 speed required to engage the scramjets for primary propulsion."

The Commander remained incredulous.

"To launch this craft you require rockets, then a switch to one type of propulsion – pulse jets? – followed by yet another power change to the scramjet engines? And both pulse jet and scramjet thrust is dependent upon these empty engine chambers? Am I hearing you correctly, Hamadi?"

"That is correct, Sir. I realize it all sounds very complex. But I do not know how to explain it more simply."

The concepts of pulse jet and scramjet propulsion remained unfamiliar to the Commander. But then, he supposed, these peculiar engines were one reason Aurora was so unique . . . and so valuable.

"Very well, Hamadi. I accept your explanation. Can we test an engine now so I may see how it works?"

Hamadi drew a deep breath and exhaled.

"Sir. To fire even the pulse jets, we would need to inject a steady stream of air into the engine housing at the speed of sound. We possess no technology that would allow us to do this. It can only be tested in flight. If we fired the pulse jets now, fire would erupt from both the front and rear of the engine cavities with unpredictable results."

The Commander drew a deep breath.

"Well, what then *can* you show me that actually operates?"

Hamadi moved tentatively to a control panel connected to Aurora with a thick umbilical of electrical wiring. He slid one of the control gliders forward. The sound of hydraulic machinery in motion filled the hangar.

Presently, the covers for the landing gear began to swing open, coming to rest at a fully flexed angle, ninety degrees to the wing and body surfaces. With a further command from the control panel, the landing gear hydraulics kicked in, lowering the wheels until they clicked into a fully locked position.

Hamadi turned to the Commander.

"You see how well the landing mechanism operates," he said with as much confidence as he could muster.

"That is all you can show me? The plane has wheels?"

"I'm afraid, Sir, this is all the physical progress we can demonstrate – except, of course, you can see that the frame of the plane itself is nearly complete."

Hamadi held his breath.

The Commander sighed. Neither the description of how the engines would operate, nor the fact that the landing gear appeared to function, provided him with any assurance that the project was on schedule. But he could think of nothing further to resolve his predicament.

"Hamadi. You realize the consequences if Aurora fails to fly on schedule?"

"I am well aware, Sir."

"And to your families as well?" He looked down the line of scientists.

"We all understand, Sir. Aurora *will be ready* on schedule. I promise you."

The Commander eyed each of the three scientists in turn.

"Then I encourage you to redouble your efforts to ensure timely completion."

With that, the Commander turned and left the scientists alone beside Aurora. They remained silent and motionless until he had disappeared from sight.

One of the other scientists turned to Hamadi, panic in his eyes.

"What are we to do, Hamadi? You know this assignment is impossible."

"Continue to pray, my friends. If there is a deliverance for us, it will be from Almighty Allah."

"Amen."

CHAPTER 17

The red 1960 Jeep CJ-3B zigzagged its way up the Caribbean slope of Venezuela's *Serranía del Litoral* mountains, its rugged tires clinging impossibly to the steep dirt tracks of what could hardly be called a roadway. The distance from the city below to this secluded retreat was a mere two kilometers, but the ascent would take the man in the Jeep nearly an hour.

The driver was a smallish but sinewy man of Caucasian descent, though his dark hair, ruddy brown skin, and coffee-colored eyes would allow him to blend in among Hispanics and Arabs as well as he had among his fellow Texans. He perspired freely with the exertion of keeping the aging Jeep true on the rustic path as it wound its way through the jungle humidity.

Nearing the end of the climb, the afternoon sun revealed a small but well-appointed villa peeking through the tropical foliage. This was "The Raptor's Nest." The sniper had chosen its name to match his clandestine identity as a high-priced gun for hire.

With his vehicle parked alongside the house, The Raptor walked behind the Jeep, reached over the spare rear wheel, and withdrew a grey, steel and rubber cargo case from the back. The package contained his most beloved possession – a .408 caliber CheyTac M200 Intervention Long Range Rifle System (LRRS).

To call this machine a mere rifle was a significant slap in the face to its artistic developers. The LRRS included a CheyTac tactical computer, a Nightforce NXS 5.5-22X scope, and Kestrel 4000 wind, temperature, and atmospheric pressure sensors. In short, it was a sniper's wet dream, developed under secret contract with the United States Military, and capable of successful soft target (personnel) shots at ranges exceeding 2,000 meters.

With baggage in hand, he nudged the building's unlocked screen door open with a foot and slipped inside.

After allowing his eyes to adjust to the interior dimness, he placed the cargo carrier containing his rifle on the dark wooden table, and patted the case lightly on top with one hand.

"We made it home agin, Angel. Home, sweet home."

In the kitchen, the Westinghouse offered a selection of several dozen long-necked brown bottles – all of them Lone Star Beer. Allowing the fridge door to slam shut behind him, he cracked open one of the bottles on his belt buckle and took a slug.

After traveling the long and circuitous route necessary for his undetected return from the Dominican Republic, The Raptor was bushed. Entering the main room, he kicked off his scuffed cowboy boots and dropped onto the sofa – a southwestern job with an apache wool blanket draped over its back.

"Sure is good to be home."

*   *   *

As he reclined on the couch, dozing with his Stetson pulled down over his eyes and a beer bottle dangling from one hand, he became aware of a low tone emanating from the stack of army surplus electronics piled in one corner. He squinted, then shook his eyes open, sending the Stetson flopping to the floor.

Awake!

The tone grew louder, and would continue to do so, he knew, until he responded to it. Frankly, he wasn't in the mood. Another beer, maybe a sandwich, and then rack time – that's what he'd had in mind. He could turn it off if he wanted to, but elected to accept the communication, nevertheless.

Rolling off the couch and approaching the "communications center," he slapped a pressure switch on the desktop . . . and the tone stopped. Still pinching sleep from his blurry eyes, a callused hand pulled out the wooden desk chair so he could sit. Almost fully awake now, he straightened himself in the chair and flipped open the army-green laptop. He typed in the password, then waited.

"Incoming TelSat Message," the screen blinked.

He spoke over one shoulder toward his rifle.

"Looks like our services are in demand, Angel. Sit tight and I'll take a looksee whether we're inter'sted."

The screen continued to blink out its message.

He looked again at the grey cargo box on the table.

"Sit tight. Be patient. Sometimes she takes awhile."

Finally, the decrypted email text appeared on the laptop screen.

R,

Senator Elbert Grossman. Red Wing, Minnesota. Saturday, November 5.
$250,000 Euros.
Respond ASAP.

Job

"Well it certainly is our month for the Egyptians, ain't it, Angel. But I don't think we're likely to go huntin' fer a lousy quarter mil of anything . . . and sure as hell not Euros. What would I do with Euros?"

He turned to the grey box as if expecting a response.

"You, too, huh? Okay. Let's see whether they'll make it worth our while."

The Raptor turned to the laptop and tapped out:

$1,000,000 US. <Enter>
Half now to usual account. Half after.<Enter>
Respond 24 hours. <Enter>
<Send>

"Now we wait an' see, huh, Angel. Let's eat while we're waitin'."

He got up and went to the kitchen to make a sandwich.

* * *

Two hours later, The Raptor was watching CNN via satellite and about to turn in when the tone hummed again.

"Well, well, Angel. Looks like we got an answer already. I'll check it out. You jus' sit tight."

After logging into the laptop, and allowing the message to decrypt, he read:

R,

Agreed.
Sending $500,000 US tomorrow.
Remainder on completion.

Job

The Raptor leaned back in his wooden chair.
"Well . . . ain't that nice!"

CHAPTER 18

At the U.S. Embassy. Cairo.

When Beth returned to her room, she found everything Hitch had promised had been done. The usual stack of encryption/decryption hardware accompanied the laptop dock on a newly arrived work desk. A note on the desktop attested to the fact that the room had been confirmed by Embassy Security to be 100% surveillance free.

When Beth checked behind the drawn curtains, she found an additional layer of plexiglas had been added on the inside to prevent any possible sonic surveillance of window vibrations.

The security folks here had been thorough, and unbelievably prompt, particularly for government employees. Beth guessed that her mission carried a high enough priority designation to warrant the expeditious service. She'd better get to work.

After docking her laptop with the high security encryption electronics, she pulled up a Word document containing further details of Rasha's attempt to contact her. After a quick review of the document's contents, she navigated to the password page for Rasha's encrypted files and entered her memorized, twenty-six digit, alpha-numeric password.

After a moment, the file listing appeared on the screen.

Surveying file names, she selected one entitled "Technical Aspects of Initial Contact," and clicked it open. She studied the information. For the most part, Hitchens had been correct in his brief analysis of the message to "Silver Star." But Rasha was definitely *not* a mere assistant. She would have to possess advanced programming skills in order to send the transmission in this precise manner. The fact that Rasha possessed additional computer knowledge gave Beth an idea.

She knew Hitchens had granted her authority to proceed without his approval. But in this case, she wanted him onboard. She planned to send a message directly to Rasha's computer at GIS – a strategy her counterparts had thus far elected not to pursue.

She rang Hitchens up on his cell.

"Ready for another chat already, Elizabeth? You do work fast."

"I plan to ping Rasha's computer at GIS, Hitch. I just wanted you to know before I did so."

Hitchens' end of the line went quiet.

"You have considered other reasonable options, I presume?"

"No . . . you did. Your people have covered all the safe advances. This is the one avenue that remains, short of kidnapping her on the street. But I think I can message her in such a way that her superiors won't detect it, and if they do, they will disregard it as chipset static. May I proceed?"

Hitchens paused again before answering.

"Yes. Proceed."

"Thank you. I'll be back in touch when I connect with Rasha."

"You have great confidence in your strategy, Elizabeth."

"Yes, Hitch . . . and so do you. Let's hope our confidence is well placed."

"Indeed, Elizabeth. Indeed. *Ciao!*"

"*Ciao.*"

Having received oral approval, although unprovable should she be called to account, Beth elected nevertheless to move forward with all haste. It had already been several days since the contact, and she didn't want Rasha to give up hope of making a connection.

Using a software program of her own design, Beth assembled a series of data packets – essentially parcels of digital information – which Rasha could reassemble into a single message after receipt. Since all information in and out of networked computers travels in similar packets, any security screen or firewall would notice nothing unusual about these, apparently random, minuscule chunks of information headed for Rasha's computer. The fact that Beth intended to send the data packets separately, as opposed to combining them into a single message, significantly enhanced their chances of passing through network security unnoticed.

Once the packets had arrived at Rasha's computer, the final packet would place a tiny silver star in the lower corner of her computer screen. It wouldn't be larger than a quarter inch from tip to tip. But if Rasha spent a lot of time at her computer, it would catch her attention immediately.

If Rasha or anyone else at her end clicked to open the star icon, the words *"Do you want to play Silver Star? Y or N"* would appear on the screen. A "Y" response would take the user to an inactive website apologizing that Silver Star was no longer available. An "N" response would minimize the star icon again.

Beth's hope was that the name Silver Star would prompt Rasha to pursue the message contents using all tools at her disposal. She would know that a game bearing that name could not be a coincidence. If she eventually got around to running the algorithm she'd employed to encode her initial message, the program would assemble the data packets, and her screen would read as follows:

Silver Star,

Call Elizabeth at 20-76-5559200.

The number was that of an anonymous Egyptian cell phone the CIA had provided for Beth's use while in Cairo. Any call to this number could not be traced.

After performing a "test send" by transmitting the data packets to her own computer to confirm the program worked as designed, she typed in the code to contact Rasha's computer, and following a deep breath, she pressed *<Enter>*.

Now she would wait.

*   *   *

It had been four hours since Beth's digital invasion into GIS Headquarters. She'd filled the time unpacking and ironing clothes, steaming suits, and checking her cell phone frequently to make sure it was functioning properly.

There still had been no contact from Rasha.

Time passed at the speed of a root canal. Beth occupied herself by making the rounds at the Embassy, introducing herself to various Embassy personnel. During her last stint here, she'd known everyone. She'd also known who were the spies and who were the diplomats . . . and who were both. None of the faces here was familiar today, save Tara's. Beth spent extra time making sure Tara knew she was valued at the Embassy . . . an affirmation Beth didn't expect Tara heard often.

As day turned to dusk and then to night, Beth became impatient. Even though she knew Rasha probably wouldn't be able to work on the decryption while her bosses were around, and even though she was fully aware that her message might be beyond Rasha's technical ability to assemble and comprehend, Beth still spent an inordinate amount of time pacing her room, willing the cell phone to ring.

At 10:00 p.m. Cairo time, Beth sent her husband a short satellite message:

Having a jolly good time. Wish you were here. :-)

Brief contact once a day was all prudence would allow her and her husband to make. They'd worked for years to establish their cover in Red Wing. She wasn't going to let contacts from Egypt destroy their anonymity. But the daily check-in would allow James to sleep better at night, knowing she was safe – so these cryptic messages were worth the risk.

Beth began preparing for bed, and most likely, another long day of waiting tomorrow. Just as she was turning down the sheets and about to crawl into bed, the cell phone rang. She wasn't sure what the sound was at first. The ringtone echoed like wind chimes in the distance, but grew louder by the moment.

I should have set the ringer myself so I at least knew what it sounded like. You're rusty, Beth.

Having determined the source of the chimes, she lunged for the cell phone, which lay atop the stand on the far side of the bed. Gaining control of the phone, she answered the call.

"This is Elizabeth."

"Can we meet?"

The voice was a woman's. It might have been Rasha, but it was hard to say for certain after so much time had passed.

"Yes. Yes, of course. You say when and where."

"There is a café on Talaat Harb Square called Groppi. Do you know it?"

"Yes. I've been there many times."

"Meet me at Groppi at 3:00 tomorrow afternoon."

"Three o'clock at Groppi. Got it!"

The phone clicked off.

Beth stared at her handset. The caller was listed as "Unknown." That was no surprise, of course. But the word served to emphasize Beth's present circumstances – she was an unknown person, in an unfamiliar land, planning to meet a woman whose identity was uncertain, to receive information, the subject of which was obscure at best.

Beth suddenly felt very much alone. Unknowns surrounded her, engulfed her, and now reached out to her on the phone as well.

Clarity would come, Beth knew, but only with time. Tomorrow she would begin killing off the unknowns, starting at Groppi's Café. The thought of standing on the brink of progress buoyed Beth's spirits. But there was nothing to be done right now . . . nothing, that is, except to get a good night's sleep.

CHAPTER 19

Back in Red Wing.

I received Beth's message at about 2:00 o'clock this afternoon. The message meant all was well, and for that, I was grateful. She had arrived safely eight time zones away. Only two days had passed, but I missed her already. I would have liked to contact her, but CIA protocol did not allow me a return message.

The protocol thing alone wouldn't have kept me from messaging Beth. I'm not a rule follower in the best of times. And I could have found a way to contact her safely. But as things stood, I had no way to find out where I might reach her . . . short of knocking on the Cairo Embassy door. I had learned long ago that, too often, bureaucracy triumphs by virtue of its inertia and impenetrability. My time would be better spent jousting at windmills than wading through institutional mire.

And thinking of windmills . . . Gunner's security project came to mind. He'd told me not to call. I didn't remember him telling me not to visit. So I hopped in the Pilot, drove the grueling six blocks to the Law Enforcement Center, and presented myself to the uniformed receptionist.

"James Becker to see Chief Deputy Gunderson, please. I believe he's expecting me."

I smiled.

"The Chief Deputy's not in his office right now, Mr. Becker. If he's expecting you, you're at the wrong place."

I scrunched up my face in abject confusion.

"I coulda sworn he said to meet at the LEC."

I assumed a thinker pose with one hand on my chin, adding additional puzzlement and confusion to my expression.

I guess I gained enough sympathy from the receptionist, because she said, "Just hold on a sec. I'll ring him up for you."

She punched up what I assumed was Gunner's cell number on the desk console.

"Chief Deputy? I got Mr. Becker here says he was supposed to meet you." A pause. "Uh huh. Uh huh."

She raised an eyebrow at me.

"I see. Certainly. Right away." She hung up the phone.

"So where can I find the Chief Deputy my good woman."

"He says he doesn't remember scheduling a meeting with you, Mr. Becker."

I needed to respond.

"Hmm," I said.

"But it seems like it's your lucky day, 'cause he says you can find him down at the St. James, scoping out the place with some out-of-towners."

"Thank you very much, Madam. You're an absolute peach."

Her expression didn't look as though she'd been shooting for "peachy."

Time to depart. I doffed my imaginary fedora in her direction and let myself out.

Two minutes later I was at the St. James Hotel, a city landmark since the days when Red Wing was the largest grain port in the world. Back then, it was a working man's hotel. Small rooms. Shared baths. Full breakfast included.

In the 1970s, the Red Wing Shoe Company had bought the hotel and embarked on a multimillion dollar restoration and renovation project. Small rooms were combined into suites. All rooms now boasted deluxe baths and showers complete with antique fixtures. The St. James was no longer a flop house for transient workers, but a hub for business meetings, small conventions, and weekend getaways for those special occasions.

My guess was that Gunner's "dignitary" would be visiting the St. James and the "foreigners" were the Congress-person's security detail.

I parked the Pilot in an open spot on the street out front, entered through the hotel's massive wooden main doors, and strode across the lobby to Hotel Reception.

"How may I help you, Sir?"

"I'm looking for Chief Deputy Gunderson. Have you seen him around?"

"I believe he's with some gentlemen on the fifth floor, Sir. Do you need directions?"

"Nope, I'm good. Thanks."

I scooted around the perimeter of the hotel's interior boutique mall to the main elevators. A minute's ride later, I stepped out into the fifth level corridor.

Since the fifth floor was devoted entirely to banquets, pub goers, and wedding receptions, the place was deserted, except for the male voices emanating from the main banquet room – also known as, The Summit. I headed in the direction of the voices.

Entering the Summit, I saw Gunner listening intently to one of three black-suited gentlemen with shiny Italian shoes. They were standing next to the floor-to-ceiling windowed wall that spanned the far side of the banquet hall, opening the room's occupants to vistas of the Mississippi River valley below.

There was a reason the architects had designed this wall of glass. The panoramic view included everything from the city's river front parks, to the winding main channel of the Mississippi, to the 1963-vintage Dwight D. Eisenhower expansion bridge connecting the great state of Minnesota with its neighbor to the east – and if one peered far enough upstream – to the haunting silhouette of the reactor containment structures at the Prairie River Nuclear Power Generating Station.

Gunner hadn't spotted me yet. Before he knew it, I was standing beside him – a part of the semi-circle of security professionals.

Gunner noticed me when the black suit who'd been speaking moved his eyes from Gunner's to mine and back again.

"Who's this?"

It seemed to me a reasonable question.

Gunner turned so only I could see his face and whispered something like "What the hell?"

I smiled.

I stepped toward Suit Number 1 and offered up a shake.

"James Becker, Attorney at Law," I said in an unusually loud voice.

The man gave my hand a firm, but not so friendly, reception.

"Why are you shouting?"

"Oh. Well . . . I wasn't sure whether you were protecting someone right now, or going deaf." I tapped my right ear.

He jerked out his earpiece.

"I hear fine. Thank you."

He looked again at Gunner.

"He's part of my local security team," he managed, with more *savoir faire* than I'd anticipated. "Just pretend he's not here, and let's continue."

Gunner had handled the situation adroitly. And his advice was sound, although pretending that I wasn't present would not be an easy thing to do.

"Okay," Suit Number 1 said. I still wasn't sure if Numbers 2 and 3 could talk. "There's too much territory out there to exclude a sniper from this direction. We've got to cover some of these windows."

"If we only cover some of the windows, do you think the Senator'll be able to avoid appreciating the remaining view with his constituents?" Gunner asked. "I don't know the Senator personally, but lots of pols tend to go where they want once they're off the leash."

Gunner sounded darned professional.

Suit 1 considered Gunner's observation.

"You're probably right. He'll mingle his ass right out to the view, regardless of how much we cover. Can we install bullet proof glass before he gets here?"

It was all I could do to stifle a laugh.

"How thick'd that have to be to stop a sniper round?" Gunner asked politely. I figured he had a pretty good idea.

"Probably four inches, give or take."

"You could sure ask the hotel," Gunner said, "but I doubt their high class restoration is gonna allow for you to put four inch thick glass in here . . . sure as hell not by Saturday."

"Then I suppose we'll have to cover all these windows with something . . ."

"Like campaign posters?" I interrupted.

Suit number 1 looked like he was considering my suggestion.

"The Senator would probably like that. But I was thinking maybe something else, like maybe cloth-covered boards that fit the window frames."

"Or . . . ," I said, "how about some sort of fabric that could somehow be suspended between the windows and the room? Like hanging down from above. Oh yeah . . . like . . .like . . . curtains."

Suit number 1 gave me the hairy eyeball.

"But I bet the Senator didn't pick this venue for its spectacular enclosed atmosphere," I went on. "I doubt he's going to let you cover all the windows and ruin the pretty view. But then . . . that's just me thinking out loud."

Suit 1 looked annoyed, but apparently agreed with my line of thought.

"So I guess we tell the Senator about the risks of these windows and a sniper bullet, and let him make the call. I can't see any way to protect against that attack avenue unless we cover these damn windows."

All three suits continued to stare at the window frames, apparently at a loss for a solution.

Gunner dared a suggestion.

"I know you guys are the security experts and all, but I was just sorta thinking . . . how about we put up one way mirror film?" Gunner tucked a thumb in one pocket and shifted his weight to project confidence.

He didn't do too bad a job of it either.

Suit 1 looked at Gunner like he'd just hopped off the bus from Hicksville. Seeing Suit 1's expression, Suits 2 and 3 joined in. Monkey see monkey do.

"Gunner, that's genius," I said. "You could coat the glass with some of that hi-tech reflective film. Hell, you could stick it right on the inside here. From the outside, the whole fifth floor would look like a mirror. I'm sure it's not something the hotel would want for its exterior appeal in the long run, but we could rip it down as soon as the Senator's gone.

"Helluva good idea, Gunner."

Suit 1 made a face like he'd just stepped in a pile of something yucky.

Then Gunner chimed in.

"You know, maybe it's just something to mention to the Senator ... since he's so security conscious and all. I bet we could probably line you guys up with summa that mirror stuff in time for Saturday."

Gunner glanced at me. I nodded.

Suit 1 tried not to look interested in the film idea.

"Give us a minute please."

The three black suits took a stroll along the glass wall to a private corner.

"Nice one, Gunner. Where'd you come up with the one way film idea?"

"I didn't just fall off the potato truck, you know. Besides, I knew the view would be a security issue, so I Googled it."

"Well done." Gunner valued preparedness as much as I did. A person had to respect that. At least *this* person did.

The suit squad was on its way back, apparently having made a decision in the huddle.

"Thanks for your suggestion. We've talked it over, and we're not so sure the light will be right for that sort of thing to work. That's why I didn't mention it in the first place."

The man needed to trade in his Italian loafers for something more appropriate to the barnyard terrain he was cultivating.

"So we appreciate your touring us around town and through the hotel. But don't go ordering any reflective film. We've got the security planning covered from here. We'll just need some of your guys to stand around during the Senator's visit. Sort of a show of local cooperation. We'll let you know when and where."

Gunner was working up a good lather, but he managed a

tempered response.

"Okay, Fellas. You're in charge. But we haven't even talked about how we get him inside the hotel yet. I was thinking his car could pull right into the hotel's covered ramp. He'd be easy to cover in there."

"I appreciate your concern. And of course, we'll take your suggestion under advisement. But I really believe we've gotten all the local input we need for today." He shot an eye dart my way. "We'll check out the exterior and make sure we've got everything covered.

"Thanks again, Deputy Gunnerman."

I put my hand on Gunner's shoulder, hoping he'd let that one pass, which he did.

"Well then," Gunner said with a shrug, "I guess my work here is done. You fellas enjoy our pretty little shit-kicking town. Ya'll come back now, ya hear?"

Before the suits could respond, Gunner was headed for the elevators. I was close on his heels.

On the ride down to first floor, Gunner shared a few choice expletives about his role in this security detail.

"I hate to tell you this, Gunner, but it wouldn't matter if you were J. Edgar Hoover, those guys have been determined to run the show from day one. They're hacks! Big shoulders. Big Guns. Big egos. Small brains."

Gunner choked on a laugh.

"In all truth, Gunner, this security planning is almost always unnecessary. I can't remember anyone killing a Congressman – except maybe his wife."

Gunner chuckled.

"But you've still gotta take your role in this seriously. Make sure you cover your ass with these guys. If the Senator's in any real danger, they'll futz it up if it's at all possible. And it's always possible. If the crap hits the fan, you can bet it'll blow on you."

"You think I don't know that? But they won't let me control anything. You got any suggestions . . . I'm all ears."

"Write up your own security plan and make sure you submit it to those private security guys, the Senator's Office, the FBI, the Sheriff, and every other place you can think of. If you suggested something that would have prevented a theoretical injury to the Senator, you've done what you could. And, most importantly, your ass is covered."

We reached the Floor 1 and exited the elevator into the mall.

"I sure as hell am glad I'm not a cop in Washington. Dealing with all this CYA political BS would drive me nuts."

"It should. It drives all the good law enforcement folks in D.C. crazy, too. I can vouch for that."

We faced each other.

"I'm gonna take your CYA suggestion, Beck. And who knows, maybe somebody'll actually take me up on some part of my security plan. Stranger things have happened."

"You just keep hoping, Gunner. And in the meantime, make sure your backside is covered with Kevlar."

Gunner laughed.

"Honestly, thanks for your help, Beck. I think I got it from here."

"Follow your instincts on that plan and you'll do just great.

"By the way, it used to just be a Congressman that was coming to visit. Now it's a Senator. And I heard the word 'constituents.' Is it Grossman?"

"Yup. It'll be in the paper and on the news tomorrow. He'll be here Saturday for a lunch address at the hotel . . . but then you already knew where, huh."

"You'd think if somebody wanted to get rid of that good old boy, they'd of done it years ago. He's probably safe."

Gunner turned toward the exit with a wave in my direction.

"I'm sure I'll be seeing you around."

"Probably a good bet. Ya'll come back now, ya hear."

I heard Gunner's laugh as he turned the corner toward the door.

CHAPTER 20

Downtown Cairo.

It was a sunny, early November afternoon. The air was warm, kept from becoming oppressively so by the occasional cool breeze. Autumn was her favorite season in Egypt, Beth remembered.

Beth's walking route to Groppi from the Embassy would take her past Mujamma at Tahrir, the Egyptian government's mammoth administration building on through Tahrir Square (which is actually a circle), and then along Talaat Harb Street toward her destination. Beth had chosen another of her Diane Sawyer outfits for this meeting – casual, yet proper and modest. So as not to draw unnecessary attention with her sandy blonde hair, she wore it up, covering it with a simple tan shawl that draped down around her shoulders and clipped together in the front.

Her appearance was properly non-Egyptian, but still respectful of the local culture's conservative dress code. She had left the Embassy at 2:30, planning to hike the half mile of downtown streets, arriving at Groppi at 2:45. She had already reached Tahrir Square and all was well.

To be honest with herself, Beth would have admitted to harboring trepidation at the thought of walking through post-revolution Egypt. But continuing onto Talaat Harb, she could see that much of the Cairo she had known in the 1980s and 90s was still there. Crowds of people still mingled and jostled along the narrow sidewalks in front of small shops.

Many of the same businesses lined the traffic-clogged street. A stubborn haze of auto and truck exhaust still hung in the air, while a grayish, filmy dust veiled everything you saw, everything you touched. Those things hadn't changed.

On the street itself, taxis, cars, and buses still jockeyed for position in a seemingly random manner – the blare of horns their constant companion. The cars, Beth noticed, were different now. The Egyptian masses seemed to favor the Korean Hyundai, likely because of its reasonable price. Yet interspersed among the aging sub-compacts, one could still see the occasional Mercedes Benz arrogantly roaming the streets among the riffraff, demanding right of way – a provoking contradiction, Beth imagined, of this country's corrupted reality. The privileged lorded their station over the working class, whose existence they merely tolerated, and when possible, ignored.

Anti-government graffiti screamed from the walls of some buildings . . . screaming loudest perhaps, after government personnel had obliterated the taggers' criticisms with large black rectangles.

Beth checked the time as she approached Talaat Harb Square (another circle) where Groppi awaited her. The architecture in this part of Cairo recalled the years of European occupation. Though the rioting of 1952's Black Saturday had gutted many first floor storefronts, upper floors retained their original European character. Groppi was one of only a few first floor businesses fronting Talaat Harb Square that had been spared the riots' destruction.

Established in the early 1900s, Groppi was once "the most celebrated tearoom this side of the Mediterranean" and had been known as the shop of choice among royalty, including princess Margaret and Queen Elizabeth of England, for gifts of fine chocolates.

During more than sixty years of military rule, like so many other proud Egyptian landmarks, Groppi had lost its former renowned stature. And like Egyptian society, the building façade had suffered from persistent decay. Yet even without its former splendor, Groppi remained a cultural icon for native Egyptians and tourists alike. All of which made Groppi the perfect choice for Beth's meeting with Rasha.

Stepping into the front alcove, Beth stopped for a moment,

admiring the ornate blue mosaic tile adorning the exterior restaurant entryway. Then with a deep breath, she continued through the open doors and into Groppi.

Once Beth was inside the restaurant proper, the raucous street din mellowed to a humming of vehicle motors mixed with muted horns of passing cars – the distinctive background sounds of downtown Cairo.

She'd visited Groppi many times in the old days. As far as she could tell, Groppi hadn't changed with the Revolution or the new repression of SCAF rule. In fact, entering Groppi was like taking a trip through the looking glass into a Bogart movie. The café's high ceiling held ancient chandeliers that only faintly illuminated the cracked white marble walls and floors. The tabletops matched the rest of the decor – cracked marble squares resting upon black iron pedestals.

Jerking her consciousness back to the present, Beth pondered her next move.

The CIA hadn't had a recent picture of Rasha in its files. Probably, because it had considered her insignificant . . . a mere secretary. Beth now found herself at a disadvantage because of that bit of laxity. She would hope that Rasha could find her. There were no other options. At least as an American, she was in the minority in this place. That should make her easier to spot. If necessary, she would uncover her blond hair.

Groppi encouraged patrons to seat themselves. Beth selected a table for two in a rear corner. A moment later, a waiter in black pants and a formal white shirt approached.

"Only one today, Miss?" he said in perfect English.

"I'm expecting a friend shortly."

The waiter offered her a menu.

"I don't believe we'll be needing menus this afternoon, thank you," Beth said. "But I'd love a slice of baklava and a cup of your house tea, please."

The waiter made a note on his order pad.

"Very well, Miss. Thank you."

Beth checked her watch, a plastic Timex she had purchased

specifically to avoid a "showy" appearance on this visit to Cairo. She found the time was ten minutes to three. As she waited for her order, she leafed through pages of the English language *Egyptian Gazette*, which she had brought with her from the Embassy. As she did so, she also took every subtle opportunity to size up the patrons already seated in the café. Groppi was a social venue. There were few lone patrons, and none that appeared likely candidates to be Rasha.

At two minutes before three, an Arab woman wearing light tan pants, a loose, white cotton tunic, and a light-toned, beautifully decorated *hijab* – a head scarf designed to cover hair and any otherwise exposed neck and shoulder skin – appeared in the doorway. Beth thought it creative that Egyptian women and taken the *hijab*, which many Westerners considered a sign of Egypt's oppression of women, and turned it into a fashion statement, albeit a subtle one.

The woman scanned the room, obviously searching for someone. At last her eyes came to rest on Beth. She watched Beth for a moment. Beth looked up, and catching the woman's eye, gave a slight nod.

The woman looked away. Perhaps this wasn't Rasha after all. But soon the woman began making her way between the tables back to Beth's corner. When she arrived, Beth motioned silently for her to sit, which she did.

In the eyes of this middle-aged Arab, Beth finally recognized the youthful page with whom she had once been a casual acquaintance. This was, indeed, Rasha. The silence seemed endless, neither woman knowing how or where to begin.

Finally, Beth said, "It is very kind of you to join me. I am alone in the city. Your company is welcome."

Beth smiled.

Then Rasha smiled as well.

"Elizabeth. I cannot say how wonderful it is to see you after all this time. Have you been well?"

"My life is good, Rasha. I am married with two grown daughters who are beautiful, strong young women. And how have you been?

Egypt has seen many changes since I was last a guest here."

Rasha lowered her face.

"I regret that all has not been well with me, my friend. I envy you your lovely children, for though I long for a family of my own, I have never married and have no children to raise up."

Rasha spoke excellent English, if accented somewhat by her British language teachers.

"But Rasha, if you want to marry, isn't it still possible to have marriages arranged through your family members? I was given to believe that such arrangements remain common here."

Rasha's eyes filled with a deep sadness.

"Rasha. We don't need to talk about this subject. I can see it is unpleasant for you."

Rasha reached across the table and covered Beth's hand with her own.

"I want to tell you, Elizabeth. It is something of great shame and I cannot speak of it among my friends. I wish you to know it, that my burden may be divided. Are you willing to hear?"

Rasha had a dark secret in her past and it would be both kind and wise for Beth to know what it was.

"Yes, Rasha. Certainly. I will share your burden."

Rasha eyed the ceiling and cleared her throat, searching for the place to begin.

Just then the waiter arrived with Beth's order, a chipped white ceramic tea cup resting upon a plain white saucer, with a small matching plate holding the baklava.

"Would you care for a menu, ya Rasha," he asked in Arabic.

"No thank you, Khalid. I will have my usual, please," was Beth's best interpretation of Rasha's response.

"It will be my pleasure, ya Rasha." The waiter bowed and left the table.

"Shall we wait until he has returned with your order, Rasha."

Rasha laughed.

"The service here is slow, my friend. The Revolution has not change this. We will have time."

"Okay. Whenever you're ready." Beth offered a sympathetic

smile.

"I was twenty-three years old," Rasha began. "I lived in my parents' home with my mother and two younger brothers, Hossam, and Amr. You know this is a common thing in Egypt, yes?"

"Of course. Families remain close, usually living together at least until marriage." Beth was familiar with the custom, which had its roots both in culture and economics.

"One night Hossam, who was age twenty at the time, returned from a night out at the clubs with his friends. He had been drinking alcohol . . . too much alcohol. When he came home, he stumbled into to my bedroom." Rasha paused as tears welled in her eyes.

"Elizabeth. He forced himself on me. He raped . . ." Her voice caught on the last word. She was unable to continue.

Now it was Beth's turn to hold Rasha's hand. Beth knew that, for Rasha to share these intimate details of her life, was exceedingly rare, especially in the Egyptian culture. But keeping a dark secret to oneself can be unbearable, regardless of customs. I was honored she felt safe sharing this extreme embarrassment with me.

"Oh, Rasha. I'm so sorry."

"Thank you, Elizabeth. Bless you. But this is only the beginning."

Beth waited for Rasha to collect her thoughts and compose herself.

"If either Hossam or I were to speak of this great shame, we might both face death at the hands of my father."

Beth was familiar with the cultural practice of honor killing, but had never personally known a family that condoned it. The fact that her brother was entirely to blame made no difference in certain parts of this culture. Rasha was no longer a virgin. In the eyes of many, her life had been devalued to the level of a discarded paper cup.

Beth continued to hold Rasha's hand and waited for her to say more, for she knew there was more to be said.

"So no one spoke of that night ever again . . . until today, Dear Elizabeth. Silence has saved my life, but at the same time, my life has been taken from me. This is why I cannot marry or have a family. In my culture, an unmarried woman without her virginity is as much as a prostitute, and would never be touched by an honorable husband. Since virginity testing is still practiced prior to marriage, I have no hope of hiding my disgrace.

"So I have made a new life for myself . . . one with no family, but with a purpose nevertheless. I am a good worker and very skilled with computers. As you may know, I am now in the employ of the Egyptian government. My work there is to maintain technology and to be an example of a woman who can have a life without children, although it may be a mere shadow of a life."

Rasha had been right about the slow service. We had been speaking for quite some time and her order was only now arriving at our table.

"Your tea and pastry, Rasha."

"Thank you, Khalid."

Again, their exchange was in Arabic. Beth was thankful that her language skills had not deteriorated to the point of worthlessness.

Now that both women had received their orders, they began to taste dainty bites of pastry on small forks, and to take occasional sips of hot tea from the ceramic cups.

"Rasha. Why have you asked to see me after all these years?"

Rasha's transformation from a sad woman, sagging in her chair, to her original confident and cheerful demeanor was immediate.

"Dear Elizabeth. There are two reasons. There is the reason I needed to contact *someone* in the U.S. And then there is the reason I had hoped it might be you. I would very much like to share the latter reason first, if I may."

In truth, Beth was more anxious to receive the valuable intel than the back story. But she had to admit, Rasha's request for her, personally, held intrigue.

"Please, Dear Rasha. As you see fit."

"You and I did not know one another well when I worked for the Ministry of Foreign Affairs delivering documents to your Embassy. But you were always kind to me in little things, even though you were busy with your own work. I respected your kindness.

"But there was a certain event, which you may not even recall, that has made you, in my mind, a woman of power and integrity .

. . a person I could trust to deal with my current information properly."

Beth couldn't remember anything in particular.

"You're right. I don't remember anything special, I'm sorry."

"Do not be sorry. I will tell you and you will then remember."

Rasha's eyes looked upward into the distance as she began to recall the event for Beth.

"One day I was taking documents to your Embassy. As I approached the main entrance, outside the Embassy compound, I saw a man in a white baker's uniform smoking a cigarette and speaking with one of the Egyptian soldiers who lined the street. It was Omar, a worker at the bakery where my family bought its bread. When he noticed me, he tossed his cigarette and walked quickly to . . ." she struggled for the word, "intercept me. I walked faster, but he still managed to place himself between me and the Embassy entrance.

"I was afraid of this man, and although he would not let me pass, I dared not meet his eyes. But I remember well his words.

" 'Why does such a beautiful Egyptian flower visit with these foreigners?'

" 'Please, sir, let me pass,' I said. But when I tried to go around him, he again blocked my way.

" 'Such a beautiful flower is meant to be plucked by a man of Egypt. You must come with me.' He grasped my elbow.

" 'No, please, sir. Let me pass,' I said. I struggled to free my arm. One soldier noticed my situation, but only smiled.

" 'You reject me? How dare you reject a man of Egypt to attend to the godless Americans! You have become one of them . . . a tease and a whore.' "

Beth now remembered witnessing this confrontation, but she hadn't recalled who the young woman was. Obviously, it had been Rasha.

"He tried to drag me down the street, grasping my back side with his lustful hand. But I got free and raced to the Embassy entrance. It was then that I saw you running up the street toward the man. You must have been returning to the Embassy and witnessed my embarrassment.

"You called to him. 'Hey, you!' And then overtook him, placing yourself between Omar and the Embassy entrance, where I awaited my document pickup.

"When you reached him, you stood with your face so close to his that I imagined you could smell his foul breath. But neither of you retreated.

" 'If I *ever* see you do something like that to another woman, *anywhere*,' you said, 'you will pray for a swift death.'

"Omar laughed into your face. 'And why should an American whore cause me to have such a wish? You are nothing more than a street prostitute.'

"I feared for your safety and wished you would end the confrontation. But you looked into his eyes without moving a centimeter from him. Do you now remember what you said to him?"

Beth nodded with a smile.

"I reached into my purse and pulled out my gun. He backed off a step and raised his hands.

"Then, if I recall correctly, I said, 'Why should you wish for a swift death?' I stepped forward and stuck my gun up under his chin. Then I said, 'Because . . .' I moved the gun downward until it was pointed below his waist and between his legs. 'I never miss what I aim for . . . no matter how small.' "

Rasha laughed.

"Very good, Elizabeth. I could see the front of his trousers growing wetter by the moment. And then you said a word I have never heard before or since. Do you remember it?"

Beth searched her memories but came up empty.

"No. What did I say?"

"You said, 'Now, git!' "

Both women laughed.

"I have to admit, I did lack a bit in the diplomacy department back then. And I carried that stupid .45. I can imagine the crazy woman with the cannon in her hand did frighten him a bit."

"And Elizabeth, here is one more thing you do not know, but you will like to hear. The next week I was buying bread for our home at this bakery where Omar worked. The owner's daughter knew I sometimes visited the U.S. Embassy. So when I was paying for my bread, she asked me if I knew why Omar refused to deliver to the Embassy any longer.

"It was all I could do not to laugh. But I just told her that I really could not say why that would be.

"After I left the bakery, I laughed and skipped all the way home. It was one of the proudest moments of my life . . . proud for you, Elizabeth, and proud for women."

Beth smiled.

"Thank you so much, Dear Rasha, for sharing that story of my foolish actions and how they inspired you for good. God works in mysterious ways."

"Indeed. Allah is merciful and wise."

I couldn't wait any longer for the information I'd come here to get.

"Dear Rasha. I apologize if I am being rude, but what is it that you have to share with me? Time may be important."

Rasha and Beth both leaned in slightly.

"Some days I work in the Director's office at the Intelligence Directorate. I fix his computer and, because I am a mere woman, I am invisible to him. Last week, I was working in an adjacent room and overheard him speaking with one of his lieutenants about a plan to kill a U.S. politician. They did not speak the name. So who it is they are plotting against, I cannot say. But I know it is not in Egypt's interest to kill Americans . . . especially not American leaders. So I needed to tell someone."

"Thank you, Dear Rasha. That information is helpful. But there are so many possibilities, I don't know how we could protect this person."

"I knew that as well. So when the Director was gone, I searched his computer. There is a back door that allows me access to his data without needing a password."

Of course, there would be. What programmer would want to have herself locked out of a computer because the user forgot his password.

"I searched his computer and, unfortunately, did not find the name I sought. But . . ." Rasha's hand crossed the table and deposited a tiny black piece of plastic under Beth's napkin. "I did find something unusual. It is unlike any other data on the Director's computer. I cannot open the file, so it carries a very high level of security protection. I am hoping that your country can reveal its secrets and that this information may help save the politician."

Beth palmed the computer chip and slipped it into her pants pocket. Actually, it wasn't a chip, but a tiny data storage device called a Micro-SD Card.

"Dear Rasha. I regret that, for the moment at least, this matter must take priority over continuing our conversation. I need to get back to my office. Will you forgive me?"

Rasha laughed.

"I would expect nothing less from the great Elizabeth Weston. Now, go. Do what is right for both our countries."

Beth wished she could promise that would be how it all worked out.

"Rasha, it is likely that I will need to contact you again. Is there a safe way for me to do so?"

Both women stood and exchanged a hug, during which Rasha passed a card into Elizabeth's hand.

"This number is safe," she whispered, "but I cannot answer while I am working."

They ended the hug.

"Thank you again, Dear Rasha. I shall do my best not to let you down."

Rasha remained at the table finishing her tea as Beth left for the Embassy, proceeding with all due haste.

CHAPTER 21

From Venezuela to Red Wing.

Even though he lived in voluntary exile from his native U.S., The Raptor was not without connections there. He would need to employ a number of "black enterprises," within and outside of America to gain entry. The greatest travel challenges always awaited him at points of entry, whether by land, sea, or air. While alone, he could travel fairly freely with his U.S. Passport. But bringing Angel along complicated matters.

For the Minnesota job, he hopped a drug plane flight from Venezuela to Tampico, Mexico. From there, he and Angel traveled under the paid protection of the Gulf Cartel north to Matamoros, near the Gringo border. From Matamoros, he caught a ride on a fishing trawler heading northeast, making sure to stay within established fishing routes. Switching vessels along the way, he took the final leg of his journey to the U.S. interior aboard an acquaintance's private yacht through the port of Galveston. Corpus Christi would have been closer, of course, but Galveston's security was much more lax. After all, who would sneak into the United States via Galveston when Corpus Christi was so much closer to Mexico?

Once on U.S. soil, with all transportation having been paid in cash with U.S. dollars, he was free to move about as he wished – Angel included.

He drove into Red Wing, Minnesota two days before the Senator, checking in at the very same St. James Hotel where his target would be speaking – if he lived long enough. The Raptor's name on the hotel registry matched his phony Texas driver's license and the name on a fraudulently procured credit card. No one would be able to trace him from those documents.

He had also arrived at the hotel wearing a Twins baseball cap and a false beard – sufficient disguise to deter any facial recognition programs, or even *ex post facto* video tape analysis.

Shortly after arriving in Red Wing, The Raptor had checked out the ballroom at The Summit, as well as possible shooting lanes through its glass windows from the river foliage below. But when he drove to the Wisconsin side of the Eisenhower Bridge, he immediately knew a shot through the windows would not be possible. Someone had coated them with reflective material. There was no way he could see inside from this angle.

A certain amount of security interference was to be expected in his line of work, so the glazed windows had not dampened his spirits. He'd next considered points of entry and exit to the hotel. If the target chose to enter through the parking garage, there would be no clear shot except through the car's windows, though Angel was certainly up to that challenge if it should arise.

He'd walked the streets of the small town, surveying building tops, industrial structures, and other potential vantage points. There were several favorable candidates for his purposes. But there was one location that stood out from the rest. It offered clear sight lines to both the hotel's front entrance and its garage portals. There would be no one around to stumble upon his position as he prepared for the kill. And the shot's trajectory would be a slightly downward angle at a distance of, perhaps, a thousand yards.

That prime location sat atop one of Red Wing's most impressive geological landmarks – Mount La Grange.

The Raptor had laughed at the name when he'd looked it up on his computer. This was no mountain. It was a hill, or a bluff, perhaps, but not a mountain. In performing his due diligence, he'd discovered that La Grange had barely surpassed someone's definition of a "mountain" by standing 1,001 feet above sea level, though it "towered" a mere 350 feet above the river.

Funny name or not, Mount La Grange provided the perfect spot for his needs. So Mount La Grange it would be. He would begin his preparations immediately . . . a successful escape from an isolated knob of ground bordered by water on one side, and local law enforcement on the other, did not happen without planning.

* * *

Later that day, he climbed the diminutive mountain to take a first hand look. Shooting lines were, indeed, exceptionally favorable. Escape would be the challenge.

There were only two options for escape from Mount La Grange – and both were on the river side. It wouldn't take the cops long to figure out where the shot had come from – at least not if they were good, and he had to assume they would be. They would seal off the land side of La Grange quickly.

The river side, predictably enough, offered only two options – upstream or downstream. La Grange was already a good distance downstream from Red Wing by boat. That made downstream the obvious choice. Why boat upstream directly into law enforcement assets rather than flee downstream and away from police density?

The biggest problem with a downstream escape was that the river valley offered few decent outlets for his boat and gear. There were lots of good spots to hide among the maze of weedy sloughs, scrub tree islands, and mucky side channels. But there was really no place to get free of the river valley terrain – at least not before any water cops might identify his fleeing boat, or find his hiding place. Even if he had access to a fast craft, patrol boats from other jurisdictions posted farther downstream, or helicopters overhead, would soon close in on him.

No. As much as the downstream route begged to be chosen, it was not feasible.

If The Raptor were to use Mount La Grange as his point of attack, the downstream failings left only upstream for his escape route. He knew there would be patrol boats in that direction. He and his craft would need to withstand a reasonably thorough search. The Red Wing harbors and landings would be teeming with cops. For him to land his boat there would be foolhardy. Then there would be further patrols if he continued north toward St. Paul. It was almost certain that police on the Wisconsin side of the river would join in the manhunt, making a safe boat landing there improbable.

No answer was obvious. But La Grange held too many attack advantages to give it up hastily. The Raptor would return to his escape play book. He would make something work.

CHAPTER 22

At the U.S. Embassy. Cairo.

Upon her return to the Embassy, Beth had immediately relayed Rasha's new information to Hitchens and Connor. If there was something they could do to avoid the alleged assassination attempt, that would have to be their job. To be honest, she doubted they would consider her new "intel" either credible or specific enough to require action.

As for the SD card Rasha had given her, Beth planned to examine that herself before giving it up to CIA minions of unknown capabilities.

Beth's computer kit contained an adapter to hold the micro SD card, allowing her to plug the device directly into her laptop. Before beginning work on the card's data, she made three separate copies of its entire contents, including its formatting and any data which might be hidden from easy view. Then she removed the SD card, placing it an anti-static bag in her desk drawer, and began work on one of the copies.

On first viewing, the card appeared to be blank. The operating system showed no files in the card's primary, and only, partition. Yet the disk scan clearly indicated something was taking up storage space on the card.

Beth employed one of her decryption programs in an attempt to discover exactly what data occupied the missing disk space. This time she had success. Her program had located a file hidden among the partition formatting. She isolated the file and converted it to a file type she could manipulate more readily.

Okay. I've got the file. Now to crack it open.

For the next ten hours, Beth tried every program, trick, finagle, and work-around she knew, but found no success in decrypting the file.

What the hell is this thing?

Beth had yet to encounter an encryption she couldn't crack. This one had her pacing the carpet and tugging at her hair.

Then it occurred to her. The file she'd been busting her backside to open was – so far as the world's best cryptographers were concerned – unopenable. It was protected by Kryptos K4, the CIA's own super code.

A message using the Kryptos code, containing 865 characters of seeming gibberish punched out of half-inch-thick copper, had been on display in a courtyard outside CIA Headquarters at Langley since 1989. The message had four parts. Three had been at least partially solved. K4 remained impenetrable.

Beth realized that the key to opening this file was beyond her reach. She must turn the data over to – heaven forbid – Simon Connor in hopes that he could locate the source of the encrypted message, and that the source still possessed the cryptographic key to open it.

She also knew the file would contain some unencrypted clues to its origin. Even if it couldn't be opened from this end, Simon should carry enough clout to solve the mystery of the file's origins and locate the author of the message that was important enough to carry this encryption in the first place . . . and yet had been found in the possession of Egypt's GIS.

She inhaled deeply . . . a long, tired breath. This package *had* to go to Simon. She began to compose the secure email that would carry the cipher to Simon's desk. She explained its urgency and sent it on its way.

She had done what she could with the information and computer data Rasha had provided. She checked her Timex. It read 2:15 a.m. Beth needed to get some sleep. She'd be dealing with Simon tomorrow.

CHAPTER 23

Back at Red Wing.

The morning of November 5th turned out to be a gorgeous day for late fall in Minnesota. It had been a sunny 35 degrees Fahrenheit when I finished my run along the river front and around Bay Point Park. The weather man predicted calm winds and a high of 60. Not bad, not bad at all.

By the time I'd finished my shower, dressed, and eaten breakfast, it was almost 8:00 a.m. Gunner had graciously invited me to accompany him on his protection detail for Senator Grossman today. Since the private security twerps hadn't allowed Gunner's team much of a role in planning or execution of the security measures for the Senator, he didn't see any reason I couldn't spectate right along with him.

We were to meet at Bev's Café for a cup of coffee. I arrived before Gunner.

"Can I help you, Mr. Becker?" It was the waitress behind the counter. The counteress?

"Just a cup of your finest brew, please."

"Every cup's our finest." She smiled a toothy smile. "I'll be right back."

I don't know how many people remember the atmosphere of a soda shop . . . or some may have called it a malt shop. But that's the ambience you got when you ate at Bev's. A dark wooden counter ran the length of the establishment, while matching, vintage booths lined the opposite wall. The classic soda machine was gone, having given way to a more contemporary version. But the malts were still here. If you ordered one, you could watch them scoop the ice cream from the slide top freezer into the stainless mixer cup, add the milk and flavorings, and finally slip the cup upward onto the pale green blender – which began blending as if by magic when the cup was properly attached. And when Bev's served your malt, you got a full glass, with a generous extra helping still waiting in the frosty stainless container.

    I perused the menu, even though the breakfast offerings hadn't changed in decades. I just wanted something to look at. Then it struck me how unusual the Bev's menu was in these times of venti mocha lattes and espresso macchiatos. In the beverage column there was a single coffee option. It was called "coffee." It cost 99 cents and came with a bottomless ceramic cup, frequently refilled by an attentive counter attendant-slash-waitress.

    If you wanted decaf – and if you looked hard enough – somewhere below "Coke," "Diet Coke," and "7-Up," there was a beverage choice called "Sanka." Now, I didn't even know whether Sanka was still in business, but when you ordered decaf coffee at Bev's, you asked for "Sanka." Whatever it was that you actually got in response to that order would come in a little packet with a side of steaming water. At Bev's, if you don't drink real coffee, you've gotta mix it yourself.

    Just then Gunner came in, causing the little bell above the door to jingle. He moseyed across the linoleum floor and straddled the wooden, rotating stool next to me at the lunch bar.

"Hi, Wanda."

"Morning, Gunner. Breakfast today? Or just coffee?"

"Just coffee, thanks."

"Comin' right up."

I just love Bev's.

I rotated my stool a few inches in Gunner's direction.

"Hey, Gunner. 'Sup?"

"How about I get my coffee first, then you can rankle my tranquility all you want."

I waited until Gunner's coffee had been poured, and mine topped off.

"I assure you, Gunner, I have no rankling in my schedule today. I just want to be here to help out." Gunner raised an eyebrow above his coffee cup. "Only if my help is requested, of course."

"Of course."

There may have been a hint of doubt in Gunner's tone.

"What table scraps have the high-priced guns tossed your way."

"Oh, there's lots of exciting stuff for us locals to cover. All the important details, really."

Sarcasm.

"For instance?"

"We get to stop traffic at the intersections as the Senator's car arrives in town. And provide uniformed presence on the hotel perimeter . . . as a deterrent, you know."

"Well, somebody's gotta do that stuff Gunner. Seems like you're staffed up for it."

"I suppose that's true. Anyway, we also get to cover all ingress and egress to town. Make sure we keep out any obvious undesirables and cover all possible escape routes for any potential doer. So I'll have cars all over creation, attending to every road in or out of town."

"That's a lot of roads, Gunner."

"Yeah, well, I'm thorough. Gimme a puddle to guard and I'll have the scuba team right there.

"We'll have three patrol boats in the river, too. And I've arranged for the Shoe Company jet to be on standby, just in case we need to track somebody in the air until some agency that owns their own aircraft can take up the duty . . . as if some killer's gonna get their plane in here without the whole world noticing in the first place."

I thought Gunner's part of this security plan sounded . . . well . . . sound. Okay, maybe a bit over the top. But hey, the man had a job to do and he was being thorough and prepared – two of my favorite things.

"Anything else?"

"Well, the dapper dandies did manage to get the mirror film up on the windows. I'm sure that turned out to be their idea in the end." Gunner turned my way. "I do appreciate your support on that one, though, Beck. Gave me a chance to shake some manure off my small town barnyard stompers in the presence of their highnesses."

I noticed that Gunner had refrained from employing his usual "cop speak" in the restaurant. "Shit kickers" would have been his normal choice. But he was mindful of his surroundings and the people he might offend with the coarser chat typical of the cop shop. I respected him for that.

"No problem. Least I could do. So is that it for your part?"

"Other than taking you up on sending out lots of CYA letters in case the fancy loafers screw something up, yeah, that's about it."

"Do you know what they've got planned to prevent a sniper from plinking the Senator from Barn Bluff?" Barn Bluff was the locals' preferred name for the river bluff officially dubbed, "Mount La Grange.'

"Geez, Becker. That'd take one heckuva shot."

Again, I noticed Gunner's slightly sanitized slang.

"True. But there are definitely folks who could do it."

Gunner thought for a moment.

"Well, if they take my advice to enter and exit through the doggone hotel garage, we shouldn't have any worries. If not, I'm outta guys. I suppose we're open to a ballistic missile attack, too. Or a Kamikaze. Can't cover everything. It's a matter of probabilities."

"D'you mind if I take a hike up on the bluff after we're done here and just see what I can see?"

"Be my guest. But if you *do* see something hinky, would you *please* gimme a call?"

"Absolutely."

* * *

After coffee, I hopped back into the Pilot for the ten block drive to the walking access path to Barn Bluff. Sheer limestone cliffs bookended the bluff, the result of constructing the Eisenhower Bridge on one end, and some other act of human origin on the other. I suspected the railroad, but wasn't really sure what. Neither cliff was suitable for climbing because the limestone fractured easily and wouldn't hold a climber's spike safely. Someone attempting a hasty escape from above could rappel down either end of the bluff, though.

Unless one cared to dare the treacherous lime cliffs, a person had two choices for ascending the bluff. You could take any number of trails up the city side, all of which were in plain view from Highway 61 and by anyone in downtown Red Wing who had even a modest pair of binoculars.

The likely approach for a sniper to take was the steeper, more treacherous, but mainly hidden, trail up the bluff's riverward side. For purposes of my recon assignment, I only needed to check out areas with sight lines to the hotel. I had no need to take the back way, so I took the easier ascent on the city side.

To call this climb "easy" wouldn't be accurate for non-hikers. I'd seen many visitors turn back before they were even a third of the way to the top. But for folks with good strength and aerobic conditioning, it wasn't a chore. I reached the summit in fifteen minutes. I was still breathing evenly and hadn't broken a sweat. Any sniper worth his salt would be in good physical condition and could certainly make this climb, even packing his rifle and gear. I assumed the same would be true if he came up the river side. Any other assumption would make my visit here pointless.

Once I had crested the bluff, I walked its entire length, searching for anything unusual – a patch of matted grass, a recently broken branch, fresh footprints on the sandy trail. I saw none of the above. Examining the tops of the cliff precipices at each end of the bluff, there was no evidence of anchor spikes or rapelling gear hidden in the brush.

I looked over the back of the bluff, toward the river. Thick woods occluded my view in this direction. But I could still see the beginning of the trail leading upward, and a good part of the river bank below. Once again, nothing seemed amiss. There were no boats in the water, and what I could see of the shoreline lay equally deserted.

My 10:00 a.m. bluff recon assignment had revealed nothing unusual, making it either a success or a failure, depending on what might happen around noon today. I had done what I could.

Continued solo surveillance of the bluff top would be futile. The area was simply too large for one person to cover.

I descended the bluff via the same route by which I had climbed it nearly an hour earlier.

*   *   *

The Raptor was glad he had taken the precaution of hiding the boat amidst the tall, dry river grass instead of beaching it, and equally relieved that he'd visited this "mountain" before sunrise to deploy the elements of his diversionary plan. The local man who'd hiked the trail up the city side was no simple visitor. He'd been patrolling the mountain top, looking for signs of intrusion . . . looking for a sniper.

The Raptor smiled to think of his own cleverness as the man had passed near him. The Raptor's camouflage uniform, coupled with the leaf-covered hollow he had selected as his hiding place, had rendered him invisible – impervious to human attempts at discovery.

Still, this intruder's last minute inspection meant The Raptor would have less time to relocate and establish his new firing position. This was not unlike situations he had encountered before. He would adapt. He would succeed in his mission.

CHAPTER 24

The target was due to arrive at noon, but The Raptor was prepared for him, whether early – which was unlikely for someone in the public eye – or late – which would be almost unavoidable for an arrogant ass. His research into the Senator's history indicated he would be the latter. But nevertheless, The Raptor had established his hunting position by 11:00. He would have done so earlier, but he couldn't risk that damn guy coming snooping along the bluff again at a time when he, himself, was vulnerable.

Pulling Angel out of her travel bag, he gave her a pre-flight inspection. Everything was A-Okay. He powered up her onboard targeting system and took aim at the hotel's front doorpost. In a few moments the screen in Angel's scope began reading out air pressure, windage, angle of attack, distance, and a host of other data crucial to a successful kill on the first shot.

Now, all he had to do was wait and watch. His opportunity would come.

* * *

Gunner and I stood on the sidewalk across Main Street from the St. James Hotel. Three of the private security guys, adorned in black and equipped with ear pieces and sunglasses, manned a cordoned area near the hotel's main door.

"Doesn't look like they're headed for the garage, Gunner."

Gunner emitted something like a growl through clenched teeth.

"Nothing you can do now," I said. "You told 'em to take the back way in. You can't make 'em do it."

Gunner's cell phone buzzed.

"Grossman should be here any minute," Gunner said. Even in

the November chill, his armpits were soaked, and his voice carried a slight tremble.

The time was 12:14.

Almost as Gunner spoke, two of his cruisers barricaded street access on the blocks adjacent to the Hotel. Soon we saw three, gleaming black limousines approaching. Apparently, the Senator didn't pack light.

The security guys guided the first car past the hotel door and to a spot along the curb. Four more denizens of The Matrix piled out and set up a soft perimeter. A soft perimeter is one that civilians are allowed to penetrate to get closer to the celebrity. But while inside this area, they are closely watched.

The next car stopped directly in front of the main doorway. I guessed this was Grossman's ride. My estimation was confirmed when four more security clones scrambled out of car number three, spinning furiously from side to side, presumably to indicate that their threat detectors were fully deployed.

Not until one of the security guards approached Grossman's car door did the Senator himself exit the vehicle.

A throng of nearly twenty people had gathered to take in the Senator's glorious arrival. Presumably those attending his presentation were already seated upstairs by this time. He popped out of the limo, hands waving and smile at full power. I wondered how excited he'd be if there were an actual crowd waiting for him.

He began his regal walk along the heavy, felt cordon, shaking hands, giving high fives, probably kissing babies, though I couldn't really see from my position.

A pair of middle-aged protesters encroached on the soft-zone hoisting "Make Love, Not War" signs and causing a minor disturbance among the security forces, who hastened the Senator indoors, insulating him from the bold effrontery of public opinion. In any case, he made it into the hotel without injury or unsuppressed mayhem.

"Well, Gunner," I said. "I think that went okay."

"Yup. My guys sure blocked the hell outta those streets."

"The Senator looked like a pretty good target to me, glad

handing with the groupies out in the sunshine. If I were a sniper, or even a John Hinckley, Jr., I think I'd've let 'er fly right then."

"Makes sense to me," Gunner's adrenaline rush was wearing off.

"Shall I grab us a couple of to-go cups from Hanisch's Bakery so we've got something to do while we wait for the show inside to get over?"

"Don't suppose that could hurt. Meanwhile, I'm gonna have my guys do another sweep of the building roofs. Maybe I'm being paranoid, but just in case. Ya know?"

"No such thing as too prepared. A little paranoid can be good in the right circumstances. I believe I'd do the same if I were you.

"I'll be back in ten."

Gunner was already on his radio directing the troops to recheck all the downtown rooftops for anything fishy, and to escort the protesters to a safer distance from the hotel.

Even though we all anticipated the Senator's departure would be as uneventful as his arrival, Gunner was still doing his job . . . and doing it with all diligence. I had to admire him for that.

* * *

"Now, now, Angel. Be patient," The Raptor whispered. "Our time is almost here. He's walkin' right toward us. I'll jus' give yer trigger a little tickle . . . ."

Just as he was about to squeeze off the shot, a plump woman and a bald man forced their way inside the soft perimeter. They carried protest signs of some sort. The idiots had completely blocked the Raptor's line of sight to the target.

"Git outta the way," he whispered. "Angel. Get 'em outta the way."

By the time security had finally cleared the riffraff from the Senator's path, Grossman was gone – already inside the hotel.

"Damn, damn, damn, damn, damn!" The Raptor was angry, but he wasn't about to give up yet. Perhaps there'd be another chance. And if not today, the guy was just waitin' to be dead another time. He'd get the bastard later if not sooner.

The Raptor lay motionless, olive and tan paint rendering even his face invisible to probing eyes. One opportunity had passed. But he hadn't survived this long in the killing business without patience, and preparedness, and diligence – the qualities the army had taught him to value long ago. He laughed to himself. *That was one set of useful skills he'd learned in the damned army. The ability to kill without remorse was another.*

"They moved them limos around back, Angel. We better make sure we got readin's out there, too." He took aim at a suitable fire hydrant behind the hotel garage, making mental note of the sighting adjustments he'd need to make if the shot had to go in that direction. But his primary settings remained on the hotel's front door post.

"They may have parked out back, Angel. But men of ego want to strut their stuff. We'll git another shot in front. You jus' wait."

* * *

I arrived back at Gunner's side with a couple foam cups of coffee, black.

"Here's your pick-me-up, Gunner."

He punched a hole in the lid and took a sip.

"Good stuff. Thanks, Beck."

Gunner's definition of "good coffee" had to be understood in relation to the swampy goo served up from his office machine. Compared to that swill, pretty much anything was "good coffee." I was appreciative of the compliment, nevertheless.

"My pleasure, Constable. You know I live to serve."

I smiled.

Gunner sipped again. I thought I saw his eyes roll.

"So anything new?" I tried.

"The troops are re-checking the roofs. Traffic is flowing again till we get the word to shut 'er down. The guys in the patrol boats say that mirror stuff is working good on the windows. They can't see a damn thing inside. Best I can tell, we're doing our part."

"You got somebody watching the bluff?"

Gunner turned halfway in my direction, and looked at me over his white cup. When he'd swallowed, he said, "Two guys take turns eyeballing it through binocs between building sweeps." He tilted his head at me as if I'd asked something stupid. "Just 'cause I don't think it's a likely threat doesn't mean I don't take it serious."

Gunner was nothing if not thorough.

"Didn't mean to offend. I just wanted to be sure you weren't relying on my recon walk this morning. Just because I didn't see anything then doesn't mean there's nothing there now."

"And you figured I didn't know that?"

"Like I said, I didn't mean to offend. Keep up the good work."

I offered Gunner a toast with my Styrofoam. He paused, but then joined in.

"To sunny skies and smooth sailing," I said.

"And to getting this pain in the ass politico out of town in one piece."

"Hear, hear!"

Gunner's phone buzzed.

"Gunderson. Uh huh. You sure? Okay. Got it." He punched the phone off.

"So what's the good word?"

"Ain't any. The idiot's coming out the front again. Why can't he just make life easy?"

Down the highway, I could see Gunner's cruisers blocking off adjacent streets. Nearer by, the three limos had turned the corner and were pulling up by the hotel's front doors. The security professionals popped out of the cars like jack-in-the-boxes. Apparently, a spring in one's step connotes greater devotion to duty.

Soon there were more security guys appearing from inside the hotel lobby. They all coordinated – using their earpieces, I assumed – and staked out a formation akin to their arrival stance.

* * *

"Git ready, Angel. He's comin' out."

* * *

After making a visual check of the onlookers, one of the security guards pulled the hotel door open. The Senator strode through like a prize cock at the County Fair. Once again, there was the glad-handing and high-fiving along the cordon – though the "crowd" was even smaller than upon his arrival.

It occurred to me that he should maybe have hired a cheer squad, kind of like they do with mourners at a funeral.

This time, Gunner's boys had relegated the peace protesters to chanting and waving their signs from across the street. As the Senator stood beside his open limo door, waving a final goodbye, his head suddenly exploded and his portly body crashed to the concrete.

Time passed in slow motion for me. Security guards surrounded the corpse, dancing a blurred twirl, searching in vain for the source of the attack. Gunner barked something into his shoulder radio. The crowd scattered.

The whole time I was counting as fast as I could in my head. *1,2,3,4,5,6,7*. There had been no sound of a gunshot when the bullet hit the Senator. When the rifle report finally reached us, by my count, the shooter had been more than 700 yards away. Given the direction of the splatter, a shot from that distance could only have come from somewhere on Barn Bluff.

I grabbed Gunner's arm. He tried to shake me off. I wasn't letting go until I had his attention.

"What the hell?"

"Gunner. The shooter was on the bluff." I pointed. "You've gotta seal it off."

Gunner had to decide whether to trust me or not. He had limited resources and needed to place them effectively.

"Get some cruisers and a boat over to Barn Bluff. Seal it off. That's where our shooter's at."

He looked at me. "You'd better be right."

"No chat right now, Gunner. You have to get that bullet before somebody else does. It should either be stuck in the asphalt about twenty yards past the limos over there." I pointed." Or more likely, it skipped off the road and ended up hitting something a couple blocks farther down."

Just then there was an explosion from the direction I had indicated. Two blocks away in a fast food parking lot, a cloud of flame and black smoke mushroomed upward from a burning car.

"There's your bullet, Gunner."

Seconds later, he was on his radio telling the deputies in the nearest cruiser to seal off the car and make sure the firemen wouldn't destroy evidence when they arrived.

"And I'm pretty sure the shooter's bullet is in or near that car," he said. "So find the damn thing and don't give it up!"

* * *

The Raptor's mission was a success, but he had no time for revelry. He knew he sat in a vulnerable spot. Chancing that the dramatic scene on Main Street would divert any binocular observation of the mountain, he broke for the back trail at full speed. With Angel in one hand and her travel case in the other, he barely slowed as he ran the steep trail down toward the river.

Livin' on a mountain of my own can come in handy, he thought as his boots deftly found sure footing.

Once at the bottom, he ran to the boat and, after placing Angel carefully onboard, pushed it out into the waters of the side channel. He needed distance from the mountain trail, and fast. The motor revved to life and The Raptor headed out into the river.

When the boat had reached a safe distance from shore, and was still running at full throttle, he locked the rudder at dead true, and stowed Angel and her case inside the large grey box, snapping the lid down tightly. Then he tossed the whole grey cargo box overboard.

The small boat jerked sharply as the rope tied to the box drew taut. If The Raptor hadn't been prepared for the jolt, it would have flung him over the side.

After a few minutes, he judged his distance from the mountain trail head to be sufficient and throttled the boat back to a five knot pace. He stripped off the camo suit and reversed it to the side that looked like the sort of coverall a fisherman might wear to stay warm, then added a bucket hat with a few fishing lures attached.

Using a mirror and a chemical soaked cloth, he meticulously removed all trace of the camo paint from his clean-shaven face. He performed a final inspection of himself and the boat. All was in order. Two fishing poles, a tackle box, a fish stringer, and a bait bucket completed the illusion.

The cargo box now trailed the boat by thirty feet and had sunk to a depth which he estimated from previous trials to be five feet. Tied to the boat at an aluminum ring below water level, the box and its rope would be invisible in the murky waters of the Mississippi. He wanted to tell Angel what a smart idea it had been for him to strap a modified surf board to the bottom of her grey box. But he caught himself before yelling out to her.

He settled at the boat's controls, releasing the rudder lock. When he checked the GPS on the "Fish Finder," he found he'd put more than a mile between himself and the accessible end of Mount La Grange. The physical part of the escape was over. Now he would rely on the psychological aspects of his plan to bring him home.

* * *

One Ottawa County Sheriff's patrol boat had been heading down river from the hotel waterfront toward Barn Bluff at full speed since receiving Gunner's order. Another had headed upstream past Trenton Island, to a point where the divided river joined together to form a single channel that would be easier to guard. The final boat would coordinate river pursuit from a location in the main channel just upstream from the bluff, beneath the Eisenhower Bridge, and near the site of the shooting.

Everyone believed that, if the shooter had chosen a water escape, this would be a race downstream – where he would have a head start from the bluff location – to catch him before he could disappear into the sloughs and rough country on the Wisconsin side of the river. But the two additional boats covered upstream, just in case the unexpected might happen.

A little more than a mile from the side channel that bordered Barn Bluff, the first patrol boat – the one headed downstream – met a small, aluminum fishing boat headed upstream toward Red Wing. Not wanting to slow his pursuit, he radioed the stationary patrol boat of the fishing boat's presence and continued at full throttle downstream.

* * *

As The Raptor's aluminum boat approached the "No Wake" zone near the Eisenhower Bridge, the Sheriff's patrol boat stationed there approached his. Observing proper boating practice, he shut down his motor as the patrol pulled alongside. He and one of the Sheriff's deputies held the two boats close together, squeezing the Sheriff's rubber boat fenders between their vessels.

"Hey, officers. Kin ah hep y'all." He poured the Houston accent on thick.

"May I see your registration please?"

"Sure 'nuf." He handed the paper to the officer, who gave it a once over. The second deputy in the patrol boat monitored the radio and scanned the river for any sign of the fugitive.

"You would be Mr. Jasper Tomball?"

"Yep. Named after my hometown. You ever heard a that? Was Mammy's idea. She never did know Pa's last name"

"I see you've got some poles in there with you. You been fishing?"

"Yessir. Tryin' to git me wonna them big channel cats y'all are so famous fer up here."

"I'll need your driver's license and fishing license, Mr. Tomball."

"They're in the tackle box. I'll fish 'em out fer ya."

The Deputy placed one hand on his holstered gun as The Raptor opened the tackle box and retrieved his wallet.

"Here ya go." He offered the wallet to the Deputy.

"I'll need you to take them out for me, please."

"Absolutely, Sir." The Raptor slipped out the licenses matching the false name on the boat registration, presenting them to the deputy.

The Deputy matched the face on the driver's license with that of the fisherman. Then noting that the correct name appeared on the current non-resident fishing license, he returned everything to Mr. Tomball.

"Where were you fishing just now?"

"I was parked out in the main channel, 'bout twenty minutes down that-a-way." He tossed a thumb over his shoulder toward downstream.

"You didn't happen to see any other boaters on your way up, did you. Maybe somebody goin' like a bat outta hell?"

"Jus' 'nother wonna you guys. Boat jus' like yours. Maybe a couple minutes ago."

The Deputy seemed satisfied.

"Where're you staying while you're in the area, Mr. Tomball?"

"I got a little trailer parked at wonna them camp grounds out by Welch. Cain't 'member the name right off."

"Okay. Thank you, Mr. Tomball. You have a nice day."

"Yessir. An' right back atcha." He saluted as the patrol boat pulled away, resuming its designated position.

The Raptor restarted his motor and smiled.

Well, kick the shit off my boots. Lookin' good so far. And he continued at no-wake speed up the main channel, passing a stone's throw from the very place the Senator had fallen.

CHAPTER 25

At the U.S. Embassy. Cairo.

After sleeping a mere two hours, Beth awoke to the sound of her secure cell chiming. The clock read 4:15 a.m. A squint at the caller ID revealed that her wake up call was from another "unknown." *Maybe Rasha?*

She sat up in bed and answered the cell.

"This is Elizabeth."

"Connor here. Hope I didn't interrupt anything." Her least favorite British accent.

Beth swallowed a riposte. He knew damn well what time it was in Cairo.

"What have you got, Simon?"

"Ah, Beth. You continue to insist on improper informality. I'm thoroughly gob-smacked."

Beth felt a headache coming on. Two hours of sleep made Simon even harder to swallow.

"Simon. No banter. What's up?"

"I've discovered the source our your bit of code . . . the one you sent me just this morning, you know."

Maybe some good news after all?

"Very good, Simon. What've you figured out?"

"The tag on the file is registered to the Joint Chiefs. Military business. Not CIA at all."

"So did you find out what the file said? Did you get the passcode to decrypt?"

"Well, that's a funny thing, Beth. There was nothing to decrypt, really. All the file contained was the ID tag . . . to the military, that is."

Beth gritted her teeth.

"So what did the military say this tag was attached to?"

"They wouldn't say, actually. Awfully close to the vest those chaps, considering we're supposed to be on the same team."

"Dammit, Simon. Why didn't you run it up the ladder until you got an answer. This could save some politician's life."

"I'm afraid that's not likely."

"How do you figure, Simon? Just maybe that file can give us some idea who the target of the assassination is. Did you think of that?"

"Oh . . . well . . . I'm afraid we won't be needing that tidbit of news. We already know the target."

How was that possible? She'd had so little information to pass along to him. How had he determined the target?

"Simon. My patience is at an end. If you don't start talking to me straight, and right now, I'm hanging up. How did you find out who the target is?"

"Senator Elbert Grossman of Minnesota was assassinated earlier today. Bloody professional job, too. Shot from nearly a thousand yards."

Beth was taken aback.

"Grossman? Why would the Egyptians want to kill Grossman?"

"We have no active theories at present."

It was hard for Beth to imagine that a Senator from her home state could have any relationship with the Egyptians that might get him killed. She didn't even recall him visiting the country. There should be a clue to the answer to this question in the Army's data files. At least she hoped so.

"So when will I have the Army's info concerning the file the Kryptos tag was attached to?"

"It doesn't appear that there is a need for it, anymore. Don't you think?"

"No, I don't think! We can't just let GIS kill one of our politicians and not do anything about it."

"I suppose you have a point. I'll tell you what, Beth. I shall see what I can find out for you . . . as a favor, you understand. Now . .

. are you satisfied?"

"I'll be satisfied when you get me the file, Simon" She nearly crushed her phone disconnecting the call.

Having no further data to work with, Beth tried to sleep – an effort that proved to be in vain.

CHAPTER 26

Back at Red Wing.

Following his successful encounter with the Sheriff's Water Patrol, The Raptor still had some artifice to execute before he would feel safe. Although it might seem desirable for him take his boat out of the river at one of the Red Wing landings, there were two reasons he couldn't do so.

First of all, law enforcement would be checking license plates and owner information on all the vehicles parked there. They had no idea where the assassin might be hiding or how he planned to escape. In their minds, the river was one possible exit route.

Secondly, The Raptor still had Angel in tow. At low speeds in shallow water she might get stuck in the muddy river bottom, attracting unwanted attention. Or a cop might notice him hauling the unusual contraption out of the water after docking his boat.

In any case, The Raptor judged that docking in Red Wing posed too great a risk. For this reason, he planned to take his boat out of the river where he had put it in – at a remote dirt landing on Trenton Island, which lay between the two principal river channels and within likely police perimeters on both land and river.

This island landing, with adjacent parking area, was fifteen minutes distant by boat from his current location adjacent to the hotel.

As he continued at "no wake" speed past the parks, coal docks, and landings of downtown he could see that the police activity on the shore was, indeed, intense. His progress past the crime scene seemed impossibly slow. But eventually, he reached the upstream tip of the Trenton Island. As he rounded the island on the way to the landing, he saw the Sheriff's third patrol boat on post about a hundred yards upstream, guarding the channel in that direction. He waved at the officers, who gave a polite, but subtle acknowledgment of his distant greeting.

Now motoring down the river's back channel, he approached his island boat landing. It remained as deserted as when he had put the boat into the Mississippi several hours earlier. Conveniently located at a remote corner of Trenton Island, away from prying eyes, at this landing he could take care of both the boat and Angel without danger of discovery.

A few minutes later, he had trailered his sixteen foot aluminum Sylvan behind a rented 1990 Ford F-150, stowing Angel's cargo crate and surf board in the truck's storage box.

Now he had a decision to make. Two police checkpoints blocked his exit from Trenton Island. One police roadblock on the back channel bridge impeded his access to Wisconsin proper. Another checkpoint on the Eisenhower Bridge blocked access to Red Wing.

If he chose the back channel route into Wisconsin, once clear of the checkpoint, he would be relatively free. But police on the back channel bridge would be diligently searching vehicles coming from his direction – from the direction of Barn Bluff – and there was great risk that someone might detect Angel in the truck box. After dragging her through the muddy river water, he was not about to stress Angel further by leaving her stranded on this island where she might be stolen by some hunter, or fisherman, or god forbid, some birder. He couldn't bear the thought.

On the other hand, if he returned to Minnesota approaching from outside the Eisenhower checkpoint, any search of his vehicle would likely be minimal. Angel should be safe. At least if she was captured, he'd be there, too, to defend her. But he would be headed into law enforcement's stronghold. There would be cops everywhere in Red Wing. His guilt could be exposed by something as minor as a traffic violation or a random stop.

The choice to return to Red Wing held one additional attraction for The Raptor. Law enforcement wouldn't be expecting him to go back there.

He had made his decision even before shooting the Senator. Departing the boat ramp lot, he and Angel drove off in the direction of the Eisenhower Bridge . . . on his way to back Red Wing.

* * *

The line of cars at the roadblock was already long as he approached this main entry point to town. The cops would be stopping and searching vehicles in an effort to prevent the shooter's escape into Wisconsin via the bridge. This activity, of necessity, caused delays in both directions on Highway 63, the road crossing over the bridge from Wisconsin.

As he neared the checkpoint, he could see the police waving cars from Wisconsin through the blockade, while those departing Red Wing were, indeed, being searched.

Isn't it wonderful how predictable law enforcement can be!

When his turn at the road block arrived, he held his breath. But as the Minnesota State Trooper motioned him onward, he relaxed enough to smile and even offered the Trooper a thank you wave.

* * *

By this time, city, county, and state law enforcement had sealed off all ingress and egress to Barn Bluff. Bloodhounds and BCA SWAT teams took the point in the search of the bluff itself. BCA was the Minnesota Bureau of Criminal Apprehension . . . the investigative division of the State Police. The plan was for the SWAT teams to sweep up and over the bluff beginning on the grassy, landward side, eventually working their way over the bluff top and down through the woods to the river, where additional armed personnel had slammed the metaphorical exit door.

Gunner and I weren't going to be a part of this search mission, though he needed to coordinate his deputies who continued to keep tight rein on any vehicles attempting to exit Red Wing.

This sniper was proving to be a potent adversary. An hour had already passed since Senator Grossman's assassination, and all the cops had accomplished was removal of his body and clean up of the crime scene.

To be fair, law enforcement had claimed one other small victory. Gunner's men had found the sniper's bullet lodged in the dashboard of the burning car. The round had had just enough momentum left after passing through the gas tank and back seat to barely pierce the plastic dash far enough for it to protrude about half an inch. It was an odd place for a bullet to come to rest. But they all end up somewhere. The dash plastic soon melted, disgorging the round onto the car floor.

The deputies had kept the discovery under wraps, per Gunner's orders. In the meantime, they'd photographed and measured as much as they could of the sniper round without disturbing it before the BCA Crime Scene Team took over. When they'd gathered all the evidence they could, Gunner gave the okay to announce the discovery to the BCA, who promptly took charge of the charred car and bullet.

The Sheriff's deputies would pass the bullet photos and specs along to Gunner whenever he was ready.

I had a feeling in my gut that this sniper had a clever exit strategy, and the cops were going to be too late to chase him down. Unfortunately, I didn't have any hot ideas on how to grab the guy either.

Maybe Bull could help. He's my American Indian friend – a big guy with some special military skills and a load of common sense, to boot. I punched him up on my cell.

"Yeah?"

"Hey, Bull. It's Beck."

"I got caller ID."

I kept forgetting that.

"Have you heard yet about the action here in town this afternoon?"

"Yeah. I got news choppers buzzing my house every two minutes. If it bleeds, it leads."

"Amen, Brother."

"I ain't your brother . . . Paleface." He laughed.

He'd meant no offense with the "Paleface" crack. It was just his sense of humor. I wished I understood Bull better. The man was inscrutable, utterly inscrutable.

"So will you help Gunner and me catch the shooter? I know it's a long shot, no pun intended. But then, you're a long shot kinda guy."

"True dat!"

"Huh?"

"Just got back from Atlanta. Picked up some street lingo."

I always wondered where Bull was when we weren't together. I wondered for two reasons. First, he always seemed to be available and close by when I needed him. How was that possible? And second, he scares the crap outta me and I'd like to have a bead on him at all times. That's not actually true. He'd come through for me in the clutch time after time. I just didn't like it when he snuck up behind me for laughs at my expense, which he'd done more than once.

"So can I call you when Gunner's free?" I said.

"We gotta work with the cops?" Bull preferred his anonymity. Cops hate anonymity. The two just don't mix.

"Yes, we do. Sorry. But I promise, you'll be a big help, and it'll be damn interesting."

"Okay. Ring me up."

Click!

"Thanks for the chat," I said, into the dead connection.

I was glad Bull was going to assist. I was sure he'd bring a unique perspective to the investigation.

*   *   *

As The Raptor drove off the bridge, making the turn onto Highway 61 into downtown Red Wing, he held a prime view of the police activity on Mount La Grange. He had to laugh when he saw the bloodhounds dragging two K-9 officers across the bluff top toward the down-river cliff. The scent trail leading to the cliff had been a delay tactic that turned out to be unnecessary. *Better too many defenses than too few.*

But it wasn't time for celebrating yet. He had a few more details to take care of before he could rest. Item one was to stow the truck and boat in the storage garages he had rented on Tile Drive, about a mile from the St. James, and well within the police perimeter. Just in case somebody connected the dots between Mr. Tomball, the fisherman, and Mr. Raptor, the assassin, he needed to eradicate Mr. Tomball from existence.

Sadly, he had no option but to leave Angel in the garage with the boat.

"Don't worry yourself none, Angel. I'll be back to getcha soon as ah kin."

He changed out of his camo/fishing clothes, lost the hat, and resumed his St. James hotel guest identity, complete with beard and Twins cap. He locked the garage doors on both the boat and truck and set off on foot for the hotel.

It would be foolhardy to tread the highway shoulder back into downtown. But there was a back route, through the neighborhoods and down Jefferson Avenue, that would work just fine. He was in no hurry now.

CHAPTER 27

Red Wing. The day after the shooting.

Gunner had suggested that the three of us meet at the LEC conference room this morning. But there was no way I was going to drag Bull in there.

"How about I ask Mr. Red Feather where he'd like to meet. You know, he's kinda weird about some of that stuff."

"He's kinda weird about everything," Gunner said. "I'd just as soon keep this whole discussion between you and me. But if you're sure Bull's an asset, well . . . a United States Senator just got killed in my County. I'd do best to take all the advice I can get. Go ahead and see where he wants to convo."

I called Bull and it turned out he thought a suitably "neutral location" would be the Tribal Council's main conference room at the Prairie River Casino, located on sovereign Dakota Indian land, just outside Red Wing. Gunner and I were accommodating. At least I was. Gunner took some convincing.

An hour later it was 10:00 a.m. and Gunner and I had crossed the border onto the Reservation.

A person couldn't really tell when they'd crossed onto the Rez. It wasn't like entering Canada or Mexico. You just sort of drove in. In fact, the tribe rather liked it if lots of folks drove in, especially if visitors made use of the reservation's top notch casino, hotel, and banquet facilities. Who could blame them?

We got out of Gunner's cruiser and approached the main entrance to the casino complex. The tribal offices were in there somewhere as well. A friendly blonde gal met us in the foyer and asked if we knew where we were going.

We had to confess ignorance, but alleged that we were to meet

Mr. Red Feather in Conference Room B.

"Who was that you're supposed to meet?" she said sweetly.

"Mr. Terry Red Feather." When there was still no sign of recognition, I said, "Bull?"

"Oh . . . Bull. He's waiting for you. I'll call an escort to take you up."

We waited a couple minutes in the foyer, enjoying the carnival atmosphere of ringing slot machines and the faint echo of a bingo caller. The casino really was a magical place, if you could afford it. Unfortunately, some people had a gambling problem and used their government debit cards to get cash from the handy ATMs to buy table chips instead of food. That was a sad situation when it happened, though one could hardly blame the Indians, especially when the State of Minnesota had ten different lotteries going at the same time. If people were hell bent on gambling, they were going to do it. This was just a very nice place to gamble. That's all.

Our uniformed security escort arrived – another young blonde woman – and we followed her up the stairs to our destination in the office section of the complex. She rapped on the door marked "Conference B," then cracked it open.

"Bull? Couple guys here say they're supposed to meet you."

"Lemme see."

She opened the door to reveal my smile and Gunner's frown. Gunner didn't like being jerked around, even when it was all in good fun.

"That's them. Let 'em in, please. And thanks for the delivery."

"You're welcome, Bull. See ya!" She departed with a flirty smile. Bull eyed her backside as she left.

We joined Bull at the round conference table.

"Isn't she a little young for you, Bull?" I asked.

He shrugged his shoulders.

"Doesn't cost nothin' to look."

I figured I should start the conversation since I was the creative soul who'd brought together this smorgasbord of experience and insight.

"You guys both know each other, right?"

Gunner and Bull nodded at me without looking at one another.

"Gunner. Can you bring Bull and me up to speed on yesterday's investigation? What'd you guys find and what conclusions have you reached?"

Gunner shifted in his chair. I figured he wasn't used to comfortable furniture. I wrote his wiggling off to adjusting to luxury, as opposed to nervous tension.

"Well, there's a bunch that we know. But so far, it hasn't led us to the shooter. And it's probably too late now. So why are we here again?"

"Come on, Gunner. You know Ottawa County doesn't have the only cops who'd like to catch this guy. Maybe we can point someone else in the right direction."

Gunner acknowledged my point with a sideways nod.

"Okay. I'll start with the security setup that applied to preventing escape.

"I had a cop car at every damn highway, street, road, and bike trail heading outta town. Even coordinated with the Wisconsin guys on Highway 63, both on the Eisenhower and back channel bridges over the river. We locked all them roads down within thirty seconds of the shooting. There's no way he drove outta Red Wing.

"We had Barn Bluff sealed off on the dry side within two minutes. I don't think he coulda got down from the bluff and past those cars unless . . ."

"Unless what?" I said.

"We found the spot we think he was shooting from. The dogs followed a trail from there all the way to the cliff at the far end of the bluff. I suppose he could've . . . just maybe . . . gone down a rope."

"You mean rappelled?"

"Yeah. Like climbers do on the way down. But we didn't find a rope, and BCA looked all over hell trying to find some hint that he'd set a peg or tied a rope around a rock or something. They came up with zilch. No rope fibers on the cliff edge either. BCA says no way he used a rope."

"Hmmph."

"Do you have something to chip in here, Bull?" I said.

"Just because they didn't find a rope doesn't mean he didn't go down that way. I could do it without leaving a sign. So somebody else could, too."

Bull glanced sideways at Gunner. Gunner did not look happy.

"Duly noted, Bull. Now, Gunner, please continue."

"So anyway, he *probably* didn't rope his way down. But he still might've used some kinda parachute or something else that maybe let him jump down quick, without breaking his neck."

Bull folded his arms across his chest and took a deep breath. I'm sure he was holding back some witticism about the parachute idea.

"I've got a little experience with parachutes," I said, "and diving off a bluff is tricky business. I wouldn't use a chute if I could rappel. Where's the gain? You know the dogs are gonna trace you anyway."

"What if the dogs were *supposed* to find that scent and follow it to the cliff?" It was Bull.

"Now why in Sam hill would the shooter want the dogs to follow his trail?"

Bull looked over at Gunner.

"I don't know . . . *yet*. What did the dogs use to sniff up his scent in the first place?"

"There was a little swatch of torn camo on a prickly ash where the gunner had laid down. They took it from that."

Bull laughed.

Gunner's face flashed red. "What's so funny?"

"That's one pretty stupid shooter. Either that or he wanted you to find that scent, maybe to slow down pursuit, or to get you to think he came of the bluff in one place, when he really came off in another.

"Did you happen to smell that swatch?"

"No. I don't go sniffin' in evidence bags. Why? Whatta ya think I would've smelled if I had?"

"Piss."

"Piss?"

"Yeah!"

"Even if I did open the bag and smelled urine in there, so what!

Maybe he had to take a leak while he was waiting for his target to finish eating lunch. It's not unusual for snipers to have to lay in one spot for a long time – maybe wet their pants in the process."

Bull looked at the ceiling as if dredging up a memory.

"True dat," he said.

Don't do this to me Bull. I winced.

"But buck scent smells like piss, too," Bull said. "Deer hunters use it to cover their human smell. Them dogs were chasing buck scent. I'll bet you a thousand American."

I could see communication between Bull and Gunner was breaking down.

"Okay, let's put that thought on a back burner for the moment. BCA can analyze the scent on the rag and they'll tell us if we need to know."

"What sort of security did you have on the river side of the bluff?"

"Like I said to you yesterday," he glanced over at Bull, "all three of our patrol boats were in the water right by the hotel. When the shot went off, I sent one down toward the bluff at full speed. Would've only taken maybe five minutes to get there. When he reached the trail head by the river, he didn't see anything so he kept on going downstream, figuring that's the way the shooter'd go to get away."

"Makes sense," I said.

Bull sat with his arms folded across his massive chest. I took his lack of an objection as agreement.

"But just in case he tried to go upstream, we sent a boat there, too. There aren't any side channels up that way, and nobody even tried to pass those guys."

Gunner again looked at Bull, who continued his stoic posture with eyes straight ahead.

"We also got the Shoe Company plane in the air. That took maybe twenty minutes. But then they flew up and down the channel for miles checking for boats. They called in a few and we checked 'em out. It wasn't long before BCA got their choppers there and took over the air part.

"We never did find any abandoned boat or signs of where he might've gotten off the river. Still, it seems like with all the swamp and weeds and trees, he probably found a way to get out somewhere downstream. That, or he's still hiding there. BCA has got more boats in the water searching with infrared and shit. And one chopper is still looking down from the air. It's possible we'll get him there yet."

"So let's see if I've got this straight," I said. "There's no way he got out of town on a road."

"Nope."

"And it doesn't seem like we can find him down the river."

"Nope."

"And he didn't go up river?"

"Nope."

Bull and I exchanged looks.

"What?" Gunner said.

"What if he's still in town?" I said.

"How can he still be in town?"

"Gunner," I said, "did your water patrol guys meet any boats at all that were headed upstream?"

He pulled his briefcase from under the table and began leafing through it.

"Here's their report. It's from the guys who stayed right under the bridge. Says there was only one fisherman headed upstream. They stopped him and inspected his ID, etcetera. He was licensed to fish and his driver's license matched his face."

Gunner flipped a page.

"Says here he was one Jasper Tomball, from Tomball, Texas. They got his local address as a campground near Welch. But if he tried to pull that boat into a Red Wing landing, he'd have been thoroughly grilled."

I had another thought.

"Did your guys make records of all the folks who left town through the perimeter after they'd been cleared?"

" 'Course. It's back at the office though."

"Do me a favor please and check to see whether Mr. Tomball left for Welch, and if not, whether you can locate his trailer there."

Gunner huffed.

"I can do that. But it isn't gonna help. The shooter's not in Red Wing. He slipped through down-river, or maybe into Wisconsin somehow. Maybe he had a small submarine or something."

Bull snorted.

"Yeah. Like nobody would've seen one of them things go into the water."

I gave Bull a stern look.

"Well, I'm sorry. But a submarine . . . ?"

Gunner was simmering.

"Gunner," I said. "Do we have any other names or leads at all?"

"Not a damn thing."

The meeting was rapidly approaching its end.

"How about your thoughts, Bull?" I said.

"I'd look hard at Tomball."

"Agreed," I said.

"Nobody here's got anything else?"

Gunner and Bull both said "Nope" at the same time.

"Well," I said, "I was hoping for more." That was an understatement. "Gunner and I had better head out and do some more investigating. I'll give you a call, Bull. Okay?"

"Yeah. You got my number."

Gunner and I let ourselves out as Bull pulled up a football game on the conference room's big screen.

*   *   *

On our way out, Gunner was pissing and moaning about me dragging him out to the meeting with Bull.

I jerked his shirt sleeve, bringing him to a halt facing me.

"Hey."

"Don't 'Hey' me, Gunner. What's the matter with you anyway?"

"Hell, I don't know. That Indian just makes me nervous. He's always so cocksure of himself."

"He's got a track record to back that up."

"Yeah . . . well that bugs me even more."

"Look at it this way, Gunner . . . if it weren't for Bull, you wouldn't have the chance to predict buck scent on the swatch before BCA finds it – which I would definitely do, if I were you. Bull is seldom wrong about such things. In addition, you wouldn't have one Mr. Jasper Tomball as a suspect. The name sounds made up to me, don't you think so?"

Gunner didn't answer. Instead he pulled open the driver's door to his cruiser and climbed in.

"Well, Tomball or not, Gunner, if the shooter is still in town, he won't be here for long, if you catch my drift."

"Yeah. I get it. Unless I have any smarter ideas, I'd better get on Mr. Tomball's trail ASAP."

CHAPTER 28

At the U.S. Embassy. Cairo.

After her 4:15 telephone conversation with Simon, Beth struggled for more than an hour to fall back asleep. Eventually, she gave up and decided to start her day at 5:30 a.m. The cafeteria was always open. She may as well have breakfast.

When she arrived there, wearing yet another Diane Sawyer outfit, she was surprised to see Mr. Hitchens already perusing one of the local English language newspapers, a cup of coffee at hand. She decided to forego breakfast for the moment, grab a coffee of her own, and join him.

On her way over to his table, she again noted his attire. His appearance was as disheveled as it had been when they'd first met. She assumed he must intentionally wrinkle and soil his clothes to maintain such a consistent look. And there was almost certainly a reason for this strategy. Beth just couldn't fathom what it might possibly be.

"Is this seat available?" Beth said as she sidled up beside his table.

She smiled.

Hitch looked up from his paper. On seeing her, he stood.

"Ah, Elizabeth. Good morning. So lovely to see you. Yes, yes. Please have a seat." He motioned to the chair across from him.

"Thank you, Hitch. I'm glad to have company. I figured the caf would be desolate this time of morning."

"A reasonable guess. But a person with my job works odd hours. I'm sure you can imagine."

She could imagine quite a lot, but was certain of nothing concerning this man.

"Hitch. I'm assuming you've heard about Senator Grossman?"

"Ah, yes. Very sad. Very sad, indeed."

"So it appears he was the target of the assassination Rasha told us about recently."

"Yes. It does appear that way, doesn't it."

He hadn't confirmed the truth of her statement, merely repeated it.

"So what then has become of my assignment here in Cairo? Is it time for me to pack up and go home?"

Hitch sipped his coffee while he thought.

"If the Senator's assassination originated in Egypt, I should think the Agency would want to gather intelligence to confirm that fact. We can't have foreign countries just killing off our government, now can we."

"My thoughts exactly, Hitch. In fact, I was hoping I could get further information about that computer file Rasha gave me. Perhaps she would be willing to dig a bit deeper if we could give her something specific to look for."

Hitch considered Beth's suggestion.

"You know, Elizabeth, accepting volunteered intel from a foreigner is one thing. Attempting to handle them in an Intel-gathering operation is quite another. I would want to give that recommendation some serious thought before pursuing Rasha as a further source of information."

Beth had to agree. But after their short meeting, Beth really felt that she and Rasha had a connection, one that went back to the "Omar incident." That wasn't the kind of story she would recall after 20 years unless its impact on Rasha had been genuine. And Rasha hadn't asked for anything from Beth in return for the risk involved in delivering the SD card to the United States. Beth's gut told her Rasha had more to offer.

"Well, I'd appreciate it if you'd think it over, Hitch."

"Let's not put the cart before the horse, Elizabeth. At present, we don't have anything to even ask Rasha to search for, do we?"

That was true.

"I say we keep you around Cairo for at least a few days more, just to see whether an opportunity to use your special gifts in this unfortunate situation arises. Is that okay with you, Elizabeth?"

Beth had actually hoped for just such an invitation. For her to have traveled across parts of three continents to get to Cairo, only to find her arrival here was too little and too late, didn't sit well with Beth. She hoped she could yet make a contribution to the Grossman murder case. Identifying the person who had ordered the hit would be at least partially satisfying.

"That'd be fine with me, Hitch. But may I ask you a favor?"

"Asking is free. Go ahead."

"You know Simon Connor at Langley?"

"We're acquainted. Yes."

"He's not trying very hard to get us further information about the file I sent him – the one relating to Grossman's murder. He says the file originated with the Army and they're not being very forthcoming with details. Is that something you might be able to help me with?"

Hitch chuckled.

"That's quite a favor you're asking. You want me to go over, or around, a Deputy Director of the CIA to gather information he declined to provide to you. That's what you're asking, correct?"

Beth knew he had posed the question in such a way that an answer of "Yes" would confirm her insubordination. But what did she have to lose? They wouldn't lock her up for insubordination, especially after her official retirement. It'd be a slap on the wrist at most.

"Yes. That's what I'm asking you to do, Hitch. How 'bout it?"

"Well, let's see. I believe I do have a few connections in various government offices after all these years. I could make some discreet inquiries . . . a fact-finding mission, if you will. No promises, but I'll peek around a bit."

That was the best Beth would get out of Hitch's mouth.

"Thanks a bunch, Hitch. You're not half the jerk everyone says you are."

Beth smiled.

"Damn. And I've worked so hard to cultivate that sonofabitch persona. Ah, well. I'm certain I'll do something to regain my reputation for disrepute."

He smiled.

Beth wasn't entirely sure it was a joke. CIA folks had a penchant for duplicity. It went with the territory.

Beth stood and Hitch began to rise also.

"Don't get up. Please."

He settled back into his seat

"Enjoy the rest of your day, Elizabeth, whatever hours you may be keeping."

Beth gave a nod, picked up her cup, and was on her way – to where exactly, she wasn't sure.

CHAPTER 29

It was the day after Beth's last visit with Mr. Hitchens in the cafeteria. At precisely 8:00 a.m., her house phone at the Embassy rang. She had been up since 6:30 and so was ready to take the call.

"Hello?"

"Good morning, Elizabeth." It was Hitch. "And how are we doing this fine day?"

"I'm feeling rather useless at present, Hitch. I'm hoping you've got something meaningful to keep me busy?"

"Indeed, Elizabeth. I have news, and I believe you will be pleased to hear it. Can we meet for a bit of breakfast in the cafeteria to chat? Say, in about thirty minutes?"

"I always enjoy a good chat. I'll plan to rendezvous with you at the usual table."

"Very good. I shall see you shortly."

Hitch terminated the call.

Beth hoped that he had found a way to work around Simon and had obtained further information that might lead to the identity of the man behind Senator Grossman's assassination.

She still wasn't sure what that information might look like though. Would it be another Kryptos ID packet? Or an email describing the files attached to the packet Rasha had found? Or possibly an entire hard drive filled with potentially, but not necessarily, relevant material that she would need to sift through for clues?

There was no point speculating. She didn't even know whether the assassination was going to be the subject of their chat.

Given that her first meeting of the day was with a man whose clothing could generously be described as rumpled, it wasn't a tough choice for Beth to go casual. Another Diane Sawyer outfit. It was lucky she'd brought a generous assortment.

It was exactly thirty minutes later when Beth entered the Embassy cafeteria. She proceeded through the food line selecting a bowl of mixed, fresh fruit and requesting a helping of scrambled eggs. She finished off by filling a coffee cup, then turned toward the table where she had expected to find her date.

He wasn't there. No matter. She was punctual. Most bureaucrats were not. She made her way to the table and took the chair Hitch had occupied during their previous meetings . . . the chair with a view of cafeteria traffic.

Eggs are not a dish best served cold, so she began to eat. By the time she'd finished her eggs, and about half the cup of coffee, she began to wonder when Hitch would appear. A check of her Timex revealed that it was now 8:50. So far, Hitch was twenty minutes late.

Beth finished her fruit and coffee, then fetched herself another cup from the commercial steel urn.

Fifteen more minutes slipped away with no sign of Hitch.

With her breakfast finished, and the appointed meeting time well past, Beth was about to get up to leave when Hitch ambled through the caf entrance and headed directly toward her. She rose and extended her hand in greeting.

"Good morning, Hitch."

He returned her shake, accompanied by an apology.

"I am very sorry, Elizabeth, for my extreme tardiness. Just as I was about to escape my office, I received a call from our friend, Simon. You know how he can drone on. Truly, I apologize."

"No apologies necessary, Hitch. Do you want to fill a tray before we talk."

"Thank you, but I shan't delay you further."

They both sat. Hitch turned his head from side to side.

"I must say, the cafeteria looks different from this perspective."

Beth laughed.

"Would you care to switch places?"

"No, no. Not at all. It's just a wonder how complacent one gets when one's point of view stagnates."

"That is true in so many ways, my friend." Beth laughed again.

"Indeed, it is." Hitch looked around once more, then focused on Beth.

"When I called you this morning, I'd planned to tell you that I'd messaged Simon with your idea about pursuing the possible Egyptian connection to the Grossman assassination."

Beth's eyes widened.

"No, no, don't be concerned. I didn't mention your name at all. I merely made the suggestion as though it were my own. Why fight my way around the bosses if I can get them to cooperate, eh?"

Beth took a breath.

"Of course. And was Simon receptive to the idea? Is he going to press the Army for further details so we have something to go on?"

Hitch looked around again.

"I *am* sorry, Elizabeth, but I feel the need for another coffee. May I refill yours as well?"

"No thanks. I'm on number two already. I'll nurse this one."

Hitch hiked up his sagging pants on the way to the coffee station.

Beth chuckled. He'd certainly nailed the "lived-in" look.

Hitch was back at the table moments later with a cup in each hand. The first thing he did after sitting was to take a large swallow of black from one of the cups.

Beth caught her breath. "Doesn't that burn?"

"Ha. I iced this one a bit. My last caffeine buzz has worn off. I couldn't wait for this stuff to cool to start my next one."

Beth rolled her eyes.

"Do you *ever* sleep?

"Hmm," he said through another gulp of coffee. The first cup was emptying. "I believe I recall sleeping. Just can't remember when."

He smiled.

Beth was anxious to talk business. If she wasn't going to be doing anything productive, she'd rather be home.

"Well, let's see. Where to start . . . . Have you had a chance to catch network news lately, Elizabeth?"

Beth suddenly realized how disconnected she'd become from the world outside Cairo . . . how easily her entire attention had focused on this Middle Eastern microcosm.

"Actually, no, I haven't. What've I missed?"

"One item I'm certain will interest you is that Senator Grossman's murder took place in Red Wing, Minnesota."

Beth gasped, covering her mouth with one hand.

"Omigosh!" Hitch waited while Beth processed the news. Her first thoughts were for her husband. "Was anyone else injured?"

"No, thank God! And there doesn't seem to be any lingering threat. But I was certain you would want to know."

"Yes . . . of course. Thank you, Hitch."

Hitch sipped his second coffee while Beth's mind raced.

"Did Simon know where Grossman was shot when he called me yesterday?"

"Yes."

"Why that ass! He knows he should have told me. What a prick!" Beth looked at Hitch's smile. "Pardon my French, Hitch. Simon has a way of getting my Irish up." Beth paused. "There's proof. I've just besmirched two nationalities in five seconds . . . that self-absorbed bastard!"

"I can see you hold Simon in the same esteem as do many of his minions, as he would call them."

Elizabeth gave a hearty laugh.

"Now if we can move along to business again . . . the only Red Wing connection appears to be that the Senator was at the wrong place at the wrong time, and he didn't follow his security team's protocols. The lecherous fool, God rest his soul, has been in a pinch before, you know. Some distraught husband brought a handgun to a parade. The Senator's men in black spotted the guy and hustled him off, so it never made the press. He's been ultra-security-conscious ever since. But not enough so, I imagine.

"Now back to Simon . . . I'm impressed at his expediency in working with the Army. They can be a bit . . . stubborn, on occasion. But it appears in this case, they gave Simon what he wanted without all the grumbles. That was the subject of our conversation this morning. He was quite proud of himself.

"He sent me a gob of computer files and a transcription that came with them from the Army. You'll get a digital copy of this, too." He reached into his hip pocket and withdrew a folded, and crumpled, piece of copy paper. He smoothed the note with his hand on the table, then handed it to Beth.

She took a minute to read it.

CLASSIFIED – TOP SECRET

To: Simon Connor
Deputy Director, Central Intelligence Agency
From: United States Army Central Command

The information you requested is Classified TOP SECRET and shall be distributed strictly on a NEED-TO-KNOW basis, only to qualified personnel, for the sole purpose of identifying the person or entity responsible for the death of Senator Grossman.

DESCRIPTION OF ATTACHED CONTENT: The files and records attached pertain to a project referred to as Aurora. Aurora is a CLASSIFIED military system.

COMMENTS: Per discussion with addressee, Aurora HAS NOT been compromised. DO NOT PURSUE possible appropriation of Aurora by foreign entities.

END COMMUNICATION.

Beth folded the paper and offered it to Hitch. He waved his refusal.

"You keep that. I can get another whenever I want."

"Do you have any idea why the Army made a point of telling Simon that this Aurora system had not been compromised?" Beth said.

"Simon can step on some toes. Maybe the Army didn't want him stepping on theirs. On the other hand, perhaps Aurora *has* been compromised, and they want him to stay away from their investigation. It's impossible to say. Simon didn't disclose anything further to me."

Beth placed the folded paper in the pocket of her olive-colored tunic.

"Your job, Elizabeth, is to examine the materials Simon sent over. Find us something that will help pin down any data GIS may have on its computers that could lead us to a kill contract on Senator Grossman."

"So we can ask Rasha to get that data for us?"

"Let's take it one step at a time. We don't know what the data might be yet. We'll speak again when we've learned more. Okay?"

"Understood." Beth didn't like being led around by a guy holding a flashlight. She wanted the big picture. Hitch wasn't going to provide it.

"I'd better get to work then, hadn't I. Will the Army material be waiting in my room?

Hitch spread his arms wide and smiled.

"Of course, Elizabeth. I am nothing if not efficient."

Beth returned the smile, but reminded herself to treat Hitch with caution. He was, after all, CIA . . . wasn't he?

CHAPTER 30

Hitch had been true to his word once again. The new data from the Army awaited Beth in the form of a portable hard drive labeled "Hitchens" which lay on her computer desk.

Beth removed her tunic jacket and hung it neatly in the closet, then sat at the desk, ready to work. Connecting the drive to her laptop, she began scanning its folders and files. She wasn't looking for anything specific at the moment – just trying to get the lay of the digital landscape on the drive. The information here had already been decrypted – at least it appeared so.

After completing the once over, Beth opened a file named "Grossman." The document contained a summary of Senator Grossman's Senate voting record and his activities on the Senate Armed Services Committee. He had chaired that committee from 2007 until his recent death.

As Committee Chair, Grossman held TOP SECRET clearance and had been "read in" on a list of military projects. With the exception of "Aurora," the names of the projects had been excised from her version of the file and replaced with series of random typographic symbols. Beth was used to dealing with sensitive information and presumed she had no need to know the names of those projects.

Reading further through the pages, Beth began to get a different picture of Senator Grossman than the one he'd presented during his many electoral campaigns. The Army had noted that Grossman "engaged in frequent extra-marital activities," and as a result, the Army had deemed him a "security risk.'

Beth realized that Grossman's position chairing the Armed Services Committee conflicted dramatically with his vulnerability to both loose lips syndrome, and overt blackmail, concerning what appeared to be multiple sexual engagements with a variety of young women – and *paid* young women, no less.

Proceeding through the abstract of Grossman's political and personal escapades, Beth came across a reference to a visit Grossman had made to an area in Nevada whose name had been excised. She presumed the visit had been to Area 51, whose existence was perhaps the worst kept secret in the United States Government. But existence was one thing, and activities were another. Very few people knew the goings on at Area 51, which were widely presumed to involve TOP SECRET military technology projects.

Reading on, Beth saw the document contained the name of the project the Senator had inspected at Area 51 – "Aurora." Once again, this name hadn't been excised. Was Aurora related to Rasha's computer data? Did Beth have a need to know of this project to pursue Grossman's assassin? This was the same project the Army had insisted in its memo "has not been compromised.'

Beth wondered how the Army had resolved Grossman's "security risk" status with his rightful demand to know about Aurora, since the Senate would have had to approve Aurora's funding. Or had they been able to resolve this problem at all?

Further on, she found her answer. On several occasions, the Joint Chiefs had sought revocation, or at least limitation, of the Senator's access to Top Secret projects. Unfortunately, the Senator had persuaded the President to intercede on his behalf in several cases. One of them had been Aurora.

The memo went on to mention additional visits to Nevada and further questionable personal activities. It also recounted an attempt on the Senator's life about six month ago. Investigators had determined the perpetrator was a distraught husband of one of Grossman's unpaid courtesans.

The man's name did not appear in the report. Nor was there information concerning how the attempted assault had been handled in the courts. Perhaps in lieu of prosecution, the Senator had elected to pay the husband an out of court settlement to keep his mouth shut about the affair. Money has a way of assuaging all manner of afflictions. It certainly wouldn't be the first time conscience had sacrificed its moral essence on the altar of bribery.

She read everything the file had to say about Grossman. There was no mention of Egypt.

In a computer folder named "Technical Specifications," Beth found numerous files whose names began with "Aurora." When she opened the first file, the screen displayed engineering drawings and numerical data, nearly all of which had been edited using digital obliteration. A few of Aurora's parts were visible, and from those she could tell Aurora was some sort of an aircraft, though an unusual one. The rest of the drawings in this file were useless in their edited state.

She continued on to the next "Aurora" file. This one held pages of tables and mathematical formulas, all of which had been rendered patently undecipherable by Army editing. After glancing through the remaining files in the "Technical Specifications" folder, she concluded that these files had been included to comply with the letter of the CIA request. There seemed nothing here of value either to her, or to anyone who might lust to steal the plans for Aurora. The entire folder was a masterwork of technobabble.

Proceeding through each folder and each file in turn, Beth found that data in the rest of the files had been similarly expunged, making their content uniformly worthless.

Nearly four hours after beginning on this data analysis project, Beth's eyes were tired, but she had identified almost nothing of value in the Army data files.

She checked the hard drive for hidden or encrypted files. The only additional file was the one she had sent to Simon in the first place – the Kryptos 4 tag that supposedly related to the content of this disk.

Beth leaned back in the task chair and stretched her arms and shoulders, finally rubbing out a knotted muscle in her neck.

Then she decided to make a list of the few tidbits of data that had caught her attention. At least she would have them consolidated for future reference:

Grossman.

Aurora.
Aircraft.
Technical Drawings.
Area 51.
Security risk.
Aurora "not compromised.'

Then she remembered the copy paper note Hitch had given her. Where had she put that? Ah, her tunic. She retrieved the note from the tunic pocket, unfolding it as she returned to her desk.

After staring at the document for at least ten minutes, she added an item to her list.

"Do not pursue possible appropriation of Aurora by foreign entities.'

Why had the Army mentioned the security status of Aurora in the note? And why had they included all of this partial Aurora data on the hard drive, but nothing that might be intelligible to a reader?

Given the information they'd provided, it was logical for the Army to assume that the CIA would pursue an investigation of Aurora in conjunction with Grossman's death. But why the prohibition on "pursuing appropriation of Aurora by foreign entities'?

If the Army hoped to hide something about stolen plans for Aurora, they'd sure picked an ill-informed way to do so. Telling the CIA not to investigate a foreign spying issue was like wrapping your fist in a porterhouse and telling a pit bull not to bite it. But the Army would know that . . . wouldn't they?

So did the Army actually *want* the CIA to investigate Aurora? Or not?

Beth's head swam. There was no way to end the double-double-double conniving wound within interagency communications, especially between two gangs of government spies, even when they worked for the same government.

Beth would give the entire hard drive another run-through after lunch, when she would have a full stomach, a fresh perspective, and hopefully, more instructive results.

Grabbing today's Diane Sawyer tunic from the closet, she was off to the cafeteria. She remembered Groppi's baklava and may have salivated just a bit. *Ah well, I'm not here for the cuisine.*

CHAPTER 31

Back at Red Wing.

After our meeting with Bull on the Rez, Gunner and I headed straight for the Cop Shop. Gunner had graciously allowed me to join him in his office while he spun the investigative wheels into high gear. I listened silently as he dispatched deputies to investigate the whereabouts of Jasper Tomball and to locate the fishing boat whose registration appeared on the Water Patrol Deputy's report. His men would interview campground owners near Welch, and scour boat yards, harbors, and adjacent parking facilities.

He'd requested copies of the surveillance video from yesterday's exit checkpoints on the Eisenhower Bridge and on Highway 61, south of town – the shooter's two most accessible entrance routes if he were actually foolish enough to return to Red Wing after the assassination.

Videos had been taken in both directions – heading in and out of Red Wing – just in case there might be some unrelated incident caused by the road blocks. It wasn't unusual for delayed drivers to become enraged and do stupid things. But Gunner wouldn't be looking for road rage. He'd be scanning for an assassin with a large set of *cojones*.

He directed one deputy to check all recent vehicle rentals made from Red Wing locations, securing renters' names, addresses, phone numbers, and vehicle data. The shooter may have switched vehicles after entering town. Gunner even detailed one squad to investigate recent rentals of storage lockers and garages. These were common locations for temporary bases of operation. There might yet be some clue hidden in one of them.

While he waited for the video, he called the BCA Crime Lab to see whether they had analyzed the scent on the clothing swatch.

"Sure. I'll wait," he said into the handset, then covered the mouthpiece with his hand. "They're checkin' with the lab folks right now. No surprise that BCA's givin' this whole investigation priority one. I should have an answer in a second."

I nodded.

Gathering facts and details aren't really my thing. I'm more of a big picture guy. I absorb the investigative details and try to bring a new perspective. Everybody has a role in the bad guy catching process. Mine is certainly no more valuable than anyone else's. And I'm grateful somebody is willing to do all that other stuff.

It wasn't long before Gunner was back on the line with BCA.

"Uh huh. Uh huh. Really? Okay, thanks." He dropped the handset onto his desk phone.

"What's up?"

"Well, I'll be damned!"

"Buck scent?"

"Uh huh. Now how the heck did that Indian know that."

"What can I say? The man knows his deer urine."

Gunner raised an eyebrow.

"Or maybe he knows how to be a sniper and get away with it. Hard to say with Bull."

Gunner leaned back.

"I don't like that guy. He makes me nervous. But I gotta admit, he does bring somethin' different to the table. Sure wish I could figure him out though."

I laughed.

"Join the club."

* * *

Gunner had managed to launch his investigative team in record time. It was only 12:30 p.m. Time was of the essence, of course. If the sniper *was* still in Red Wing, he wouldn't be here for long. The road blocks had long been disassembled and traffic now moved freely in and out of town.

Just as Gunner and I were deciding what to do next, a uniformed officer knocked on Gunner's open door.

"Yeah. Whatta ya need?"

"We got the video from the bridge here now. The rest is coming. You wanna start looking at it?"

"Thanks, Kyle. Can we set it up in here?"

"Yeah. We could. But it's all set to go on the big screen in the meeting room."

"Better yet. Get 'er all queued up to where the Senator gets shot, and I'll be there in a second."

Kyle departed with a "Yessir."

"You're welcome to stay and watch the movies with me, Beck. Maybe you'd spot something I'd miss. Can get pretty darn boring, though."

I couldn't think of anything else useful to do, so I accepted the Chief Deputy's request and we moseyed off to the screening room. There's a lot of moseying goes on around Gunner's office. I think it's a small town cop thing.

When we arrived, the flat screen was lit up and the flick was set to roll. Kyle gave Gunner the remote for the DVD player.

"You guys need anything else in here?"

"Thanks, Kyle. Bring us a couple mugs and a pot of full-strength coffee."

"Yessir." And he was gone.

Gunner punched on the video and shut off the lights.

"No snoring," he said.

"Then keep me entertained."

I could imagine Gunner's eyes rolling in their sockets.

The video started with Sheriff's cars and barricades lined up along the bridge shoulders. The screen was split to show separate views of traffic approaching and departing Red Wing. There was no audio. I'd been hoping for a talkie.

Our eyes barely left the screen when the coffee arrived. I wasn't surprised that Gunner could pour coffee in the dark. He could probably do it in his sleep, too.

I took my mug and cozied into my metal chair. No chance of falling asleep here. Maybe that was the point of the ridged furniture.

A short time after we had our coffees in hand, the cruisers on the screen swung into motion. Lights flashed as they maneuvered to block all bridge traffic. The deputies allowed no one in or out. Prodigious lines of vehicles grew on both sides of the roadblock.

"Can we fast forward to where they start letting cars go through?"

"Good idea." Gunner took aim with the remote and depressed a button.

The screen flickered and deputies paced comically at high speed. In a moment, one of the cop cars vacated its position, preparing to allow the bridge traffic a single lane to pass by. At first they allowed only inbound traffic. But as additional law enforcement personnel arrived – some Red Wing Cops and some additional deputies – they began searching outward bound cars, eventually granting them passage at the rate of an IV drip.

"Do you think we could just look at the incoming traffic? Your guys searched the cars headed out. Right?"

"Right."

Gunner beckoned for assistance with the technical maneuver, and Kyle soon had us zoomed in on incoming traffic only.

We stared at the crawling vehicles, mostly small cars and oversized pickups, for what seemed like hours, though the time counter in the corner of the video confirmed that only fifteen minutes had passed.

"What're *you* looking for Gunner?" I asked, my eyes still locked on the screen.

"A boat."

"Me, too. Don't you think we could speed this show up a little and still see a boat when one came through?"

There was a pause.

"Do you want this controller? 'Cause maybe I ain't doing it just your way."

I said nothing.

"Okay. You're right. Let's move it along." Gunner switched the video back into fast motion.

At this speed it wasn't too long before we saw our first candidate. There weren't a lot of fishing boats on the river in November, let alone on the road.

I looked at Gunner as the boat moved closer.

"I got it," he said, as though he'd sensed my gaze.

As the red pickup towing a small aluminum fishing boat approached the camera, Gunner slowed the video to normal speed. When the truck was as close to the camera as possible, he froze the shot.

"Kyle. Get in here," Gunner hollered over his shoulder.

"Kyle appeared as though he'd been awaiting just such a summons.

"Yessir."

"Where's those Water Patrol guys who were under the bridge yesterday?"

"Hanson's out searching trailer parks. Birch is just down the hall."

"Well get me Birch then, and make it snappy!"

Kyle raced out the door and toward the front of the office section.

"That Kyle sure does a good job of 'snappy,' Gunner. Do you guys award a pin for 'snappiness' ? Or is that the Boy Scouts I'm thinking of."

"Just shuddup and quit flapping your lips."

"That's redundant."

Gunner turned toward me, his profile eerie in the side-lighting from the flat screen – his features like something out of a black and white horror movie.

"I said it twice and you still didn't shut your face."

"Good point," I said. I saw no reason to pick a fight.

Snappy Kyle came trotting in with Birch in tow.

"I got Deputy Birch, Chief."

"Yeah, I see that, Kyle. Thanks. That'll do for now."

Gunner stood and shook Birch's hand.

"Dan."

"Gunner."

"Did you get a good look at that guy in the fishing boat yesterday? What's his name . . . Tomball?"

"Yeah. I took his license and info. Why?"

"Dan, take a good look at the guy driving that red Ford pickup." Gunner gestured at the screen. Birch stepped around our table to get a batter look.

"Could that be the guy?"

Surveillance cameras seldom have the desired resolution. It's just not practical to record terabytes of HD video on every security camera. Reduced image quality saves storage space. Simple as that.

Birch looked hard at the man in the pickup.

"Yeah," he said. "I think that's the same guy. Can I see the boat?"

Gunner stepped the video forward until there was a clear shot of the trailered fishing boat.

"That's the boat, for sure, Boss. A sixteen foot Sylvan with a Johnson 50 horse. Blue carpet. Even looks like the same tackle."

"Thanks, Dan. That's all we need."

Birch turned to Gunderson.

"Did this guy have something to do with the shooting? "Cause I cleared him. There wasn't anything suspicious about him or the boat."

He looked anxiously back and forth between Gunner and me.

"Don't worry about it, Dan. We're just playing hunches here. Maybe this guy saw something and we'd like to talk to him, is all," Gunner said.

"Thanks for your help. Now get back to whatever I told you to do last."

"Calling car rental places. I'm about half way through. Damn Blue Laws have got all the dealers closed for Sunday. I'm having to drag folks outta their homes to get the records we need."

"Keep at it, Dan. Fill me in when you're ready."

"Got it, Boss." Birch departed the screening room.

"Looks like that's our guy, Gunner."

"Yeah . . . that's a guy who was fishing while the Senator was shot. There's still nothing saying he's the shooter."

"You got any other hot leads to work at the moment?"

"Not so much."

"So what do we do now? Yell for help?"

Gunner laughed. "Pretty much. BCA's gotta enhance this guy's pic and license plate. Maybe we'll get lucky and find him that way."

"Like Thomas Jefferson always said, 'The harder I work, the luckier I get.' I'm a believer."

"Yeah. Me, too. I gotta get this to the BCA, pronto.

"Kyle!"

CHAPTER 32

At the U.S. Embassy. Cairo.

After filling her lunch tray with spinach and feta cheese salad, Beth turned to face the tables. There, in his usual spot, sat Hitchens, drinking a cup of coffee and reading the *Wall Street Journal*. For a man who claimed long working hours, he certainly seemed to spend a lot of time in the cafeteria.

Before approaching him this time, Beth considered whether he had been informed in advance of her visits to the caf. That would mean he was spying on her in her room. She shuddered at the thought.

Pretending not to notice the frumpy . . . what? . . . diplomat? Or agent? . . . she chose a small table across the room from Hitch and prepared to eat her lunch.

Just as she tasted the first bit of spinach salad, his voice came from behind her.

"Ah, Elizabeth. We have to stop meeting like this."

"Quite a coincidence, isn't it, Hitch, especially given your odd hours and all."

"And you don't believe in coincidences. Do you, Elizabeth. So you suspect that I am 'stalking' you?"

"I wouldn't have said it just that way, Mr. Hitchens. But you do have an unfathomable knack for following in front of me."

"May I join you, Elizabeth?"

Beth considered sending him away and enjoying her meal in peace. But that was no way to gain cooperation from a co-agent, if he was one. And in truth, she hoped for further insight into this man.

"Pull up a chair," Beth said, and forked another portion of

greens into her mouth. The salad was passable, but could have benefited from a few Greek olives.

Hitch maneuvered through the tight space between Beth's table and the adjacent one (which currently stood vacant), set his cup down, and took the seat across from Beth.

"I'm afraid I must begin with a confession."

"Really?" Beth rearranged some spinach on her plate.

"Yes. You are correct that I have been . . . ah . . . monitoring your movements within the Embassy. But I assure you, I have acted in complete discretion. All my information comes from *outside* your room. The inside is quite secure."

"Indeed. So you're not behind the digital trace that has been dogging my computer maneuvers?"

"Well, honestly, I am. But you seem to have blocked those efforts quite successfully . . . that is, unless the Army encoded nursery rhymes in their data."

He smiled.

"You're not a Bo Peep fan, I take it," Beth said. She eyeballed Hitch, but did not return this smile.

"And is that the full extent of your 'monitoring' activities? Or do I need to shower in my bathing suit?" Beth raised skeptical eyebrows.

Hitch laughed, then caught himself.

"No, no, no, Elizabeth. There is nothing further for you to be concerned about. We have already covered all my surveillance efforts. And I shall terminate them immediately. You have no need of further concern."

"Really? I can't tell you how relieved I am, Mr. Hitchens, that after having been caught in your pursuits, you now vow to desist. Quite admirable."

Beth returned to rearranging salad.

"Elizabeth. I was only following orders. Will you please forgive me? Surely, my actions were no more invasive than the video cameras in the hallways. I just happened to add an extra sensor to your door so I knew when I could interrupt you.

"Don't you think our cafeteria meetings have been quite

convenient?"

Beth had to admit she preferred that Hitchens work around her schedule rather than the other way around. And she was certain that his lame attempt at cyber-espionage had revealed nothing. She'd seen to that.

"Some folks would email or message me to set a date," Beth said. "That's a convenient approach to scheduling meetings that might be considered a bit more conventional. You should give it a try."

Hitch didn't reply, though his expression was suitably apologetic.

"So the fact that you're here right now would imply you hoped to meet me this afternoon," Beth said. "What have we to discuss?"

Beth continued with her meal.

"Yes. You are correct, Elizabeth. I wanted to know your progress on the Army data, and perhaps to share my own thoughts as well. You've not been the only cyber-guru assessing this information."

That was no surprise. In fact, Beth welcomed any help she could get in scouring the data.

"Okay, Hitch. Whatta you want from me?"

"A summary of your findings thus far, Elizabeth. That's all."

Hitch had been properly contrite, if a bit tardy in presentation. It's much easier to admit one's faults, and to apologize for them, when one has already been caught. Just ask any police investigator.

Still, in the context of the CIA world, his sins could be forgiven, though not forgotten.

Beth dabbed her mouth with a paper napkin, then placed it on her plate.

"Okay, Hitch. I forgive your unwelcome and undeserved surveillance activities. You may consider us even on that score."

Hitch's face remained calm, but his eyes twitched at Beth's implication.

"Now . . . you want a summary of my findings. Here you go.

"The data contained numerous references to Aurora, but all mentions of any other classified projects had been excised. It appears Aurora is an aircraft of some sort . . . an Area 51 project. And Senator Grossman was connected to Aurora in his capacity as

Chairman of the Senate Armed Services Committee. He certainly possessed more information about Aurora than the Army would have liked. It's unclear whether he also possessed unedited copies of Aurora's drawings and specifications corresponding to the excised ones I viewed on the disk. That's all I know about Aurora, except for the contents of the transmission you shared with me at our meeting this morning."

Beth paused to allow Hitch an opportunity for questions. He motioned for her to proceed.

"As far as Grossman goes . . . the Army considered him a substantial security risk. They detailed the Senator's numerous inappropriate intimate contacts – liaisons that rendered him vulnerable to blackmail, or bribery, or both.

"That's about it for the data."

Hitch considered for a moment.

"Have you reached any conclusions about this information, Elizabeth?"

"Only preliminary. While it seems the Army was happy to connect Grossman with Aurora, they gave us little more to go on. And then there's the enigmatic demand that the CIA *not* pursue possible foreign compromise of the Aurora project. Did the Army really expect the CIA to leave that one alone? Or did they know we would investigate further, and that's the real reason they told us not to? In my opinion, it could cut either way."

Hitch had finished his coffee and needed another cup.

"May I get you coffee as well, Elizabeth?"

"Yes. That would be great. Thank you."

"Cream or sugar?"

"Black would be fine."

Was Hitch's coffee service a subtle attempt to regain her favor? Beth wondered. In any case, it would take more than a cup of java to win back her good graces.

He returned with the cups a few moments later, setting one before Beth, then retaking his chair. He took a sip before speaking.

"Elizabeth, have you considered that the Army may be equally satisfied with either CIA action, or inaction, on this Aurora matter?"

This was a line of thought Beth and not pursued. Why would the Army mention the possible "foreign compromise" of the Aurora project at all if it didn't care what the CIA did?

"Are you suggesting the Army might have something to gain by dangling the Aurora issue, regardless of whether the CIA obeys the Army's demand that we leave it alone?"

Hitch raised one eyebrow.

"It's merely a question, Elizabeth. If there is an answer, it would resolve your quandary about the Army's intent."

Beth knew that Hitch had his own opinions on this subject. But he wanted hers as well.

"Hitch. That scenario is something I will need to contemplate further."

"I understand completely. This question presents no obvious solution."

Beth began tidying her tray.

"Don't leave just yet. Please. I believe there are actions we can take on our current information to locate the persons responsible for the Senator's death."

Beth pushed her tray aside and settled in her chair.

"Tell me more." Beth found Hitch's suggestion that she might be able to make an immediate impact in the Grossman investigation attractive.

"We already have key words from the Army data that are likely to link Grossman's assassination to Egypt . . . *if* we can gain access to the GIS network."

"Are you agreeing to allow Rasha to help us?" Beth said. "Because I think she'd be willing. She believes the decision to kill the Senator was not in Egypt's interests. I have a good feeling about Rasha. I *know* she can help."

Hitch took a breath and tugged at his already loosened tie.

"I'm afraid I still have several concerns about using your Egyptian friend to gather data for us. First of all, *you* may trust her, but *I* have no reason to do so.

"Secondly, how can we be certain she has the technical

knowledge to efficiently search the GIS network, locate the data we want, and then remove it from the premises?"

Beth massaged her forehead. She had to admit that, were she in Hitch's place, she wouldn't want Rasha to be in control of this cyber-invasion. And his observation about Rasha's abilities was valid, too. She might be able to enter programs and files through the "back doors" she had created, but such a method was cumbersome, and would need to be applied one file at a time. If Beth could crack the GIS internal encryption, she could search many files concurrently.

"But without Rasha's working from the inside, how in the world can we gain access to GIS internal data?" Beth said. "The Egyptians may not have the same level of cyber-security as the CIA, but they're no fools either. Sensitive portions of their network will be air-gapped, so we can't probe with a Trojan Horse. The entire building has to be insulated from any sort of carrier wave we might use to attempt access that way. And they *must* scrub unwanted frequencies from their power source, so we couldn't use a digital-over-power attack. How do you propose we gain access to the Egypt's most secure computer network?"

Hitch leaned in, while Beth followed his cue. Hitch spoke in hushed tones.

"There is a means of access to the Intelligence Directorate's computer network. We have known of it for some time. But it will provide only a short window of opportunity, and can be used once before GIS discovers the access point and seals it. With your expertise, I am confident that our present assignment would make good use of this one-time vulnerability."

"Go on."

"You are correct, Elizabeth, about the security measures GIS has employed to defend their network. But they have left a small hole for us in their power supply. While they do, indeed, scrub the frequencies entering the facility via the usual power lines, they have not applied the same diligence to their backup power generator."

Beth was following.

"So if we can tap into the auxiliary power lines serving the building while the primary power is down," Beth said, "we could still use a broadband-over-power, or digital-over-power, attack to gain access to their interior power wiring."

This was a plausible method of attack. Yet there were many details that had to fall into place for it to be successful.

"How do we get the digital transceivers clamped onto the power lines from their generator?"

"There is a team of Seals that has been conducting classified operations in Cairo for awhile now. They would be at our disposal to make the connection to the power lines between the generator and the GIS building. The distance between the generator and the building wall is approximately 100 feet. And to make things more convenient, Elizabeth, the Egyptians have constructed a sound barrier around the generator. They don't want to hear the diesel while it's running. Our operatives can work in relative safety inside the sound walls."

Hitch had clearly been thinking about exploiting this vulnerability for a long time. And he'd had the benefit of someone's computer skills as well. Hitch did not strike Beth as a computer guru.

"How about re-transmission? We'd need to have a WiFi router near the power line access, and a wireless receiver not too far away."

"That is very astute of you, Elizabeth. I propose that we hide a small computer inside the walls of an adjacent building to receive the primary signal, and use that computer to forward information to us via a wired or satellite connection. There are many computer wires already buried beneath Cairo's streets. I have confidence we could find one that is suitable for our needs. This would allow you to conduct the invasion from the safety of your room here at the Embassy."

Hitch's plan was flawed.

"Hitch. You can't expect me to hack an encrypted network through some proxy server in a wall next door. I would need direct access to the network. I trust you won't require me to explain why this is so."

Hitch frowned.

"That does present a challenge."

"And the digital-over-power approach will only work once we have a network 'wall wart' connected inside GIS. Otherwise, our digital signal will never reach the network computers. You can't just send digital commands through a computer's power supply unit."

"I *had* considered that issue, Elizabeth, though I have no simple solution. I thought perhaps someone more computer savvy than I would be able to plug that hole in my plan."

Beth thought about Hitch's invitation for her input.

"Rasha," she said. "Rasha would be the perfect person to install the wall wart where we need it. She maintains the GIS Director's computer and could probably make our connection right in his office. This assignment wouldn't require technical expertise beyond what Rasha has already demonstrated."

"I don't know, Elizabeth. I still have my concerns about Rasha's loyalties."

"Then I'm afraid *you* will need to solve the puzzle on your own. I've given you my solution. But we still need to discuss how I can maneuver within GIS from a safe distance."

"I shall put my best minds to work on that issue, and the wall wart problem as well. If I can resolve these concerns to your satisfaction, will you consent to perform the attack? You are certainly the most qualified person to carry it out."

Beth hesitated to commit to any suggestion made by this man . . . especially without all the details in place.

"I promise I will give your plans my most favorable consideration."

Hitch laughed.

"Spoken like a diplomat, Elizabeth. Perhaps you missed your calling."

* * *

Beth returned to her room after the lunch visit with Hitch harboring mixed feelings. She was enthusiastic about hacking into

Egypt's most well-guarded computer network. But the problems remaining to be resolved were considerable, particularly if Hitch wouldn't agree to engaging Rasha's help. For the remainder of the afternoon, and into the night, Beth sifted through the Army data, plotting the particulars of her part in the cyber-attack – assuming an attack could be successfully mounted. And as her husband had said so often, there was no point assuming anything else.

By 10:30, Beth felt confident she had gleaned as many inferences from the Army info as she was likely to get. She also had her cyber-invasion plan ready – the decryption programs she would need, the network hacking software, the specifications for encryption of the data she was able to mine, and the appropriate protocols for re-transmission of her findings to a secure communications satellite. All she needed now was a way into the GIS network. She hoped Hitch and Co. would either come up with an avenue of attack that she'd overlooked, or that Hitch would agree to use Rasha,

With nothing further on her to-do list for today, Beth decided to turn in. If she'd be hacking into GIS, it would probably be tomorrow night. She would need to get what sleep she could this evening. After sending off her daily message to her husband, she crawled between the cotton sheets and instantly fell asleep.

When Beth awoke, it was after 7:00 a.m. It had been too long since she'd enjoyed a good night's rest, but last night had done much to restore her energy.

After rubbing the sleep from her eyes, she noticed the red light on her room phone was blinking. No doubt Hitch wanted to see her. She thought it was decent of him to leave a message rather than to awaken her – or spy on her.

Still wearing her silk pajamas, Beth picked up the handset and dialed the Embassy Operator.

"Operator. How may I assist you?"

"This is Elizabeth Weston. Someone left me a message on this extension. Could you retrieve it for me please?"

"Please hold, Ms. Weston." The operator clicked off, then on again. "Playing your message now. Thank you."

Hitch's recorded voice came on the line.

"Are you up for breakfast this morning, Elizabeth? My timing is flexible. Please call me at extension #4575 when convenient. Thank you."

Did that man never sleep?

She dialed Hitch's extension.

"Good morning, Elizabeth. I hope you are available for a breakfast chat. I have something for your consideration."

"I'm certain I'll be mesmerized by your proposal. Shall we say 8:15 at our favorite table?"

"That would be lovely. I shall anticipate your arrival."

* * *

Beth wasn't sure who she'd be meeting with today . . . besides Mr. Hitchens, that is. Best to dress for success. She selected one of her dark, Egyptian-style power suits, complete with buttoned-up neck, black pumps, and slim black leather briefcase. A few subtle touches to hair and eyes and she was off to the cafeteria.

She found Hitch at his usual table, still dressed as though his washer and dryer might be on the fritz. She filled a cup of coffee and joined him. He stood upon her arrival.

"Ah, so nice to see you again, Elizabeth. I trust you slept well?"

After shaking hands, they both took their seats.

"First decent night's rest since I arrived at your hotel of dubious slumber." Beth smiled.

"The time difference between here and Washington does tend to muck with one's circadian rhythms. You'll get used to it, that is, if you stick around long enough."

Beth preferred the sleep disturbances to the prospect of remaining away from home until her system adjusted. She tasted her coffee.

"Good batch of brew this morning."

"It's all a matter of timing. But then, who can afford to schedule their day around the coffee maker. Just enjoy your good fortune when it comes calling."

"Duly noted." Beth took another sip from her cup. "So what've you learned since yesterday?"

"I'm pleased to say that we have been able to refine our access plan. I believe you may approve. Shall I expound?"

"Feel free."

"Well, first there was the problem of planting the wall wart. By the way, I'm told in the twenty-first century they're referred to as BPL modems. Broadband over Power Lines. I guess the wall wart term was too ugly to stick around."

"Got it. So how do you propose to embed our BPL modem into the GIS network."

"As it turns out, there is a certain young Egyptian gentleman who has been valuable to us on inside assignments in the past. He's a delivery boy and would have access to a number of network connections where he could surreptitiously connect the BPL modem. As you said yesterday, Elizabeth, it's not a challenging undertaking. All he needs to do is locate a suitably discreet network jack with power nearby and plug the device in at each end. It's not even possible for him to attach it backward. It only fits one way."

"Yes. I'm aware how a wall wart . . . excuse me . . . a BPL modem attaches to a network." Beth ran her finger around the rim of her cup. "I'll offer a few thoughts on your connection plan in a moment. But first, tell me how we deal with the limited range of the wireless transmission from the router. That was a concern as well."

Hitch showed no indication of offense at Beth's request to hear the entire plan before commenting. In fact, his expression revealed nothing at all about the thoughts that lurked inside his CIA-trained brain.

"My techies tell me that we can stretch that signal up to 1000 feet using a wireless bridge. That would allow us to infiltrate the GIS network from a reasonably safe distance."

Beth practiced her own impenetrable countenance.

"And when you say that would allow 'us' to remain at a safe distance, you're referring to *me*, correct?"

"Well, yes. You have the best qualifications."

"A thousand feet doesn't give me all that much comfort, Hitch, especially since about 500 of it will be inside the GIS compound."

"I thought you might say that, Elizabeth. So I inquired of my computer experts as to whether we could install a series of these 'repeaters' to gain a greater perimeter for your protection. They indicated that this was, indeed, possible."

"Did they also say that daisy-chaining unmonitored repeaters or boosters frequently results in dropped signals? Under our circumstances, losing the network connection in mid-hack would be catastrophic."

Hitch rubbed his chin.

"They didn't actually mention that. No. So is one repeater okay? Or are we back to a location directly across the street from GIS?"

"One should be all right, assuming you're prepared to get me into my operation center without notice, and out before the bad guys arrive at my door."

Hitch laughed.

"That goes without saying, my dear Elizabeth. But you had another concern?"

"Yes. How does your delivery boy know he's connecting our broadband to the right GIS network? I'm certain they have one highly secure loop, and probably two or more that are less so. If we don't get into the Director's encrypted stream, the whole mission is shot."

Hitch lifted his cup, staring into space as he drank.

"Why don't these computer 'experts' ever know what they ought to?"

"Oh, gimme a break, Hitch. You know 'expert' is a relative term. These days technology's more art than science. And that's true in spades when you it comes to cyber-espionage. Your people are okay."

"This is yet another reason why you are the only person for this job. But now we are back to an unresolved issue. How do we plant the BPL modem?"

"Rasha," Beth said, speaking over the brim of her cup.

Hitch eyed the ceiling.

"You realize, Elizabeth, if she screws us over, there'll be hell to pay. And the shekels are *not* going to be mine!"

Beth couldn't resist a hearty laugh with coffee still in her mouth.

"Aggh. I hate it when coffee goes up my nose."

She laughed again, at herself, and at Hitch.

"You never had any shekels in this game to begin with, Mr. Hitchens. Your backside's clad in steel. You've got Simon above you, and me and probably a dozen other scapegoats below. You're wallet's safe."

Now it was Hitch's turn to laugh.

"I do suppose that's so, isn't it? You are exceedingly perceptive, Elizabeth. I can see now why you chose to leave government employ."

Elizabeth leaned forward and locked eyes with Hitchens.

"So may I speak with Rasha? At least to see whether she's willing?"

Hitch paused for a breath, then locked his hands behind his head and stretched.

"Talk to her, Elizabeth. But please be discreet."

Beth covered her eyes and shook her head, then looked up at Hitchens.

"I shall do my best."

* * *

Beth arranged to meet Rasha later that day at Groppi. This time, Rasha arrived first. She greeted Beth with a formal hug.

"Rasha. I'm grateful you could meet me today."

Rasha held a cup of tea, her thumb, worrying its ceramic surface earnestly.

"It is my pleasure to visit with you again, Elizabeth. But I must confess to some worries at the cause for our meeting. I trust this is not entirely social?"

Beth wanted to ease Rasha's concerns, but she didn't think her proposal would offer anything to relieve Rasha's distress.

A white-shirted waiter arrived to take Beth's order.

"Would you care for a menu, Miss?"

"No thank you. I'll just have a cup of your house tea, please."

"Very good."

After the waiter was gone, Beth decided the direct approach would be best.

"Rasha. I don't know whether you've heard, but it seems your employer's target was a United States Senator. The man was killed by a sniper's bullet this past Saturday."

Rasha squeezed her cup so hard Beth though it might break.

"I had not heard this. So my information was too late to be of help. I am so sorry, Elizabeth." Sadness welled in her eyes. Her chin rested on her chest.

Beth gently pried one of Rasha's hands free from the tea cup and held it in her own.

"Rasha. It's not your fault. It's the men who think themselves above all standards of decency, the corrupt men who should never be leaders, and yet lead. It's their fault."

"I tried to do what was right." Rasha's voice was close to a sob.

"Yes. You *did* do what was right, for Egypt and for the United States. Most importantly, you did what was right in your heart. You can't blame yourself for the end result."

Rasha was not yet ready to speak.

"I need to ask you something, Rasha . . . not that you haven't already done more than many would have in your position. And we are grateful for your information. But now, with the Senator dead, we need to know who is responsible. Your government also needs to know who is acting outside their authority."

Beth still held Rasha's hand.

"And you can help us prove the identity of that person. But your help would not be without risk to your own safety."

Rasha looked up. She searched Beth's eyes for . . . Beth wasn't sure what.

"This thing you would like me to do, would you do it if our places were exchanged?"

"My safety will also be at risk in this matter. But I can't tell you what to do, Rasha. You have to choose for yourself whether to help us bring the murderer to justice."

Rasha leaned over the table and whispered.

"You know it is the Director, do you not?"

"Yes. We expected that was the case from the data on the card you gave me when we last met."

"In your opinion, am I able to do this thing you want me to do?"

"You have the knowledge and the skills. You have already shown you are brave. I can't guarantee that we will achieve our goal, even with your help. But without your assistance, Rasha, our hope of success is slight, indeed."

Rasha did not hesitate.

"Then you must tell me what I should do. I will help you prove this man's guilt."

* * *

After explaining to Rasha that Beth was not at liberty to discuss details, Beth and Rasha hugged goodbye, and Beth returned to the Embassy, where she hoped Hitch would now accept Rasha's assistance.

CHAPTER 33

At the underground research lab. Three weeks ago.

Seated on stools around a lab table, the three scientists eyed the second 1/30th scale Aurora model before them.

"Gentlemen, the time is fast coming when we must present this aircraft for a test flight."

"But Hamadi," another scientist said, "you must believe, as we all do, that this test will not go favorably."

Hamadi reach out and stroked the sleek, steel prototype.

"She is beautiful, though. Is she not?"

"Yes. And if it were this tiny replica that needed to fly, I would have no concerns. A couple electric servo motors would take it aloft. But our true challenge hangs in the great room below. Tell me, Hamadi. What is your honest assessment? Is there any way in the world that thing will fly?"

Hamadi exchanged meaningful looks with the other two men.

"We have followed the plans precisely. Everything appears as it should appear. We have documented as much, for we know we will be called to answer for any failure.

"But have the alloys cooled correctly to meet stress specifications? Will our castings expand and contract as they must for success? Will the combustion chambers compress the air sufficiently to fire the empty engines? Will the computer programs and complex electrical connections all function per design? Will the hydraulics operate at extreme altitude and temperature? Will the heat shielding on the leading surfaces suffice to prevent the craft igniting in mid-air?"

Hamadi looked to each scientist for his answer when he asked, "What do you think?"

CHAPTER 34

At the U.S. Embassy. Cairo.

When Beth returned to the Embassy following her second meeting with Rasha, she immediately phoned Hitch to tell him Rasha was available to help.

"Her willingness gives us one more option to consider, at least," Hitch said.

"What do you mean 'one more option'? We have no other options that I've heard of . . . unless you've come up with something new since breakfast."

"No. Nothing new, Elizabeth. But if we are to consider using a GIS employee for this sensitive assignment, I'm going to need clearance from someone farther up the chain of command."

"Simon?"

"Yes, Deputy Director Connor. I can ring him up right now. If you'd care to join the conference, you're more than welcome."

There was no way Beth was going to be left out of this discussion if she had a choice in the matter.

"I'm in. Should I just hang on the line while you give Simon a jingle?"

There was a moment of silence on Hitch's end.

"That would be fine, Elizabeth. He should be in his office by now. Please hold while I see if he's available."

There was a click, and then an empty echo in the phone line. Beth hoped he hadn't disconnected her. In any case, she would wait with patience.

Every sixty seconds a recorded voice spoke through the handset.

"We apologize for the wait. Your call is very important to us. Someone will be with you shortly."

At least she hadn't been cut off.

She'd heard the message repeat five times before Hitch's voice returned.

"Ms. Weston, are you still on the line?"

"Yes, I am, Mr. Hitchens. Has Deputy Director Connor joined us?"

"Good morning, Beth. So lovely of you to join Mr. Hitchens and me on the phone."

Beth ground her teeth.

"Good morning, Deputy Director. Has Mr. Hitchens briefed you on my request to employ our Egyptian friend in the pending assignment?"

Beth assumed that Hitch and Simon had already covered this territory in her absence, but she still needed to know their decision.

"Yes, Beth. He's told me all he knows about this woman. He and I are both reticent to employ her services in this matter. Yet I am given to understand that you place great faith in her trustworthiness."

"I do, Deputy Director. And in addition, there seems to be no viable alternative to engaging her assistance if we are to proceed at all. I've explained this to Mr. Hitchens."

"Yes. So he told me. Seems that we're in a bit of a sticky-wicket. We can place the operation's success in the hands of this foreigner on your say so. Or we can risk losing our single chance at success by our own man failing to make the correct network connection."

"I'd say that sums it up . . . Sir."

For a few long seconds, no one spoke. Then Simon continued.

"You realize, Beth, that if we expend our single opportunity to access this particular data source, and your friend fails us, you will need to take full responsibility for the result. You do understand this, do you not?"

Simon's statement was exactly what Beth had expected from the bureaucrat. Hitchens would distance himself from any political fall out as well. Of course, if the operation turned out to be a spectacular success, Beth's role would diminish exponentially.

Beth was ready with her answer.

"I accept responsibility for Rasha, and for my role as hacker and code-cracker. But the rest of this operation is on you two. Agreed?"

Beth was certain that neither Hitch nor Simon was accustomed to this sort of demand from their 'underlings.'

"Please hold a moment, won't you Beth dear," Simon said. "Mr. Hitchens and I need to discuss your request."

The line went quiet again as the bosses excised her from their discussion.

Three "someone will be with you shortlies" later, the two men reconnected with Beth.

This time it was Hitch who spoke.

"We've considered your request and find it to be reasonable. So long as your 'helper' and your computer skills don't fail us, no blame for any unfortunate result will fall upon you."

Beth noticed they hadn't acceded to her request that they assume responsibility. But they had at least said *she* wouldn't be the scapegoat. Beth also realized that a verbal assurance from a career CIA wonk like Simon wasn't worth the paper it was written on. But she was clear in her own mind concerning her role. If someone else dropped the ball, her conscience would be clear . . . even if her CIA record might not.

"So I have permission to take my friend up on her offer of help?"

"Yes." Again, it was Hitchens.

"And yours as well, Mr. Deputy Director?"

"You don't need my approval, Beth. Hitchens has authority to proceed as he deems fit. Now if I have sufficiently micro-managed your little glitch, I have more important matters demanding my attention. Good luck to you both."

Simon hung up. Beth and Hitch remained on the line.

"I'll contact Rasha right away so I can get her the BPL modem. Then she'll be ready to move when we are."

"Very well, Elizabeth. And I do hope you have judged this woman correctly."

"Me, too. I'll be in touch soon. Good bye."

Beth wasted no time in calling Rasha on the secure cell. There was no answer. Beth checked her watch. Rasha was probably still at work. She'd see the missed call and return it when she could.

Then she called Hitch again.

"So soon, Elizabeth?"

"Yes. Hitch, I need the exact computer I'll be taking with me on this assignment delivered to my room ASAP. I want to make sure everything is working right. And I need to get all the programs installed. It'll take me a few hours minimum. So I might as well get that detail out of the way."

"Very good. You will have the laptop shortly."

Beth was getting excited about the assignment. She'd hacked plenty of computers over the years, and decrypted all varieties of security code. But she had always done so from a safe distance. This mission placed her in harm's way. If she hadn't bought into the mission goals wholeheartedly, she wouldn't have considered exposing herself to the dangers this assignment entailed. But she couldn't condone Egypt, or any other government for that matter, assassinating United States citizens . . . let alone a Senator . . . on U.S. soil. If this act went unpunished, the U.S. lack of response would embolden other actors . . . countries and terror groups alike . . . and the slippery slope would become precipitous. If she could play a role in bringing the assassin's employer to justice, the mission justified the perils.

Fifteen minutes later, there was a knock on Beth's door. It was her combat computer . . . army green, bash-proof, with a monster battery and titanium casing.

The sight of the military computer brought home the nature of the assignment. Beth was entering a potential combat zone without an army to protect her. She said a quick prayer, then sat down to work.

*   *   *

Early that evening, Rasha called Beth on the cell.

"Hello?" Beth answered, not wanting to use Rasha's name in case her phone had been compromised and someone else was calling.

"Hello, Elizabeth. It is Rasha. I hope you will now tell me how I can assist you."

"That is precisely the reason for my call. Here are the details."

Beth outlined as much of the cyber-attack as was necessary to assure that Rasha would make the correct network connection, and no more.

"And we must meet tonight so I may provide you with the small piece of equipment you'll need."

Beth made arrangements to pass Rasha along Talaat Harb Street at a certain time that evening, where they would hand off the modem.

CHAPTER 35

Egyptian Intelligence Services Directorate. Cairo.

GIS Director Muwafi had just received a message from one of his operatives. The information was vague, almost to the point of being useless. The message read:

Director:

Information indicates that the Americans plan to infiltrate government computers in Cairo within the next week. Exact location unknown. Exact date unknown.

The Director wasn't particularly concerned with this information. He assumed that the Americans, and the Israelis, constantly attempted to access his government's classified information. Appropriate measures had been taken to ensure those attempts would not be successful.

Nevertheless, he passed the message along to the SCAF and advised his own personnel to raise their level of awareness regarding such an attempt. He wasn't about to have this information in hand, and not make someone else responsible for dealing with it.

CHAPTER 36

Back in Red Wing.

While Gunner tried to maneuver the BCA into prioritizing his digital enhancement project, I decided to take my leave of the halls of law enforcement and work from a more comfortable location. For now, that location would be the front seat of my grey 2004 Honda Pilot.

I was concerned that the tension between Gunner and Bull might have squashed any chance of getting my savvy American Indian friend to help out in this investigation. I hoped that wasn't true.

I rang Bull up on my cell.

"Yeah?"

"Hey, Bull. How's it going?"

"Who is this?"

"What? When I introduce myself you crab that you've got caller ID. Now I just dive in and you bitch about that, too."

"I'm kind of a pain in the ass, huh."

I could hear him smiling over the cell signal.

"Okay. So I can't win. I'll live with that."

"Good."

"Are you going to stick with us on this Senator assassination thing? You were a little hard on Gunner this morning."

"You know I don't like working with cops."

"That's true. But there *is* such a thing as common courtesy. You could be polite. We did haul ourselves all the way out to the Rez to meet you."

"I suppose. It just doesn't feel . . . normal."

I raised my eyebrows and consulted the ceiling.

"Next item. Same as the first. Are you going to help us or not?"

"I'll pitch in. But I've gotta work this my own way. I don't play well with others."

Now *there* was a shocking revelation.

"Okay. You help however you want. We do need you if we're going to catch this guy before he leaves town though. Maybe it's already too late."

"I don't think so."

I waited for further explanation. Nothing.

"Why not?"

" 'Cause I would still be here for another few hours if I was the shooter."

A momentary thought that maybe Bull *was* the sniper flashed through my mind. I dismissed it – not because he couldn't do it . . . he certainly had the skills. The Army Rangers had seen to that. He just had no reason. And money wasn't a motivator for Bull. He was just so infuriatingly impenetrable. One could never rule anything out . . . at least not one hundred percent. But then again, that's what made him Bull.

"So you say you're trusting your gut."

"Yup."

I had some experience with gut feelings. They were the sort of thing that one developed over years surviving in difficult, if not impossible, situations. I trusted my gut when it spoke to me. I sensed Bull's gut was equally reliable.

"Well, that's good then. It means we've still got a chance to grab him up."

"True dat!"

"Bull, I wish you'd cut out the ebonics. 'True dat' just doesn't work for you."

"I was thinking the same thing. But it's so damn efficient."

Sometimes, despite Bull's economy of words, it was nearly impossible to move the conversation forward.

"Okay. Now I need you to be quiet for a minute while I tell you what Gunner and I have been doing and what we think we know. Okay?"

No response.

"Okay? I repeated.

"I thought I was supposed to shut up and listen."

I took a cleansing breath. Then I relayed to Bull the various assignments to which Gunner had tasked his deputies, from finding Tomball, to locating the boat, to checking rental cars and storage lockers, to finding the lone fisherman.

"I don't think Gunner buys it yet, but my gut tells me that Mr. Tomball, the fisher cowboy, is our man. Anyway, he's our only suspect at present."

Bull remained silent.

"You can talk now."

"I think you're right about Tomball."

"Why's that?" I wanted to hear if Bull had better reasons than a feeling in my gut.

" 'Cause of that last thing you said."

I searched my memory. What was the last thing I had said?

" 'Cause we've got nobody else to chase right now."

Ah, yes. Sometimes it's just as practical as that. If you only have one suspect, he's the one you go after. Who could argue with that logic? Certainly not me. I'd said it first, after all.

"So where do we go from here, Bull? Got any hot ideas?"

"You and the cops keep doing what you're doing. Those things gotta be done. Better them than me."

I had to remember to tell Gunner that Bull had approved of his investigative approach.

"And you?"

"Keep me posted. I'll figure out my job on this end."

Click.

"No need to coordinate our efforts, I'm sure. I'll try not to shoot you by accident," I said to the dead phone.

That's Bull. Hard to read, but damn handy when you needed him. I hoped he'd be there if we needed him today.

* * *

As I idled around the streets of Red Wing, wishing something helpful would jump out at me, my cell rang. It was Gunner.

"Maybe we just got a break." His tone was animated. "My guys found a rental car and the boat and the truck and . . ."

"Hold on. Slow down. What's the upshot? We haven't got time to waste."

"We think he's still in town. We got a good face shot from BCA and my guys are looking into the hotels and motels and such. You know, to see if anybody recognizes him."

"Excellent! Any way I can help?"

"Yeah. You and me are gonna go check out the St. James. Doesn't seem likely the guy would have the balls to crap right where he eats. But you never know. We're checking everywhere."

I thought for a moment. If the sniper was sophisticated enough to divert the bloodhounds, bluff the Sheriff's patrol boat, wave at a cop as he drove through a road block, and convince almost everybody he was long gone, why not stay at the hotel? It'd be the ultimate in bravado.

"Gunner. The St. James is the perfect place for the sniper to stay. He'd get a front room so he could look down on the scene of his recent kill. Man, this guy's got a pair!"

"Well, whether he's there or not, I got a picture I'm gonna show to the desk clerk in about two minutes. If you wanna come along, you meet me there." Gunner disconnected the call.

I looped around the block and headed straight for the St. James. My gut was more convinced than ever that, if we were going to find this guy, the St. James would be the place.

When I reached the hotel a couple minutes later, Gunner's cruiser was parked illegally in front. I parked right behind him and charged through the hotel's heavy front doors.

* * *

The Raptor had his bags packed and was enjoying a last triumphant view of the stained sidewalk below his window at the Hotel. He chuckled to himself.

They kin clean it, but they cain't never get it out.

The sight of the Sheriff's cruiser pulling up outside the front doors jerked his mind back into sniper mode. This cop probably had nothing to do with him. Still, he hadn't survived this long in the sniper business by making favorable assumptions. He had to assume the cop posed a threat.

He acquired the Colt from his smallest bag. Holding the handgun at his side, he turned the knob on the old oak door, then peered through the crack. Seeing nothing amiss, he dared a step into the hallway. The only signs of life were the maid's cart in the hall two doors down and the sound of her vacuum cleaner. He closed the door and hurriedly revised his exit plan.

* * *

By the time I arrived at the front desk, Gunner had already approached the acne-faced Sunday desk clerk to see whether he recognized Mr. Tomball's picture as someone staying at the hotel.

"Look at this picture and tell me whether you've seen this man."

The boy squinted ta the picture. "I don't think so. But I'm only here on Sundays. Maybe you should talk to the manager."

"Well go get him then. *Tout de suite!*"

The clerk hustled into a room behind the counter.

"You're so authoritative when you speak French," I said.

Gunner turned toward me.

"What?"

"*Tout de suite*. It's French."

"Will you just for once shut up!"

"Hey, just trying to keep you loose. You look a little jumpy."

"That's because I *am* jumpy," He whispered. "You got me believing I'm gonna come up against an international assassin in a couple minutes. Damn right, I'm jumpy."

"Well, take a breath. And for Pete's sake, don't shoot *me*."

The clerk and the manager returned. The manager spoke.

"May I help you Deputy?"

Gunner handed him the 8 x 10 glossy.

"You seen this guy around here in the last week or so?"

The manager studied the photo.

"We have one guest who looks sort of like this gentleman. But he has a beard, and almost always wears a baseball cap, at least when I've seen him."

"Do you have a record of what kinda car he's got parked here?"

"I'll check. One moment please. If he has parked a car in our garage, I should have that information."

The manager punched up a few screens on his computer.

"Yes. Here it is. This gentleman parked a 2005 Toyota Corolla with us."

Gunner's eyes raced down his list of rental cars. A match!

"Okay. What's this guy's name?"

"I'm afraid I can't . . ."

"Don't give me that confidentiality crap. This 'gentleman' may have shot the Senator. Now give me his name and his room number. *Tout de suite!*"

Gunner gave me a stare. I held my tongue.

The name was not Tomball, but the room did overlook the front sidewalk, as I had predicted.

"And this guy is still here?"

"He hasn't checked out and we don't have his key card back yet. That's all I can tell you."

"Make us a key for his room, and hurry it up. Time's a wastin'."

The manager did as Gunner asked. On our advice, the manager remained at the front desk to divert other guests into the lounge for a complimentary cocktail while we cleared the building.

"You got some more guys coming soon, Gunner?"

"Dammit, Becker. I just ran my whole squad on double overtime all day yesterday and half of 'em again today. They're all detailed out." Gunner contacted dispatch requesting backup, but neither of us felt we could afford the luxury of waiting for it to arrive.

With key card in hand, we raced up the steps to the third floor room the manager had indicated. The hallway was empty except for a cleaning cart.

Gunner led the way as we approached the room door. The "Do

Not Disturb" sign hung on the knob. With one of us on each side of the doorway, Gunner rapped the gold knocker twice and announced, "Hotel Manager.'

"Whatta ya want? I'm sleepin' in here."

"I'm sorry, sir. It is about your bill. Something is wrong with your credit card. If you could just provide us another, I'm sure everything will be just fine."

I thought Gunner did a pretty good impersonation of the manager.

"I'll fix it when I check out. Now go away!"

"Ottawa County Sheriff. Open up or we'll kick this door in."

"Jiminy Christmas. Why didn't ya say so in the first place. I'm comin."

There were some shuffling sounds inside the room. Then the door opened a few inches and the duck-taped head of the maid appeared.

"Now come on in," the man's voice said. "And hurry it up. She spoils quick. And guns better come in here first."

Gunner and I couldn't leave the maid alone with the guy. Our chances were better to help her if we followed the sniper's instructions.

We each tossed our handgun through the partly open doorway.

"The other ones, too. Hurry up!"

We retrieved our secondary weapons and threw those in as well.

"Now git in here!"

The door opened slowly, always with the maid's face in view and no direct look at the shooter.

"Now, close the door, nice an' easy."

I pushed the door with my fingertips until it closed and latched.

Now we could see the killer, his Twins cap pulled down low over empty eyes. I could tell his beard was fake, but it would've fooled most people. His worn denim trousers and flannel shirt could have belonged to any fisherman in the area.

"Now we ain't got no time to waste, fellas. You, in the uniform, take this here rope and tie Missy Maid to the bedpost, good and solid. I know my knots, so don't ya dick around with me."

The shooter pushed the maid at Gunner. He caught her as she fell forward. Her arms and hands were bound with more grey tape. Gunner sat her on the bed, and using the rope the sniper had provided, tied her hands firmly to the bedpost.

"Now git over here by yer buddy. I wanna check yer knot."

Gunner moved sideways toward me, keeping his focus on the gunman.

After giving the knot a quick look, he pronounced it, "Jus' fine."

"Okay. Now. You guys are gonna help me out. I might jus' need a little escort outta town since you prob'ly got friends on the way. So yer comin' with me."

The gunman motioned us around the room until he reached the spot where our guns lay on the floor. He picked up my Beretta .40 caliber. Now he carried a potent weapon in each hand.

So far, I hadn't seen a chance to take on the sniper without risking the maid's life. I assumed Gunner had decided the same, since both of us remained docile and compliant.

If we could get him to take us out of here and leave her behind, then the danger was solely to our own lives. We could decide for ourselves what risks to take.

"Now, Mr. Deputy, you take a look-see out the door an' make sure the coast is clear. Then khakis and boat shoes is gonna follow you. I'll bring up the rear. We're headed for the garage elevator. Got it?"

"Got it," we both said.

Gunner opened the door. Since the coast was, indeed, clear, we exited the room and the gunman hastened us along to the elevator. From here we would go directly to the parking garage where, no doubt, the killer's car awaited.

On the ride down, he held both guns . . . one at the back of my head and one at the back of Gunner's. Neither of us dared move without imperiling the life of the other.

As luck would have it, the elevator made it all the way down to the second garage level without stopping for passengers at any floor. That was just as well. We didn't need more bystanders engaged in this mess.

When the elevator came to a stop, he shoved us both out, establishing a safe distance between us and a quick dive for his weapons.

"Straight ahead. Fourth car on the right. Keep movin'."

When we had passed the second parked car, I stopped.

"Git movin, I said!"

I turned to Gunner. "Say, Gunner. Don't they teach in self-defense classes that you should never go anywhere with the bad guy? Whatever he'd do to you where you're at, he'd probably do worse if you went along with him?"

"Dammit. I said git!" The assassin waved one gun in our direction, still keeping his distance." The gunman was beginning to get flustered. Maybe he didn't want to make a loud, gunshot sort of noise just now.

I nudged Gunner's toe.

He looked at me.

"You know. I believe that *is* what they tell you at them classes," Gunner said.

"Yup." I turned to the sniper. "Sorry, Sir. You'll have to surrender to us right here."

"What the hell . . ." was all he got out before an unknown force launched his feet from under him and his head hit the concrete. Hard.

Before he could reorient himself, he was on his stomach, with guns out of reach, one side of his face acquiring a cutting case of road rash.

With his available eye, he looked up to see what had happened. Straddling the sniper's back and pressing firmly on his head was a very large Indian, his long black hair framing broad cheekbones and an evil stare.

"Damn!" he wheezed. "Where the hell'd you come from?"

Bull leaned over the prostrate sniper.

"Shh. Don't talk. You'll hurt yourself."

"Wh-what happened?" He was still dazed.

"Indians beat the cowboys this round."

CHAPTER 37

Following Bull's Blitzkrieg assault on the sniper, Gunner had applied the cuffs and we all escorted our suspect to Gunner's cruiser out front. Once a couple of Gunner's backup deputies arrived to lend aid, I hustled back up to the room to rescue the maid and reclaim our weapons. Once I'd freed her, I released her to the custody of a pair of deputies who had been sent to secure the room.

I suspect that the St. James Hotel housekeeping department may be in need of a replacement maid. This one looked as though she'd rather not set foot in the place again. Her uncontrollable sobs confirmed my suspicions. Who could blame her!

By the time I'd reached the hotel lobby, the place was crawling with city cops and Sheriff's Deputies and a growing press contingent. No doubt BCA, and probably the FBI, were on their way. Gunner had departed to incarcerate the perp, while Bull had vanished entirely.

I decided I deserved to remain in the loop. After all, I'd been the one who'd nearly got us shot in the parking garage. That should count for something. I drove the Pilot to the LEC hoping to find Gunner back in his office.

Once in the LEC lobby, I didn't have to wait long for the Chief Deputy to make his entrance through the doorway that led from the jail cells. No doubt, he'd wanted to see the gentleman behind bars with his own eyes before tackling the requisite paperwork.

"Hey, Gunner. Congratulations! That's one big fish you got frying in there."

Gunner couldn't restrain himself from displaying a big grin.

"Damn straight. I never figured him to still be in town. I only went along with you guys to be thorough, you know. Never figured you'd be right."

"Thanks a bunch, Gunner." I feigned offense.

"Oh, c'mon. You know what I mean. You gotta admit, the odds seemed pretty thin."

"And yet . . ."

Gunner was losing his grin.

"Never mind, my friend," I said. "I was just kidding around. The only reason any sane person might've agreed with Bull and me is because he didn't have any other options. If the sniper was gone, he was gone. End of story. But if not . . . why not do what you do best, Gunner."

"And what's that?"

"Your job. And in this case, that amounted to being utterly thorough and following every possible lead, regardless of how unfounded it may have seemed."

Gunner hitched up his belt on both sides.

"You're right, dammit. I did my job. And lookie what we got. A damn Senator killer. Not bad."

"And don't forget, if the Senator and his security dream team had listened to you in the first place, the Senator would've entered the hotel through the garage, and a sniper on Barn Bluff would never have had a shot."

"Good point. I'll remember to mention that in my report."

I'd stroked Gunner's ego enough for one day. Not that he didn't deserve it . . . it's just not good for a law man to get a big head.

"I think I'll leave you to your paperwork, Gunner. I'm going to head home, pop a cold Bud Light, and find a John Wayne movie on cable."

"Whoa there. Hold on. I've gotta know a couple things about what happened back at that hotel garage."

"Like what?"

"Why'd you stop walking and start talking about that self-defense stuff? You know that advice about not leaving with the bad guy doesn't really apply to this kinda situation. So what's the deal?"

"It's pretty simple actually. I needed the sniper to stop moving for a few seconds."

"Don't tell me you knew that Indian was gonna sweep his legs like that. I didn't see any sign of him at all till he sprang out from behind that car."

" 'Course I knew. Why else would I stop moving and chance getting us shot."

Gunner tilted his head. He still had no idea how I knew about Bull.

"How'd he even know we were at the hotel?"

"I called him on the way over. He was already in town."

"And how'd you know he would be in the garage?"

Gunner was persistent.

"Bull's red Cherokee was parked in the second spot from the elevator doorway. I made sure to walk close enough to the parked cars to give him a shot. That's all."

"If that's true, and Bull had a bead on him the whole time in the garage, why didn't Bull just shoot the bastard? That sniper had a spare hostage. He could've plugged either one of us at any moment and still had the all the leverage he needed."

"You'd have to ask Bull. But I've got a couple guesses."

"Fire away."

"Well, for one thing, if the sniper ends up dead, we can't question him and maybe find out who he's been working for."

"Okay. That makes sense."

"For another, Bull doesn't like getting involved with cops. If he shoots somebody, there's no telling what kind of trouble he might get into. You saw how he acted out at the casino."

"Yeah. He can piss a guy off all right."

"And finally, shooting people is a choice of last resort for Bull. He did plenty of shooting back in the . . . back in the day. He much prefers to overwhelm his opponent with muscles and dexterity. He says it's the Dakota way."

"The Dakota way?"

"Hell, I don't know. You've met Bull. You explain him to me when you get him figured out."

Gunner folded his arms across his chest.

"I reckon you got a point."

"Damn straight, " I said.
Gunner chuckled.
"Damn straight."

CHAPTER 38

While Gunner wrote up his reports, the expected jurisdictional infighting had already begun between the various governmental entities vying to try the sniper in their courts.

Since the assassination had been carried out entirely within Ottawa County, the Ottawa County Attorney claimed primary jurisdiction. The Minnesota Attorney General's Office contended that such a high profile case as this one could, indeed, be tried in Ottawa County, but his office must handle the prosecution. The Federal District Attorney asserted superior jurisdictional authority because this was an attack that had clearly been commissioned and planned entirely outside the county. Besides, the case involved the murder of a sitting United States Senator – patently, a federal crime.

While I normally let the bureaucrats resolve their own urination competitions, I held a vested interest in keeping the sniper, who had been identified as Monroe Burton, originally of Tomball, Texas, within my own reach. While the attorneys concerned themselves with who might try the case, I had greater interest in finding out who had ordered the hit, and in the other deaths this man might be responsible for. While Burton remained in the Ottawa County Jail, I was certain I could convince Gunner to allow me access to the deranged gentleman.

I didn't have any potent contacts at the BCA or in the Justice Department. But I did have one card up my sleeve – a card named Dan Trew.

Dan and I had served together on a number of black ops assignments during my tour of duty. He'd departed the Team sooner than I to make a career for himself in the FBI, where he'd succeeded fabulously. His official FBI title was Executive Assistant

Director for National Security Branch/Associate Executive Assistant Director for National Security Branch, Counter-Terrorism Division. It was a mouthful. But Dan hadn't forgotten his roots on the Team. He was one of very few people in the world I trusted completely.

Sitting on the red leather sofa in my livingroom on Jefferson Avenue, I propped my feet up on the wooden drum case that served as our coffee table, and punched up Dan's office number. It would be about 11:00 a.m. Monday morning in D.C. I figured Dan'd be up to his armpits in weekend emergencies. But it was still worth a try.

A female voice answered.

"Executive Assistant Director Trew's office. How may I direct your call?"

Dan had already learned my new identity, so I didn't hesitate to drop the name.

"James Becker calling for Dan Trew, please."

"And what may I say this is regarding?"

"Personal business."

"I'm sorry, but I'll need a bit more information before I put you through."

She wasn't being rude. It was part of her job to screen out the stock and bond salesmen, the contractors seeking FBI business, and the kooks who just wanted someone to bitch at.

"Please tell him my name, and remind him I saved his life."

There was silence at the other end of the line. I didn't imagine she'd heard that line before.

"One moment please. I'll see if he is available."

One had to admire an effective staff person. I'd employed some truly excellent administrative help at my law office, and some not so . . . effective. I could tell the difference. Dan's phone person was top notch.

The other end of the phone line connected and I heard Dan's muffled voice.

"Hold my calls, Lynn. I don't care if it's the Vice President. I am *not* available."

"Well, Mr. Becker. Nice to hear from you again. I trust you've been well."

"Thanks for clearing your phone line for me, Dan. Yeah I've been peachy . . . couldn't be peachier, really."

"Well that sounds just grand. Wish I could say the same. Counter-terrorism has got me all jammed up trying to get their hands on this guy that shot the Senator. You've heard about that, I trust."

"You might say so. The guy got himself shot in *my* home town."

"So you're at ground zero. Red Wing, huh?"

"Yup."

"You say he got himself shot. Is that more than an aphorism? Did the Senator screw up his own security?"

"Yes. And had he followed the advice of my local Deputy Sheriff – who the private guns practically shoved off the map, by the way – he'd still be drawing breath today."

"Lemme guess. The Senator just *had* to have some public face time on the way into the hotel. Your guy told him no, but he went ahead and did it anyway."

"Exactly . . . except it was on his way out."

"Wow. Some people are just hard to keep alive."

"You know it."

I knew that my interests and Dan's on behalf of the FBI might be in conflict concerning the favor I was about to ask. But I learned a long time ago, if you don't ask, you don't get.

"Dan, I've got a huge favor to ask."

"I'm shocked. And usually you just call to chat." He laughed.

It was true that I only called Dan when I needed a favor. But he knew I was always available to him if he ever needed me. So I wasn't shy about it.

"Yeah. I'm definitely a sad case."

Dan laughed again.

"So show me what you got."

"The local Chief Deputy, my good friend, and I were the guys that caught the sniper when everybody else figured he'd blown town. I don't know if you heard, but the day after the shooting, he was in a guestroom overlooking the Senator's blood stains on the street."

"No shit. I knew he'd been caught in Red Wing. I wondered how all that went down. Pretty savvy policing, Mr. Becker."

"I sure can't take all the credit. But I was a part of it. And I hate to ruin my humble image with you, Dan, but if I hadn't been there coordinating local law enforcement with . . . less conventional resources, Mr. Burton would've waltzed outta town Sunday afternoon and he'd be gone for good."

"I'd say that's something worth mentioning . . . all heed of humility aside. Congratulations."

"Thanks. But there's method to my immodesty. I'd really like to keep the sniper investigation in local hands for just a couple days. I know that's not what your people, or the Justice Department, have in mind. But I've got a plan I think will not only get him to confess to shooting the Senator, but give us info on his other kills as well."

Dan's phone was silent for a few long moments.

"You're asking a bunch, my friend. I've got friends in Justice, but I seriously doubt whether they'd be willing to play ball by your rules."

"Dan. All I'm asking for is forty-eight hours. I'm sure the potentates can fill the time with press conferences and video histories of famous sniper attacks. Just two days. I'm begging here."

Dan sighed audibly.

"I'll do what I can, Becker. But no promises. It's all uphill from where I sit."

"I'm eternally grateful, Dan. I couldn't ask for more."

"No. You really couldn't." It was only half joke.

"Please ring me up if you find out something. I'll work the best I can from my end. And I *won't* mention your name."

"Okay. Look, I gotta go. Lynn's waving her arms at me like the place is on fire. I'll be in touch. So long."

"Bye."

* * *

I was just pulling into the LEC parking lot when I caught a glimpse of Gunner marching out the front door. I jumped out of the Pilot and waved.

"Hey, Gunner. Where you headed?"

"Out." His voice was curt.

"Great. I was just on my way there myself."

He and I reached opposite sides of his cruiser at the same time. I opened my door and got in. Gunner did the same.

"Mind if I come along?"

"Do I have a choice?"

"Sure. You gotta gun . . . ergo, you gotta choice. But I think you're going to want me along."

There was a sigh from the Chief Deputy. He started the motor and slammed the transmission into gear.

"Fasten your belt."

I obliged. I would've worn the seat belt anyway. I always do. It's just plain stupid not to.

Gunner peeled out in the lot and squeaked the tires rounding the corner onto Sixth Street. He was taking his agitation out on the squad. I sat quietly, allowing him to simmer.

When he reached Highway 58 heading south out of town, Gunner flipped on the lights and siren and picked up speed. We'd cleared the city limits and topped 90 miles an hour when I spoke.

"This is fun. We should do it more often." I looked at Gunner's profile and smiled.

He continued a staring contest with the roadway ahead.

"Gotta blow out the carbon every once in a while."

"Yeah . . . if this is a 1970 Crown Vic. All you need these days is a bottle or two of injector cleaner." I returned my view to the dashed center line, which had merged into a single white blur somewhere around 100 mph.

Gunner said nothing, but continued to press the car's limits around a few gentle corners.

"Let me know when you wanna chat. I'll be ready. Oh, and I've got some news that just might cheer you up a bit."

Gunner and I hurtled forward into the valley between the last rows of bluffs and then climbed the final grade to the open prairie above. At this point Gunner slowed the car to the speed limit and shut down the flashers and siren.

Approaching the small town of Goodhue, Gunner took the first street into town – there were two – and followed it until we reached the high school athletic field. There he pulled into the gravel parking lot, facing the expanse of baseball diamonds and football fields and the flat farmland beyond.

"Are we 'out' yet?"

Gunner laughed one of those laughs you employ when you'd just as soon be crying.

"Just look out there. The grass is mowed. Goal posts are painted. The corn fields are nice and tidy, ready for spring planting. If we got outta the car we could smell the fresh manure from here. Now *that* kinda shit I can deal with. Lawyers drive me frickin' apeshit." He looked over at me. "No offense."

"Of course. None taken." I paused for effect. "They drive me apeshit, too."

Gunner laughed again, this time like he meant it.

"Okay. Now that my pulse is back down to around a hundred and my jaw's loosened up, you said you had some good news. I could use some. Let's have it." He beckoned with four fingers, as though inviting a fight.

"I got somebody working on keeping Mr. Burton in Ottawa County Jail for at least a couple more days."

"That's your good news? Two more days of lawyers bitching and wrangling all over my cop shop?"

I hadn't really thought of it that way.

"Yeah . . . but here's the really good part. You get to be the one to break Burton, convincing him to admit the totality of his nefarious deeds."

"Speak English. I ain't got the patience for Shakespeare."

"We can get him to tell us all the guys he's shot. And you can take the credit. You deserve some credit, right?"

Gunner considered.

"Credit *is* hard to come by in this job. Whattya got cooking?"

I explained my plan to interrogate Burton and how Gunner could come out the hero.

He smiled.

"Let's do that."

CHAPTER 39

The next day, I had everything ready and Burton was still incarcerated in Ottawa County. The most challenging part of my due diligence had been to convince Bull to set foot inside a jail. But after a mostly one-sided chat, he had consented to participate in my plan.

The three of us – Gunner, Bull, and I – planned to meet at the LEC at 10:45 a.m. From there we'd visit Mr. Burton in the jail interrogation room . . . a small space with a wooden table and hard wooden chairs. There were also fittings to attach Mr. Burton's chains to the concrete. Gunner didn't want to chance an escape. Personally, with Bull in the room, I thought Gunner's extra security measures amounted to overkill.

After confirming the role that each would play in this drama, the three of us joined Mr. Burton for interrogation.

Burton was already locked down and seated on the side of the table facing the two way mirror. There were cameras on the mirror wall, too, to ensure the prisoner didn't claim police brutality during questioning.

Gunner and I took the two chairs on our side of the table. Bull stood in a corner directly beneath one of the cameras. The attorneys in the observation room could still see Bull's back. But he was otherwise out of sight. It was convenient that, owing to Bull's size and intimidating stature, the lawyers had actually requested that he "keep his distance" from Burton.

Burton was a scraggy guy – short, unshaven, his hair had barely been finger-combed. Where his hands and arms protruded from the rolled sleeves, you could tell by small muscle movements that his physical condition was better than his scrawny appearance implied. Muscles twitched in his neck and face as we came in.

Gunner started out by reading Burton his rights.

"Do you understand these rights as I have read them to you?"

"Git me my lawyer."

"You misunderstand, Mr. Burton," I said. "We're not here to question you. We just want to talk to you. You listen. We talk. You see, our friend Mr. Bull back here . . ." I motioned in Bull's direction . . . "can read minds."

Burton scoffed and leaned as far back in his chair as the chains allowed.

"It's a skill he learned from his great grandfather," I continued. "You don't need to believe in it. And it's not admissible in court, of course, but still useful for investigative purposes."

Burton started to speak. Gunner shut him down.

"No talking Mr. Burton. Your lawyer's not here. So you gotta keep your mouth shut. Understand?"

Burton nodded. He retained his cocky, laid back posture.

"Now, Mr. Burton," Gunner said. "I'm gonna read a bit from your file. You just sit there and let Mr. Bull watch you."

Burton's eyes flickered. He shifted in his seat, trying to look away from Bull.

"That's a good start," I said. "Body language is helpful, too."

Burton altered his posture to face straight ahead at his reflection in the two-way mirror.

Gunner began to read.

"You were born in the city of Tomball, Texas on May the 19th, 1968. Your parents were Angeline and Ronald Burton, both presently deceased." Gunner paused.

Burton glanced at Bull. Bull had his arms crossed and eyes closed. He opened them suddenly, as if he could feel Burton's gaze.

Burton gave a start.

"You've been married twice, divorced twice and have two kids you visit at holidays. You've never paid child support. But for some damn reason, your kids have told us they love you anyway."

Gunner looked up at Burton. Burton smiled, then glanced at Bull, who glared back with black marble eyes and a maniacal grin. Burton looked away, but couldn't help stealing a peek at Bull every few seconds.

I stifled an urge to laugh.

"You've been a hired gun since your dishonorable discharge from the Army in 1992, when you struck a superior officer for embarrassing you in front of a young lady."

"That sonofabitch . . ." Burton started. I shushed him.

"We're going to have to put tape over your mouth if you won't be quiet . . . unless you want to waive your right to counsel."

Burton scowled and shook his head.

I looked over my shoulder at Bull.

"How're things going back there, Mr. Bull?"

Bull gave me a smile . . . at least I think it was a smile . . . and flashed two thumbs up.

"Good. Would you like to proceed Chief Deputy?"

"Sure. While in the service, your weapon of choice was a .408 caliber CheyTac M200. Your sergeant rated your shooting skills above average, but your demeanor as 'unstable.' "

Gunner looked at me. "Huh. Wonder why that was."

We both laughed. Burton pounded the table. His eyes flashed, but he kept his mouth shut.

"Your daughter, Angela, lives in Los Angeles with her husband and two kids, ages eight and five. I guess they'd be your grandkids."

Gunner turned to me again. "Damn dangerous in Los Angeles with all them street gangs killing each other and even innocent bystanders."

"That's what I hear," I said.

Burton glanced again at Bull. He was blowing the smoke off the end of his finger gun. He held out one hand, the hand that was off camera, to indicate the heights of an eight-year-old and a five-year-old. Then fired off two finger shots in their direction.

Burton pointed frantically at Bull. When we looked, he had resumed his arms-on-chest pose. I got up and turned one of the cameras to show Bull's innocence, then returned it to its normal position.

"And your other kid, Gerard, lives in Soho with his gay buddies." Gunner looked up at Burton. " 'Course he ain't married. But that damn AIDS is really killing off the gays. Hope he uses protection. Drugs is bad for that stuff, too."

In the corner Bull fired off more finger-gun rounds. Then injected himself in the forearm.

Burton waved and pointed at Bull again.

Gunner and I made sure we were on camera when we looked over at Bull.

"I don't get what your problem is with Mr. Bull," I said. "Are you a racist or something?" Burton motioned palms out that he was definitely okay with Indians. " 'Cause otherwise, I'd think you guys would have a bunch in common. He used to be a sniper, too."

"Ranger," Bull said from off camera, making sure to use a calm voice. While talking, he fired yet another finger round at Burton.

Burton tossed himself back and forth in his chair. "Let me outta here!"

"Well, now, Mr. Burton," Gunner said, a sly expression on his face. "That ain't the way it works in *my* county. I decide when you come and when you go. And we ain't done yet. I hope you understand."

Burton was running out of gas. He sighed, then nodded.

" 'Course we could finish up with a few quick questions and let you go grab a nice warm shower and some grub if you'd agree to waive your right to counsel. I got a form right here."

Gunner shoved the paper and pen half-way across the table. Burton shook his head.

"Now, let's see. Your grandkids go to school at Greenvale Elementary, 44500 Greenvale Drive, in LA. I bet they're good students, too."

I don't know what kind of face or gesture Bull made this time, but Burton grabbed the paper and signed.

"There. Now let me outta here."

Gunner retrieved the signed Waiver of Counsel.

"You sure you understand that this means we can question you without your lawyer present? You know that, right?"

"Yeah."

"And that's okay with you, right?"

"Yes, dammit. Now lemme outta here."

"You're almost on you're way," Gunner said. "Just a couple more things. You wanna talk now Mr. Becker?"

"Thanks, Chief Deputy."

I reached beneath the table and produced a clear plastic evidence bag, complete with official chain-of-possession label. The baggie contained a .408 caliber bullet, though not the one the sniper had fired. The BCA wouldn't give that one up.

"You know we found this bullet in a car down the street immediately after you shot the Senator. It's a .408. The markings match the rifling in your CheyTac – we found it in the trunk of Mr. Tomball's rental car. FBI confirmed that, too."

"Not mine," he said.

"Now I haven't asked anything yet. So just wait, please. I'll get to the question."

Burton glanced at Bull again, then seemed eager to please.

"And we know you're Mr. Tomball, the Water Patrol Deputy has positively identified you." I returned the evidence bag to my case below the table, and retrieved a crisp sheet of white paper.

"This is a copy of the Minnesota Statute regarding capital crimes – murder, that is." I passed it across the table and Burton grabbed it. "It says that Minnesota doesn't have the death penalty. All you're going to get in the Minnesota courts is life without parole. That doesn't sound so great, but compared to lethal injection, it's not so bad."

I had Burton's attention.

The Federal Government, on the other hand, reinstated the death penalty for capital crimes – like murder, treason, and terrorism – a while back. If you're convicted in Federal Court, you're going to die, my friend. You killed a sitting U.S. Senator. You can't do much worse."

Burton kept his eyes on the Statute in front of him.

"I don't suppose you know how these jurisdiction things work out in the real world, but if we can't settle your case here in Minnesota right now, the Feds are going to throw their weight around and you'll be headed to Federal Court with no way back to

Hicksville."

"Now," I said. "Pay attention because this part applies to you."

Burton tried to look cocky, but sweat traced streams down his temples.

"If you and the Chief Deputy and the County Attorney can reach an agreement as to your guilt in the Senator's shooting, we can sentence you here in Minnesota and you head off to a nice air conditioned prison cell. Hell, the way people feel about politicians, you'll probably be a cell block legend.

"But . . ."

"But what?" Burton said.

"But . . . . Here's the tricky part. We Minnesotans have gotta convince the Feds to sign on to any plea agreement. Otherwise, they'd just try you again in Federal Court and you'd be dead anyway. So we gotta give them something . . . something they couldn't get without your cooperation."

"Yeah. Like what?"

"I'd say if you'd provide information about who you've killed and who ordered all your hits, that'd be mighty tempting."

"I s'pose it would. But if I'd killed anybody . . . I said 'if' . . . I prob'ly wouldn't even know the name of who hired me. It'd prob'ly all be done, electronically, ya know."

We had Burton where we wanted him.

"I think the lawyers would understand that you can only give up the information in your possession. But I bet whatever information an alleged hired killer might possess would be worth plenty to cut a deal."

Burton's wheels were turning. He had to know he was screwed. And he had to believe he'd get the death penalty when he was convicted – because he would.

Burton looked at Bull again. Bull was cleaning an imaginary musket . . . or . . . oh hell, I don't know what he was supposed to be doing, but it seemed to scare Burton enough.

"How . . . how would I go about discussin' some kinda deal, like the one ya'll said"

"That's a piece of cake," Gunner said. "I'll get the shysters . . . I mean lawyers . . . together right now. All of them – Fed, State, and County . . . your guy, too. I bet they'll be in here to chat in not long at all."

"Then be quick about it. I don't wanna end up in federal custody afore this deal is done, signed, and sealed."

Gunner and I stood.

"An' don't ya'll leave him in here alone with me. Ya hear!" He indicated Bull.

I picked up my case and we buzzed the jailer to be let out.

"Did you get everything you needed, Mr. Bull?" I said.

Bull nodded. "Good to go."

The door opened and Gunner held it for the rest of us.

"Now don't you go nowhere. I'll be right back," Gunner said.

"Well, hurry it up. Dammit. Now I gotta pee, too."

Gunner laughed.

"I'll send somebody to help you out with that."

CHAPTER 40

In and around Cairo.

Two days after the technology handoff to Rasha, Hitchens told Beth to prepare for the operation to commence at 2:00 a.m. the following night. All personnel were prepared. She should instruct Rasha to connect the device whenever it was safe to do so, then confirm with Beth that Rasha's mission had been accomplished.

* * *

As the appointed hour approached, all seemed ready. Rasha had reported planting the BPL modem in the GIS Director's office. Beth felt confident that his network connection would offer the information she sought.

Beth had also completed the remainder of her preparations. The networking devices to be planted by the Seals were all working properly and contained sufficient internal battery power for the duration of the cyber-attack. The repeater bridge was powerful enough to transmit the GIS network signal to Beth's hiding place, in a second floor flat half a block outside the expansive Intelligence compound. She had requested a perimeter check to assure there were no extraneous radio waves in the area of GIS that might interfere with her receiving a clear signal from the modem. And she'd personally prescribed the installation method the Seals would use to connect the BPL modem to the backup power lines from the auxiliary diesel generator.

Beth had installed the required computer programs on her Army-issue laptop, and would carry with her any gadgets necessary to accomplish her role – and nothing else.

For tonight's work, Beth would wear neither her formal suits, nor a Diane Sawyer combo. Her outer clothing consisted of a dark, drapey cotton robe with matching *hijab* to cover her blonde hair. Underneath, she wore a pair of black Puma tennies and loose, black poly-fiber shorts over skin-tight black spandex top and pants. If she needed to run for her life, she didn't plan to be encumbered with culturally sensitive garments that might slow her down. She hoped she wouldn't need to make use of the running gear. She wouldn't, if all went according plan.

At precisely 1:25 a.m., a white Toyota van arrived at the Embassy's main gate. Its driver appeared to be native Egyptian and was dressed as such. Carrying her gear, and decked out in her conservative Egyptian clothing, she and one of Hitch's male agents, also dressed as a native Egyptian, climbed in the back seat.

At 1:30, the same van departed the Embassy through the main gate. After driving several blocks and negotiating numerous turns and switchbacks, a voice crackled in Beth's earpiece telling the driver he hadn't been followed and was clear to proceed.

The trip to the flat near GIS Headquarters took them twenty-three minutes. The building had a rear entrance. Beth and the male agent availed themselves of it, climbing the eight short flights of interior stairs to the fourth floor. Beth's flat, and temporary operations center, faced the building behind hers.

Arriving inside the room, she confirmed that the equipment, spare batteries, duplicate network hardware, and other equipment were present. All was in order. Beth dismissed the agent.

"Thanks for the ride. I'll be seeing you soon."

"Good luck, Ma'am." He closed the door with a click.

Beth laughed to herself. This kid was no more than twenty three years old, and he probably knew more ways to kill a man than she did to hack a computer. Beth felt old.

Immediately, she fired up the Army laptop and set about connecting it to the peripherals. In less than five minutes, all was ready. It was 2:03 a.m.

Beth pulled back her *hijab* for comfort. All contact would be encrypted.

"Red Dog, this is Garfield. I'm ready. Over."

"Garfield, this is Red Dog. Confirmed. Out."

Now Beth needed to wait – for the Seals to install the network clamps over the auxiliary power lines and connect the BPL modem, for the main power to go down, and with a little luck, for the GIS network to become available on her screen.

* * *$*_1$

Once the order arrived, the team of four Seals swung into action.

Because access to the unprotected backup power line was a one-time-only opportunity, they had not yet entered the GIS compound nor begun work installing the BPL connections to the power lines.

It was convenient that no one wanted an office near the noisy backup diesel generator, so it had been banished to a remote corner of the GIS compound, where it was easily accessed through the low-tech wire fence. A dozen or so snips and the wire lay far enough open to allow one Seal and a black rubber umbilical cable to slip through.

The cable carried high voltage electricity and low pressure water. It was part of a portable laser cutting device the military had developed for covert operations during the early years of the 21st century. The same technology was available in the industrial marketplace, but these machines were bulkier and carried cumbersome shielding that made them useless for a cutting assignment such as this one.

Having successfully breached the perimeter fence, the Seal now used his clipper once more to remove the padlock from the generator's wooden enclosure fence. It had taken thirty seconds from first movement to arrival at the power access point.

Mounting the laser-water device to the metal electrical conduit leading to GIS headquarters, the Seal contacted his counterpart outside the fence, requesting power to the laser. If anyone had been listening for this 60 Hertz hum over the thousands of other electrical devices on the block humming at the same frequency, they might have been able to pick up the increase in volume when the laser operator flipped its power to the "On" position. As it was, no one noticed.

The laser cut was precise and swift, slicing a four inch oval from the conduit, without damaging the wires within. There was no need to remove insulation before connecting the BPL clamps and battery-powered modem.

The intrusion was behind and beneath the generator. Unless someone was searching for this precise incursion, it would go unnoticed at least until daylight, perhaps longer.

The Seals departed the compound as swiftly as they had arrived, soldering the severed fence wires on their way out. Less than five minutes after receiving the "Go" command, these men had completed their part of this mission. They disappeared into the blackness of Cairo's back streets.

Several blocks away a third Seal in a dark, unmarked delivery truck prepared to inject the neighborhood power grid with half a Megawatt of extraneous power. He had completed his connections an hour earlier. So when his order arrived, he was set to throw the switch.

When he did, the radio frequency remote triggered a power surge that flashed across more than a square mile of power grid, frying circuit breakers on electric transformers as it went, and plunging the vicinity into total blackness.

* * *

Inside the Egyptian Intelligence Service Directorate office building, the night watchman noted the power outage, communicating it to his superiors. There was a protocol for dealing with such occurrences.

Of course, the battery backup power for all crucial systems was automatic and instantaneous. The computer networks didn't even register a blip. But he needed to start the diesel backup generator to ensure continuous power in case the outage persisted.

The chief of maintenance on duty at GIS that night followed his written procedures and engaged the diesel generator. Momentarily, his control board registered that the generator was running and had stabilized its power flow. It was ready to take over supplying electricity to GIS.

*   *   *

Beth's computer registered the presence of the BPL modem as soon the Seals turned it on. A few minutes later, she received the modem's signal that electric power was present in the backup power lines. Her fingers fluttered above the keyboard. The wait seemed unbearable. There were so many things that could go wrong. She'd addressed the variables within her control. But there were always unpredictable elements that could bring the best laid schemes to naught.

Just as Beth was about to give up hope of connecting to GIS, her screen flickered and the network login screen appeared, in Arabic, of course.

Beth set about applying her decrypting arsenal to gain access to the network. Each program required precious seconds to execute. On her third attempt, the network firewall fell and she was in. She could only hope that this was the correct network and that she could now find the information that would lead her to proof of the man behind the Senator's death.

It didn't take her long to locate the Director's computer, which confirmed that she would, indeed, have access to the sensitive information she needed.

Thank you, Rasha!

Beth next employed her battery of data analysis software to scour the Director's computer for information pertaining to Grossman, Aurora, and the other keywords she had previously identified. In a matter of minutes, her computer displayed a list of files containing the pertinent content.

At this point, there was no substitute for manual review of the files. She needed to be certain she possessed enough evidence to positively establish both the origin of the assassination order and the person who had given the command. It was unlikely that the GIS or the SCAF as an entity had approved the killing. She needed to identify the rogue operator to make U.S. political pressure on Egypt effective.

Messages and emails were most frequently the best sources of incriminating evidence, so Beth scanned those first. It took only a few minutes for her to find the communications she sought and upload them to the Embassy via the satellite connection.

Her mission was complete. She had identified the source of Grossman's assassination order and provided her country with the documentation to prove it. She contacted the Seal operations center to let them know she was ready for extraction.

"Red Dog, this is Garfield. I'm ready for a ride. Over."

To Beth's surprise, the voice that rang in her earpiece belonged to Hitchens.

"Garfield. We have a small change of plan. Over."

Beth's heart sank. What did Hitchens want now? She needed to get the hell out of the hot zone.

"Red Dog, I have delivered the complete package and repeat my request for a ride. Over."

"Negative, Garfield. Remain engaged and collect information on the bird. Do you copy? Over."

The bastard wanted her to dredge up additional details on Aurora.

"Red Dog. I strongly object. Over."

"Garfield. Proceed to collect information and contact us when you have completed your new task. Red Dog out."

Damn, damn, damn!

Beth wanted the hell out of here, and now! But she'd been offered no choice in the matter. Her only option was to collect the additional Aurora data as quickly as possible, and hope the Egyptians didn't find her in the meantime.

After revising her search logic to focus on Aurora, Beth located several folders with a huge amount of data pertaining to her new target. Once again, focusing first on examination of direct communications, she soon learned that GIS possessed stolen plans for Aurora and a project to construct the aircraft had been underway for nearly two years.

She uploaded these communication files to the satellite. Because the files were small, this process didn't take very long.

The remainder of the Aurora data consisted of CAD/CAM files with detailed engineering drawings and specifications. These files were huge compared to the ones Beth had transmitted thus far. It would take quite a while to squeeze all that data through the slow BPL modem connection and up to the satellite. She contacted the op center again.

"Red Dog, this is Garfield. Over."

"This is Red Dog." It was Hitchens again. "Go ahead Garfield. Over."

"Red Dog, I have sent several additional packages your way. I would like my ride, please. Over."

"Negative, Garfield. We need all the packages that are available. Keep working. Out"

Beth was generally not a person to use coarse language. But she considered a few choice words that she'd like to pass along to Hitchens right now. He knew there was more information to be had, and despite Army direction to the contrary, he wanted it all.

Beth began the tedious process of copying and uploading the massive Aurora data files.

* * *

Beth's Timex read 4:15 a.m., and there was at least another half hour of file copying to be completed, when a man's voice, not Hitchens', whispered in her ear.

"Garfield. This is Angelfire. You've got company on the way. Execute Bravo Zulu immediately. Over."

Beth's worst fears had been realized. She would not escape from the apartment in time to avoid capture. But she had no time to ponder the consequences. She had duties to carry out.

"Copy that, Angelfire. Executing Bravo Zulu. Out."

Bravo Zulu was the plan to destroy any evidence that might disclose the reason for Beth's presence in this flat. Among other measures, the hard drive which held her hacking programs and a history of the data she'd just stolen, would be destroyed. Beth scratched out the keyboard command to destroy the drive.

There was a high-pitched grinding noise as a metal plate covered with steel spines pierced the hard drive's spinning platters. Once the plate had driven the "bed of nails" through the drive, no technology or expertise could recover the information that once resided there.

Next, operating from the laptop's secondary hard drive, Beth sent remote commands to the modem and repeater, signaling both to power down and cease transmission. She unplugged the satellite jack from the laptop and tossed a blanket over the small stack of communication electronics in the corner.

She knew she'd need to crush the ear piece as well, but she would wait until the last possible moment to do so. Without the radio, she'd be isolated from all hope of last minute rescue.

When she had purged all connections to her snooping activities, she called again for assistance.

"Angelfire. This is Garfield. Bravo Zulu complete. Are you coming? Over."

Beth held her breath.

"Negative, Garfield. They're at your door. Out."

Beth heard the loud clunking of boots on the stairway. She ripped the radio from her ear and crushed it with a Puma-clad foot.

Beth's heart pounded in her ears as the boots got closer.

Remain calm. Cooperate. Breathe. You will survive.

Someone in the hall kicked her door open and four men in black Egyptian State Police uniforms, armed with automatic rifles, burst inside. Beth stood in the center of the room with her hands in the air.

One of them searched her roughly, and without regard for personal modesty.

"No weapons," he reported in Arabic.

Now the apparent commander of the team spoke to Beth in English.

"Your troubles have only just begun."

CHAPTER 41

Back in Red Wing.

Before my next chat with Gunner, I wanted to see what, if anything, Dan Trew had discovered . . . or accomplished. I called his office.

After wheedling my way past his office defenses, I reached Dan.

"Hello, Mr. Becker. Calling to catch up on recent events?"

"Yup. You know me so well, Dan. But in case you haven't yet heard, the perp is ready to give up all his victims and employers in exchange for life without parole."

"You Minnesotans work fast. I haven't even heard back from Justice yet. So if you've gotten that far, what do you need me for."

"I figure the U.S. Attorney is going to be reluctant to take the death penalty off the table. A Senator's assassination is a big chance for 'tough on crime' publicity. I don't know whether Justice will endorse the deal. And if they're still going to hang the guy, he won't be talking."

"Hmm. I see your point. So you'd like me to try to talk some sense into Justice and get them to sign off on life without parole."

"That's about the size of it."

"I'll do what I can my friend. I'm going to have to assure the Justice Department and my guys here at the FBI that they'll get their share . . . well, more than their share . . . of credit."

"That goes without saying, Dan. Good luck. And thanks again."

"Same to you."

Now it was time to pay Gunner a visit and see what he knew about the legal wranglers and whether they'd negotiated a settlement among themselves. Hell . . . the criminal was ready to talk, and the prosecutors had to haggle over who got the credit. It's times like these when I'm glad I operate independently.

After the usual routine in the LEC lobby, Gunner ushered me into his inner office. I glanced at the Mr. Coffee. It was dry as the Mojave.

"Been hitting the sauce pretty hard today, eh Gunner?" I tilted my head at the coffee machine.

"That's the truth. Should probably be mixing some Irish in there with it . . . calm my nerves."

I laughed.

"What's the latest on our willing confessor and the legal eagles?"

"Frickin' lawyers should all get life without parole! We had the guy all primed and ready to confess yesterday, and they're still trying to figure out which one of them can get the biggest piece of glory pie."

"I'm sure the Ottawa County Attorney and the Sheriff are all set to go with the deal. Who's the biggest hold up?"

"Damn Feds. They haven't done one single thing in this case 'cept try to screw up our confession, and they want all the credit. The only way they can see to make a contribution at present is to try the guy and stick him with a needle."

"That can't really be a surprise."

Gunner snorted.

"No. I'm not surprised one bit . . . just pissed."

"I wonder if anyone has pointed out that there'll be plenty of FBI work and federal prosecuting to do once Mr. Burton turns over his info about the other killings. I know he said he didn't have names, but there are ways to trace communications to home in on the bad guys."

"You can bet I mentioned that to the Sheriff. Whether he relayed the good news to the Feds is anybody's guess. At least they seem to be content to leave the doer where he is till they hash out the plea thing. I should probably be grateful for that."

"Settle for the crumbs, Gunner. You'll be a lot happier for it."

Gunner laughed.

"Ain't that right."

*   *   *

Two days later, the powers that be had finally agreed to accept the sniper's information. I'm sure Dan had something to do with that, and I'll make sure to thank him. Gifts to federal officials are illegal, otherwise I'd send him something nice.

Once the plea deal was signed, all the attorneys, including Burton's defense guy, filled the counsel tables in the largest courtroom in the Ottawa County Courthouse. Local, national, and international press overflowed the remaining court room space into the hallways, and even stood outside in the chilly November air.

The judge accepted the plea and applied the agreed upon sentence, to be served in a Minnesota maximum security prison. After the plea was entered, everybody took turns giving interviews to the media . . . well, everybody but Gunner.

The Feds hailed the "participation" of local law enforcement in apprehending the sniper, while extolling their own wisdom in negotiating a plea deal that would not only ensure this criminal "would never see the light of day again," but would also lead to "justice for victims of other murders Burton had committed.'

Gunner did actually show up in a lineup of "also participatings" at the rear of a few newspaper pictures and news videos. That would be the extent of his fifteen minutes of fame for this case.

On the other hand, his work did not go unrecognized within the Sheriff's Department. Without the burden of a press release or undue fanfare, the Sheriff presented Gunner with the "Distinguished Service Award for Law Enforcement." This was the highest honor the Sheriff of Ottawa County had authority to bestow.

As far as "crumbs" go, this award amounted to nearly a whole sandwich. Gunner took my advice and enjoyed this prestigious, if unpublicized, honor. He was actually a cheerful guy for a full week afterward.

That ended my involvement in the sniper case. I assumed that between the FBI and the CIA, someone had located his primary base of operation in a non-extradition country, and had begun poring over a wealth of information that would lead to uncomfortable times for a good number of bad people. I took some satisfaction in that thought.

*   *   *

That night was the first on which I had failed to receive our agreed upon message from Beth confirming her safety. I would allow an additional twelve hours for operational delays. After that, I would be demanding answers.

One door closes and another opens. I was hoping it wouldn't be hell in the hallway.

CHAPTER 42

Somewhere in Cairo.

Before removing her from the flat, Beth's captors cuffed her hands behind her back and tied a hood over her head. Unless this was going to be a short trip, it would be impossible for Beth to determine her ultimate destination.

The State Police loaded her into the back seat of a four door car and drove off. Apparently, some other personnel would be inspecting and analyzing the technology she'd left behind.

Beth kept track of probable distances and the order of turns the vehicle made as it wound its way through the narrow streets of Cairo. But the route was well planned and executed, with frequent curves and backtracking. Soon, Beth had no idea of her whereabouts. She was completely at the mercy of the dreaded State Police.

When the vehicle reached its destination, nearly an hour, Beth guessed, after departing the flat, it passed through a security checkpoint and over a set of speed bumps. Beth could hear the raising of the access gate as they waited to proceed. Since the single warning in the apartment, no one had spoken a word, to her or otherwise . . . at least not that she was able to hear.

The car proceeded into an underground receiving area of some sort and came to a halt.

"Place her in the lower level cell block," a male voice told her abductors in Arabic.

Despite her passivity, her handlers continued to handle her roughly, often touching her in areas she would have preferred had remained private. Her anger built and she longed to lash out. But this would not help her, she knew.

Remain calm. Cooperate. Breathe.

After a walk down a long and echoing hallway, the men shoved her into a prison cell, where she fell to the concrete floor. Two of them stood her on her feet and removed the hood. It took a few moments to adjust to the illumination. As she tried to get her balance and assess the situation, one of the men removed her bonds and lifted the long robe off over her head.

There were three of them. They whistled at Beth's body as revealed in the skin tight running suit.

She suddenly felt naked.

The men jeered and mocked her in English.

"Whore," "slut," and "prostitute" were three of the less graphic taunts.

Beth found a concrete bench against the back cell wall and huddled upon it. She drew her knees up and wrapped her arms around them, searching in vain for a position these men might consider modest. The last thing she wanted was for their behavior to escalate beyond the verbal barrage.

When they tired of harassing her, they departed the cell, closing the grey steel door behind them. There was the unmistakable buzz of an electronic lock. One of the police eyed her momentarily through the door's wire-reinforced window. She refused to meet his eyes, choosing to remain motionless in her fetal position on the bench until she could tell he had left.

Remain calm. Cooperate. Breathe. You will survive.

CHAPTER 43

Back in Red Wing.

The extra twelve hours passed without word from Beth. One minute later I was on the phone calling CIA Director Holford. His receptionist was also a thorough vetter. But when I insisted that she just tell Director Holford that Mr. Elizabeth Weston was on the phone and it was extremely urgent, she consented to looking into the Director's availability.

About thirty seconds later, Director Holford came on the line.

"Mr. Weston? How may I help you?"

"Thank you for taking my call, Director. My apologies, but I need to ask. Is this line secure?"

"Yes, it is."

"Director, you don't know me from Adam, but the woman you know as Elizabeth Weston is my wife. She is working a mission for you folks right now in Cairo, and she's in trouble."

There was a pause.

"What kind of trouble and how do you know?"

"I don't know exactly the nature of the situation, but I can assure you that it is serious. Elizabeth and I have an ironclad agreement that she would contact me every twenty-four hours while she was away to assure me that she was okay. Elizabeth and I are not ordinary people with casual experiences. She has contacted me religiously every day since she left . . . but now has not messaged me in the last thirty-six hours.

"Sir, she is in trouble, I promise you. I know that Elizabeth holds you in high regard. It is for this reason that I have contacted you directly. I need to know Elizabeth's situation and I need to know it now. I'm hoping your agency will assist me."

"Mr. Weston. I can assure you that I've heard nothing to indicate that Elizabeth is anywhere but on the Embassy grounds. However, because I also hold Elizabeth in high regard, I will make a call to confirm her situation. Would you mind holding for a minute or two?"

"No. Not at all. Thank you."

The minutes ticked by on my wall clock. Eventually, the Director returned to the line.

"Mr. Weston. I have Deputy Director Simon Connor with us on the phone right now. Tell Mr. Weston what you know, Simon." The Director's voice cut with an edge of irritation.

"Mr. Weston. I have just been . . . I was just now made aware of the fact that Mrs. Weston's whereabouts are presently unknown."

I had no patience for CIA double-speak.

"What the hell does *that* mean?"

"Yes, Simon," the Director said. "What *does* that mean exactly?"

"Well . . . ah . . . Mr. Director. She was participating in an operation two nights ago in Cairo, and disappeared from her station during the assignment."

"So someone kidnapped or arrested her. Is that what you're saying, Simon?" The Director had taken the words right out of my mouth.

"Ah . . . yes it seems as though that may be the case, Sir."

"And what measures, exactly are we taking to locate her and return her to the safety of the Embassy?"

"We're pursuing the usual channels of intelligence vigorously, Sir. I'm confident we will locate her soon."

"Is that it Simon? That's really all you have to say to this woman's husband? You're pursuing the usual channels?"

"Well, yes, Sir. I mean, I am sorry that your wife is currently missing, Mr. Weston."

My blood boiled. Beth had probably been arrested by a brutal Egyptian regime and this Simon had no idea what to do to get her back.

"Simon," I said, "you are a complete ass. Director, may we speak privately?"

"Goodbye, Simon. I suggest you find Ms. Weston soon and unharmed by any and every means possible."

I heard Simon's connection click off.

"I'm very sorry Mr. Weston. It was never my intention to place Elizabeth in danger. It seems Simon has overstepped his authority once too often. I assure you, he will suffer appropriate consequences.

"Now, besides exploiting every connection I've got to find Elizabeth, is there something else I can do?"

"Yes, Director. As a matter of fact there is."

CHAPTER 44

En route to Cairo.

The CIA had been kind enough to hook a ride for Bull and me on a Lockheed C5 military cargo jet headed for Ramstein Air Base in Germany. The Air Force shuttled us to Hamburg, where we took a Lufthansa flight which would be depositing us at the Cairo Airport at approximately 8:00 a.m. local time.

Director Holford had been extraordinarily helpful in coordinating CIA, diplomatic, and military support in the effort to locate Beth. After 48 hours of wasted time I hoped, with Holford's assistance, Bull and I could yet find and rescue Beth. She had to be okay. Any other assumption was worthless.

It was plain from the CIA briefing we'd received en route from Minnesota to Germany, that Beth had been captured by a military element of the Egyptian government. Though the SCAF was supposedly in command of all military and State Police operations, the CIA advised that both governmental and opposition sub-groups operated independently of SCAF control.

The soldiers who had taken Beth wore the uniforms of the State Police. But even uniforms were not determinate in this new Egypt. Another faction might well impersonate the State Police simply to divert blame from themselves.

The CIA had also told us that, pursuant to direction from her CIA superiors, Beth had been engaged in a remote computer attack on the Egyptian Intelligence Services Directorate at the time she was captured. Navy Seals involved in the operation confirmed that black-uniformed riot police had taken Beth from her operational location in an unmarked, dark blue Toyota Camry.

Unfortunately, the Seals weren't equipped for vehicle pursuit, and they were unable to confirm her destination.

I was anxious to find out what rescue efforts the CIA team on the ground had already tried. Whatever, they were, Bull and I would find another, more successful, approach. We had to.

Bull slept during most of the night flight to Ramstein. He'd forced himself to do so to assure maximum effectiveness upon our arrival in Cairo. Normally, I would have done the same. But this was no ordinary operation. Beth's life was at stake. I found myself unable to sleep.

We arrived in Cairo a few minutes early. After passing through customs and immigration using manufactured names and passports, we picked up our luggage and rental car. Bull drew more than a few stares as we hiked the airport passageways.

Although we had a room reserved at the Ritz Carlton on Tahrir Square, we headed straight for the U.S. Embassy. The CIA must have told the guards to expect us, because they gave a cursory inspection to our documents and waved us through. A valet appeared at the front entrance to park our Nissan. Since we hadn't been able to bring any special equipment with us through customs anyway, Bull and I exited the car and gave the young woman the keys.

As we climbed the steps to the Embassy door, a page met us. He said that Mr. Hitchens was expecting us and we should follow him. Hitchens, I recalled, was the name of the CIA agent in charge of the botched operation that had gotten Beth captured. I took several calming breaths on our way to the meeting room. I would've liked to introduce myself to Hitchens with a right to the jaw, but I knew that wouldn't help Beth's situation. So I resolved to keep emotion in check and try to coordinate this rescue as efficiently as possible.

The page ushered Bull and me into a well-appointed conference room. The man in the black power suit would be Hitchens. He was flanked by a large, dark-suited man and a small woman with a pen and clipboard. One of them was, no doubt, Embassy security . . . the other, Hitchens assistant.

The page announced us as Mr. Becker and Mr. Red Feather, then backed out and closed the door.

Hitchens approached us and offered a hand.

He wore his greying hair slicked back, his tie too tight, and his cologne in excess. I would've disliked the man under any circumstances, more so this morning.

Bull and I shook Hitchens' hand.

"Welcome to Cairo, gentlemen. I'm pleased your travels were safe." He smiled.

"If we could dispense with the pleasantries, Mr. Hitchens. We'd like to get down to finding my wife."

The smile disappeared.

"Yes, of course. Please take a seat and I will be happy to answer any questions you may have and provide whatever assistance you require – though I believe you will find that we have been quite thorough in our search thus far."

Bull and I took seats at the far end of the rectangular conference table from Hitchens and company. Hitchens took the head of the table.

"We've been briefed concerning the details of the situation, at least as far as CIA Langley knows them. What have you done so far to locate Beth?"

"I can assure you, Mr. Becker . . . may I call you James?"

"No. Proceed."

Hitchens didn't flinch his practiced poker face.

"We have engaged the State Department to communicate with Egyptian Foreign Affairs and to make a formal protest concerning the unwarranted arrest of a U.S. citizen. Thus far, Egypt denies any knowledge of Elizabeth's situation and assures the Ambassador they will investigate."

I nodded.

"Director Holford has also contacted the Joint Chiefs. Several of their generals have worked with the Egyptian military for many years, and have some chance of finding a sympathetic ear via that route. The Egyptian generals may also know of a rogue element inside Egypt whose activities might include taking captives."

"And here in Cairo," I said," what've you done to find Beth?"

"Quite a lot, actually. We've searched her room here at the

Embassy and scoured her cell phones and computer for anything that might help us out. We've also attempted to contact Rasha – Beth's contact within GIS – to see if she can assist, but she doesn't answer her phone."

I interrupted.

"Is cell phone the only way Beth contacted Rasha?"

"Yes. Except when they met in person at Groppi."

"Groppi?"

"A local restaurant."

"And you've been monitoring Groppi in case Rasha might show up there, right?"

"Ah . . . actually, I'm not positive that we have. I shall make sure that detail is covered immediately, if we haven't already done so. But I should also mention that it is entirely possible that this Rasha betrayed Elizabeth to her captors."

Hitchens knew damn well that they hadn't watched for Rasha at Groppi. He was trying to excuse his omission. It was probably too late now.

"And your other efforts?" I kept my voice level and firm.

"When we felt it was safe to do so, we examined the room from which Elizabeth was taken. It had been stripped by her . . . by someone. All our equipment was gone. We looked for any clues Elizabeth might have left us, but found nothing."

I didn't imagine that Beth could have left any useful clues, since she would've had no idea where they were taking her.

"Continue."

"Our operatives are monitoring Egyptian communications, hoping to find a mention of Elizabeth, or of any new prisoner. No results there so far. And our human intelligence appeals have been similarly unsuccessful."

So neither his spies on the ground nor his signal intelligence resources had been helpful in finding Beth.

I was growing weary of Hitchens' lack of creativity in conducting this search. By this time, when routine measures had failed, the situation called for a more innovative approach. I hadn't heard any inspired techniques yet.

"Anything else?"

"I believe our further endeavors would amount to mere elaborations on the efforts I've described so far. But we've been very thorough. Very!"

Bull hadn't contributed to the conversation . . . which was to be expected. But I was impressed at his self control in not making faces or uttering derisive grunts at Hitchens' report.

At Hitchens' last statement, however, Bull had been unable to avoid offering his opinion. He looked at me, with eyebrows raised and head cocked to one side.

"Very thorough," he said, then flashed a glare at Hitchens.

Hitchens recoiled slightly at Bull's look, but he chose, nevertheless to respond. In my estimation, it was a sign of poor judgment on Hitchens' part.

"I suppose you have a better approach to finding Elizabeth?"

"Maybe."

"What is that supposed to mean?" Hitchens slapped both hands on the table in front of him

It seemed to me he had lost his composure rather suddenly. I imagined he wasn't accustomed to unabashed insubordination and mockery.

"How'd Beth contact Rasha the first time?" Bull asked. His tone was serious, but not confrontational.

Hitchens exchanged whispers with the small woman.

"She used her computer to message the Egyptian. But as I said, this Rasha may not be on our side."

"Or she might be," I said. "Did Beth trust her?"

"She seemed to."

"Then I trust her, too. Besides, what have we got to lose by contacting her? If she's a dead end, so what. The Egyptians know we're looking for Beth. They already know that. Contacting Rasha should be priority one."

Hitchens searched for a rebuttal.

"We have tried calling her on Beth's cell, but she doesn't respond. Don't you think that means she doesn't want to talk to us?"

"Has Rasha spoken with anyone here besides Beth?"

"No."

"So if she knows Beth is locked up somewhere, and that her phone may have been compromised, what would you do with your cell if you were Rasha?"

Hitchens knew the answer, but didn't want to admit it.

"I suppose I'd ditch the phone so any internal investigation couldn't connect me with Elizabeth. But we can't just send someone to meet Rasha on the street, or in her home. If she's suspicious of the Egyptians, she'd sure as hell be suspicious of us."

Hitchens leaned back, with arms across his chest.

"Contact her in a way only Beth would know." It was Bull.

"And just how do you propose we do that? If only Elizabeth knows it, how can we know it?"

"I already told you," Bull said.

"What the hell are you talking about? And why is this guy here anyway?"

"He's here because he's going to help find Beth . . . and your Director agrees. Now, why don't you listen to him?"

"But he's not saying anything that makes sense!"

"He asked you how Beth contacted Rasha in the first place. Have you tried duplicating her contact procedure?"

Hitchens remained silent.

"Well then," I said, "let's get your best computer people on Beth's computer and find out what she did and how she did it. Then if this Rasha is friendly, at least she'll know the message is from Beth's friends."

Hitchens was apparently reluctant to respond.

"All right then. If you won't act, I'll take Beth's computer and we'll send its contents to my military contacts. I promise you, they *will* get us an answer."

Hitchens had no idea whether I could make good on my threat. I probably could. In any case, it got Hitchens off the dime.

"Andrea," he said to his assistant, "please see to it that we have our best people working on Elizabeth's computer immediately."

"Yes, Director." She arose and left the meeting.

"Now," I said, "let's try the common sense approach. Bull." He turned toward me. "If Beth was abducted while executing a cyber-attack on a certain government agency in Cairo, whom would you suspect of grabbing her up?"

"I'd guess it would be that agency she was screwin' with."

"Gee. Me, too." I turned to Hitchens.

"What sort of beefed up surveillance have you got going right now on the GIS compound?"

"Our usual surveillance assets are quite thorough."

"So . . . none. I suggest you work with the Navy to get their people to beef that up a bit. Will you do that for me, please?" I still hadn't shown anger, but my tone had become demanding.

"If the Director will authorize the contact, I will request additional surveillance on GIS."

"The Director's already given it a green light. Please engage the Navy right now."

"I will act as quickly as possible. Is there any way I can be of further service to you gentlemen?"

I'm pretty sure it was sarcasm, but we needed guns and technology.

"Yes. Bull and I need weapons, communications gear, and other equipment. If you would contact your munitions clerk and see that we get what we ask for, that would expedite matters. Thank you."

Bull and I stood. Hitchens and his man followed suit.

"I've got your cell number, Mr. Hitchens. I won't hesitate to call if I need something further."

Bull and I turned and left.

As we walked alone down the hall, Bull had a comment.

"Dick!"

"Yeah," I said, "but he's *our* dick, and our best connection to Beth right now. We'll have to see whether he follows through."

"Still a dick!"

"No argument from me."

CHAPTER 45

Although Beth had no watch and couldn't see daylight from her cell, she nevertheless was able to keep rough track of time by observing the routines of her captors. She estimated that she had been in this prison for just over twenty-four hours. Thus far, she had had no direct contact with anyone since her arrival yesterday.

Various uniformed guards would peer through the small window in the door from time to time, usually wearing a lascivious grin on their faces. She refused to meet their gazes.

She was thirsty, hungry, and tired, but she kept her mind occupied with thoughts of escape. She would need help, she knew. But help would come. It was only a matter of time. By now, she was certain that her husband would have missed her daily message and would be coming to Cairo to search for her. She also knew, that he would leverage every contact he had in the military to support his efforts.

Every few hours, Beth would stretch her legs on the bench, and again against the wall. She did push-ups, abdominal crunches, leg lifts, and assumed various yoga positions. She also allowed herself a few hours at a time of fitful sleep. And she prayed . . . a lot.

As often as possible, she would remind herself that her captivity *would* come to an end. She needed to hold onto that thought.

A guard appeared at the door, his presence followed by the electronic buzz of the door unlocking. When the door opened she saw two men. Both wore the same black uniforms as the men who had taken her freedom from her only a few short hours ago.

"Up," one guard said, in English.

Beth uncoiled from the fetal position she had adopted whenever she was within view of the guards, and stood up, her arms at her sides. She had no hope of covering her female form in this running suit while standing. She may as well stand proud.

One of the guards, grabbed her arm and jerked her out of the cell, while the other led the way through the corridors. When they arrived at the interrogation room, the same guard pushed her roughly into a steel chair. She wasn't resisting. The guards' actions were either out of disdain for her, or intended to frighten her. She refused to allow either possibility to affect her state of mind.

The two guards left her alone and unbound, seated at the grey metal table. The electronic lock buzzed as the door closed. The room held only the table and three chairs – two across from her. The door was similar to her cell door, with a small wire-reinforced window. One wall held a large mirror, which Beth assumed was two-way glass.

As she waited for her interrogators to arrive, she steadied her breathing, closed her eyes, and pictured her home on Jefferson Avenue. The trees would be bare of leaves at this time of year. Her crafting room in the attic would be just as she'd left it, a plain denim jacket hanging on its rack, waiting for her to apply her artistic flare. She smiled.

The door clicked open and two new men entered. One was portly, grey-haired, and wore a fine linen suit. The other wore an army uniform, khaki tan, with pocket and shoulder decorations indicating that this soldier was a leader of men.

The grey-haired suit pulled out a chair and sat, while the officer stood behind and to his side.

"You are Elizabeth Weston," the man in the suit began, speaking in English. "You work for the United States Department of State in the Embassy here in Cairo. Until recently, you had been retired. Now you have been called back to your former position in the Embassy communications area."

Apparently, he'd pulled her Embassy file from Egyptian Foreign Affairs.

"Tell me Elizabeth. What brings you back to Cairo after all these years?"

Beth looked straight into the man's eyes, while his wandered over her upper body.

"I was following orders," Beth said, speaking in an even tone. "Shortages of personnel to work abroad. Foreign wars have taken their toll. You understand these things, I'm sure."

Beth glanced at the officer. He stood at parade rest, watching her face intently. No lewd grin. He was all business.

"Certainly, I understand, Elizabeth. But the timing of your arrival here is curiously coincident with a recent attempt to attack our computer systems at the Intelligence Directorate. You were found in a room not far from the Intelligence office building, and in possession of a good deal of electronic equipment. Don't you find that odd?"

"I don't have an explanation for the coincidence."

"Ah. But I do, Elizabeth. You were hacking into our computer systems. You were looking for something."

Beth remained stoic.

"I don't see how that is possible. My computer is half broken and the rest of the equipment I know nothing about."

"Then tell me. How did you happen be visiting that particular flat, so near to my headquarters, in the middle of the night?'

"A friend told me the apartment was vacant and I wanted to be alone."

The man leaned forward.

"A decent woman does not walk the streets of a large city alone after dark. All manner of evil may wait to befall her." He grinned.

"I can't tell you how much I'm enjoying our chat. But I have friends who will be coming here soon to bring me back to the Embassy. I would appreciate it if you might return my clothing and hail a cab so I can be on my way. You wouldn't want to illegally detain an American diplomat once you've identified her. And I am, indeed, who you say I am."

"Alas, we have seen no diplomatic papers. We have only guesses at your true identity. And your State Department has made no request concerning you whatsoever. I'm afraid we can't allow a potential . . . terrorist . . . loose in the streets of Cairo. That just wouldn't be responsible. I am certain the Americans would agree."

"Then I have no more to say to you. Why . . . I don't even know who you are. Perhaps, it is I who am speaking with a terrorist."

"Then let me show you my credentials, my dear, that you may know the peril in which you have placed yourself."

The GIS Director reached into an inner pocket, produced his Intelligence identification card and held it toward Beth.

She leaned in and scrutinized it closely.

"Well, Director. It is an honor to meet you. Now that I am assured you are not a terrorist, I know you will contact my Embassy and send me on my way promptly."

The Director laughed. The officer remained solemn and silent.

"Saed," the Director said, his eyes locked with Beth's, "what is the punishment for espionage against the State of Egypt?"

"Death, Sir."

"Death."

"If you think I'm a spy, then send me to your courts of law. I will prove my innocence. Otherwise, I must demand that you release me *now*."

The Director sat back in his chair and grunted.

"You are a saucy one, Miss Elizabeth. Let me be direct with you, before it is too late."

"Yes. Please be direct." Beth leaned forward.

"What have you stolen from our computers, Ms. Weston?"

"Nothing. I don't know what you're talking about."

The Director studied Beth's eyes.

"Tell me about . . . Aurora."

He was clearly searching for some tick, some quiver that would give her away. But Beth met his stare.

"Borealis or Australis?"

"What?"

"Those are the two aurora's of which I am aware. One in the northern sky and one in the south. Now, I'm done talking until you release me."

"Tell me about Aurora!" He now stood, his voice approaching a yell.

Beth remained silent.

"Let us go, Saed," the Director said. "She will say more once she has lost the false American pride."

Saed preceded the Director to the door and rapped twice. The locked buzzed open and the two guards appeared to return Beth to her cell.

* * *

Back inside the GIS Director's office, the Director spoke to Saed.

"What is your opinion? Shall we extract her information by more forceful means?"

"Sir. We have only speculation that she was even able to access our files. There is no evidence other than her proximity and the satellite beacon in her flat. I agree that she may have been attempting to attack our computers. But our experts say there was no intrusion. Our security remains intact."

"How do they know this?"

"They tell me they can determine when any file has been read or copied and they have found no evidence of unusual activity. They are confident our information is safe. If we attempt to extract a confession from the woman by torture or drugs, and she knows nothing, there is no telling what she will say to appease us."

"But if she does know," the Director said, "she will divulge her knowledge."

"This is true, Director. However, if our computer systems remain secure, what can she tell us? That she suspects we have Aurora? And what good are suspicions? I am certain the American CIA suspects us of everything possible, including terrorism. I don't see what we gain by torturing the women. And once we do so, we could never return her to the Americans, saying she was lost in our bureaucracy."

"What you say makes sense, Saed. And we can always torture her once the Americans have forgotten her . . . presumed her dead, the victim of unknown crime."

"Yes, Director. I agree that, for the time being, we should wait."

"That is my decision, Saed. For now, keep her alive. We will deal with her when the appointed day arrives.

"In any case we have a triumphant launch to attend in a few hours. I anxiously await our mutual victory, Saed."

"Yes, Sir. And as far as the American girl goes, I will make it so."

CHAPTER 46

From the secret Aurora facility to Egypt's Deversoir Air Base, northeast of Cairo.

The three Egyptian scientists had done all they could to ensure Aurora's success in its first test flight. Over the past two weeks, the Egyptian Air Force had constructed a roadway from the development facility to a main road. Now the overhead cranes lowered the massive aircraft on to a specially built truck bed. Covered in tarpaulins and great drapes of thick foam rubber to disguise its true shape, Aurora was ready to see daylight.

Two huge Caterpillar bull dozers towed the unique vehicle up and out of its hangar, across the newly built road, and to a transfer platform adjacent to the existing highway. Here, the dozers gave way to a diesel truck to ferry the payload the rest of the way to Deversoir Air Base, a few kilometers distant.

A convoy of military vehicles from machine-gunning Humvees to towed missile arrays, to covered troop trucks accompanied the valuable cargo, creating an impenetrable barrier in both front and back. Additional troops, tanks and missile launchers punctuated the roadside terrain along the entire route. The thudding of attack helicopters filled the skies.

The Egyptians were taking no chances with security.

Of course, the move was made under cover of dark, and the entire length of highway from the lab to Deversoir, as well as adjoining several miles of intersecting roadways had been blocked off to all traffic since dusk.

The going was slow. Despite the specially designed suspension on the trailer, no one wanted to risk damaging Aurora during transit.

Arriving at its destination around 4:00 a.m., the truck rolled directly into a fortified hangar. The remaining vehicles, including a van containing the three scientists, assumed their pre-determined positions. The deserted air base had suddenly sprung to life in Aurora's presence.

* * *

It was now mid-morning. After troops had dragged Aurora's camouflage and tarps away, and newly installed overhead cranes had relocated Aurora from the truck bed to the concrete hangar floor – an operation requiring no mean skills nor patience – the scientists were ready to inspect their baby's condition.

Everyone else stared at Aurora as the three white-coated men inspected every inch. Aurora was no longer shiny steel, but dark grey and black – her previous opalescent beauty replaced by an imposing, powerful shadow . . . a weapon exuding astonishing power and deserving of utter awe.

After the inspection, the scientists gathered alone in a corner.

"I can identify no flaws which would absolve us of responsibility for the craft's condition," Ahmad said. "Have either of you noticed anything?"

"Regretfully, no. The transport was entirely successful."

Commander Saed approached their group.

"I trust all is ready for the test flight?"

"All appears in order, Commander. We have found no damage in transport."

"Good. The Director is here to experience his crowning glory – the theft of plans and successful construction of the Aurora craft. The entire SCAF will also be present, as well as representatives from Russia and China, who are most interested in purchasing our technology. See to it that you do not fail us."

"Yes, Commander."

Saed left to coordinate with the Director.

Aurora held seating for two pilots, though only one was needed to operate the sophisticated and intuitive controls. The brave men who were selected to fly this miracle craft stood beside the engines, peering into their emptiness.

The pilots had never seen Aurora . . . at least not the outside. They had practiced extensively using a mock cockpit with training programs designed by the Americans. They knew the chances of a successful first flight in such a revolutionary craft carried great risk. And yet, they and many others had competed for today's honor.

"I don't suppose there's any point in waiting longer," Hamadi said. "Let us have the ground crew prepare the plane for flight."

The other two nodded. All three looked skyward for their deliverance.

*   *   *

Aurora waited at the end of the two mile long runway, her oversized booster rockets anticipating ignition, and her fuel tanks fully pressurized with methane. All dignitaries had assembled at a safe distance, anticipating the takeoff.

Aurora remained eerily silent. Her engines unable to ignite at speeds below Mach 1.

At last the countdown rang over the loud speakers.

"Ten, nine, eight . . ." The scientists held their breath. The Director nudged a Chinese General as if to say, "Now watch this." ". . . seven, six, five . . ." the booster rockets ignited with a growling roar, but had not yet reached full power. Aurora remained motionless, her brakes locked for a few more seconds. " . . . four, three, two . . ." The rockets had reached maximum power – their nozzles twitching.

" . . . one, takeoff."

The pilots released the wheel brakes and Aurora started down the runway, slowly at first, but rapidly accelerating on the solid booster's combined 250,000 pounds of thrust. Aurora lifted off a mere half mile from its dead start, then began climbing on a near ballistic trajectory. Within 15 seconds, Aurora was no longer visible to the naked eye.

The dignitaries applauded the successful launch, while the

scientists continued their prayers.

Mere seconds after the boosters had rocketed Aurora to Mach 1, the pilot dropped the dead booster shells and prepared to engage the pulse jet engines.

His voice rang through the speakers on the airfield below. "Engaging pulse jets . . . now."

The PA system immediately turned to loud static. Observers who had been following Aurora with telescopes felt their hearts jump into their throats. There had been an explosion.

A few seconds later, everyone saw a the small cloud, far down range, spraying white tails like a jester's hat.

The scientists prayed even harder.

CHAPTER 47

After collecting guns and other essentials from the armament storage room at the Embassy, Bull and I retrieved our rented Nissan and checked in at the Nile Ritz Carlton, not far from Tahrir Square in downtown Cairo. The accommodations were extremely high end. This location was popular among wealthy Americans, and our presence here should draw less attention from the local police.

At 1:30 that afternoon, our first in Cairo, we were expecting a meeting with a representative from a Navy Seal Special Ops Team attached to the U.S. Sixth Fleet, which routinely patrols the Mediterranean. The Captain did not disappoint.

At precisely 1:30, my cell phone rang.

"James Becker."

"Mr. Becker," a male voice said, "I'm your date for this afternoon. Where'd you like to get together?" His accent was Midwestern. It'd be like talking to Gunner.

"Room Number 1407 at the Ritz would be great. See you . . .?"

"Two minutes."

I summoned Bull from the adjoining room. I think he'd worn the carpet out in there with all his pacing. His concern for Beth was one of few emotions I had ever gleaned from that Native American visage.

Presently, there was a knock at our door. I checked the peephole to see an Arab-looking man dressed in white linen and sandals.

I opened the door.

"Mr. Becker?" he said. There was the same Midwestern accent I had heard on the phone. It seemed odd coming from this fellow's mouth.

"Yes. Please come in." I swung the door wide and directed him into the room. He took two steps, saw Bull, and stopped short.

"He's with me," I said. "You'll like him when you get to know him . . . or not. Doesn't really matter. He's all in." I closed the door.

"I'm Captain Smith from Bravo Group." He shook my hand. "Pleased to meet you Becker." The Captain was about five feet nine inches, 170 pounds. I supposed he would blend in better with the natives if he wasn't too tall. His stature probably made Bull appear all the larger.

"Please call me Beck. Everybody does."

"Right, Beck."

He extended his hand to Bull.

"And you would be?"

"Bull."

The Captain looked at me. I nodded.

"Pleased to meet you, Bull."

Bull shook the Captain's hand.

"Have a seat, Captain," I said, indicating the largish table and three chairs I had requested from housekeeping.

The Captain removed his head wrap.

"Thanks."

Bull sat as well, while I grabbed three bottles of water from the mini-fridge, setting one on the table by each of us.

"Thank you, Sir." The Captain opened the bottle and toasted in my direction.

"Bull. Beck. I've been briefed on your situation, and my Team is at your disposal. Do you have an extraction plan?"

"Bull and I have discussed several, yes. But a lot depends on where Beth's being held."

"CIA ain't got that nailed down yet?"

"No. But Bull and I are assuming she got grabbed up by GIS and is being held at their compound somewhere."

"If that's right, they've got their main holding cells in the basement. Kinda got a whole prison, actually. They don't normally have lots of prisoners at any one time though. Just when they snatch up a bunch of demonstrators or something."

"Beth got captured while she was working a covert operation affecting GIS. Some Seals helped out with parts of that deal, so you may or may not know about it."

"I heard things were taking a lot longer than my guys expected. She was close to the GIS compound and some riot police homed in on her. Probably the satellite transmissions. They're hard to hide if somebody's looking for them."

"Any idea why somebody'd be looking for a satellite transmission around GIS in the middle of the night?"

"No, Sir. But for what it's worth, the Egyptians had increased security at all of their government buildings this week. Some before your wife disappeared. Some after. My opinion? They were looking for somebody to come at 'em."

I thought of Rasha. If Rasha had broken Beth's trust, she would've known the target was GIS, wouldn't she? Why the heightened alerts all over?

"The wiring and hardware and stuff you guys used to connect Beth up with GIS . . . is it all still there?"

"Sir, I'm not sure. It certainly is possible . . . everything but the repeater and your wife's hardware."

"So someone might be able to re-establish the hack?"

"Can't say for sure, Sir. Seems like it'd be worth a shot though. If it's still in place, a short hack shouldn't be too risky."

Yet another way the CIA could have been looking for Beth, and hadn't. *Dammit!*

"Well, Captain. Let's the three of us go over what Bull and I've been chewing on, and then we'll see if you can help us adapt it to wherever Beth's at. That sound reasonable?"

"Ten-four. Let's have at it."

* * *

Following our conference with Captain "Smith," I called Hitchens' cell.

"Hitchens."

"Have your computer geeks figured out how Beth contacted Rasha in the first place?"

"Yes. Indeed they have. A very clever contact it was, too."

"Yeah. That's exactly how my wife would do it, Hitchens! Try to reach Rasha and get her a cell number to Mr. Elizabeth Weston. Got it?"

"I will make the request."

"Don't make the request. Make it happen. Let me know when she calls you."

I hung up.

Bull and I needed to go back to the Embassy to see whether we could re-establish the network hack at GIS. It was after 4:00. I wanted us to get Beth *tonight*.

CHAPTER 48

After Hitchens connected us with the computer gurus at the Embassy, I found that there were two who knew something about Beth's operation, and had some ability to hack a foreign network. A man and a woman, both in their early twenties, both Caucasian. Their knowledge, combined with the information Beth had transmitted as she worked her way into the GIS network, seemed to provide hope for another successful hack.

"One thing we can't figure out, though," the woman said. "Your wife had a program that could enter and exit files without leaving a trace. I'm sure the program is on her computer, but we don't know which one it is, or how to use it if we found it. Hacking is a very personal pursuit."

"So my wife tells me . . . often. But you think you could get in? Maybe find out if there's something there about Beth's location? I don't really care if you leave a trace."

"We can try. That's all I can promise."

The man nodded.

"That's all I can ask. Can you be ready tonight?"

They looked at each other like a pair of treed raccoons. I was sure their comfort level didn't extend far beyond this computer lab.

""Yes, we can, Sir. We'll get on it now."

"Good. Stay available and at the Embassy. I'll be in touch if and when we need your help."

* * *

It wasn't long after the CIA had pinged Rasha using the "Silver Star" code word that she was on her new cell and returning their call. She wouldn't talk to Hitchens, instead demanding to speak with "Mr. Elizabeth Weston.'

Hitchens forwarded me the call.

"Rasha my name is Beck. Elizabeth is my wife. I've come from the U.S. to bring her home."

Rasha paused.

"Tell me the word that Elizabeth would use to describe you to me."

Damn. We didn't have a signal or code word for that one. I'd have to wing it.

"She'd say I was a cowboy. I kinda do things my own way."

There was a pause.

"I believe you are Elizabeth's husband. She would marry a cowboy. She has been captured by GIS and is in prison in the GIS headquarters. Please. Can you get her out?"

"I think I can, with some help. But there might be some bloodshed if I have to force it. I'd rather use finesse, if you know what I mean."

Rasha was silent for a moment.

"I am not sure what you mean. But do you ask for my help? If so, you have it."

"That is exactly what I was hoping for, Rasha. Can you meet me at the Nile Ritz Carlton in one hour? Room 1407."

"I will be there. Give me your direct cell number please in case I am delayed."

I gave her my Egyptian cell.

"Thank you, Rasha. I'll see you then."

* * *

The hour before my meeting with Rasha gave Bull and me time to coordinate and refine the plan we had discussed earlier. It was much easier to do so now that we had confidence Beth was being held in the GIS building. We scheduled our incursion for early the next morning. Captain "Smith" would bring personnel and technology that would lend considerable aid to our hope of freeing Beth with minimal bloodshed.

* * *

At precisely the appointed time for my meeting with Rasha, there was a tentative knock at my hotel room door. Seeing a fortyish Egyptian woman through the peephole, I opened the door and welcomed her.

"Please come in. I'm Elizabeth's husband. Call me Beck."

Rasha shook my hand lightly as she scanned the room. She wasn't a spy by training. I was certain the present situation made her very nervous. But I had to give her credit for facing her fears to help Beth.

"Hello, Beck. Are we alone?"

"We are for the moment. But there is someone I want you to meet. He's a good friend of Beth's . . . that is Elizabeth's . . . and he has come to Cairo with me to help free her. Don't be afraid. Okay?"

It never helps to tell someone not to be afraid, but sometimes there's no other option. I moved to the connecting door and rapped on it twice. Bull opened the door from his side and stepped just far enough into my room for Rasha to see him.

She covered her mouth at the sight of the big Indian who was now dressed in denim jeans and a black cotton T-shirt, stretched tightly over his muscular bulk.

"Rasha," I said, "this is Bull. He's not as scary as he seems."

That last statement might have bent the truth a tad. But Bull was certainly no danger to Rasha.

Bull remained beside the connecting door and extended his hand toward Rasha, who was still a good distance across the room. She would have to come to him.

Rasha looked at me, then at Bull again. Finally she approached him and accepted his hand.

"It is my pleasure to meet a friend of Elizabeth's. Thank you for coming to her aid."

Bull was gentle with the handshake and even bowed a bit.

"The pleasure is mine." He smiled the most genuine, friendly smile I've ever seen from him. Honestly, I didn't know he had a smile like that. I'd log that thought away for future consideration.

"Well," I said, "now that we've all met, we need to get down to business. Shall we sit?" I swept my hand toward the round table and three chairs. Bull and I waited for Rasha, then we joined her.

"Rasha, we hope to free Elizabeth tonight."

"So soon? But I will not be able to enter the building again until morning." She probably assumed her assistance would be similar to placing the wall wart in the last operation.

"That's okay. We don't need you inside the building. We've already got a plan for entry, and some exceptional personnel are onboard to assist."

"Okay. Then how may I help?"

"There are two areas in which I hope you will be able to lend us aid. First off, we need to know where in the building Elizabeth is being held, and the route we must take to reach her. I have an outline of the GIS building. You can show us where we'll run into security guards and locked doors, etc. Can you do that?"

"Yes. But my information will be incomplete. I am seldom permitted in the building after normal work hours."

"That's okay. Whatever you can tell us will be a big help."

Rasha nodded.

"Then there is the second thing I hope you can do for us . . . or I should say, *with* us. Here's what we need . . . ."

CHAPTER 49

At 1:15 a.m. that night, the Navy Seals were in position and Bull and I had holed up in the bushes beside the busy thoroughfare known as El Mokhabarat Street (Intelligence Street), which ran between the Egyptian National Intelligence Complex and the Presidential Palace grounds. The entrance to the underground garage was near this street.

"Red Dog, this is Mesa Five. Over," I whispered into my headpiece. I was Mesa Five and Captain "Smith" was Red Dog. Bull was call sign Tomahawk.

"Roger, Mesa Five. You've got Red Dog. Over."

"Tomahawk and I are in position. Is the repeater in place? Over."

"Roger, Mesa Five. Up and running. Still awaiting word about transmission. Over."

The repeater was working but the BPL modem under the diesel generator was still dead. I needed to check with our pod of computer experts, including Rasha.

"Tech Pot, this is Mesa Five. Over."

"Ah . . . this is Tech Pot."

"Tech Pot, I need you to establish target contact now. Let's see if we can get her up and running. Over."

"Okay, Mesa Five. Pinging to engage."

The computer nerds weren't exactly up to speed on radio communications etiquette. But that wasn't important. The transmissions were encrypted anyway. The call signs were more habit than necessity.

Minutes passed.

"Tech Pot, this is Mesa Five, you still there? Over."

"Ah . . . sorry Mesa Five. We just woke up the repeater and the exterior . . . ah . . . modem. It should connect to the network for us as soon as the Aux power starts flowing."

I laughed.

"Well done, Tech Pot."

"Red Dog, this is Mesa Five. Did you copy that? Over."

"Mesa Five, this is Red Dog. Five by five. Over."

It was time to begin the attack.

"Red Dog, this is Mesa Five. She's all yours."

"Roger, Mesa Five. Commencing operation Indigo."

Phase One of Operation Indigo was to take out the electric power in the entire Palace Dome neighborhood. The Seals were ready at a nearby power substation. The weapon they would use was called a graphite grenade. One of the Seal team would use shoulder-mount launcher to send the grenade about 100 feet above the electric substation, where the grenade would explode, showering the transformers and high voltage equipment with graphite filaments.

Red Dog gave the order. His man launched the grenade.

The weapon was tiny – the results dramatic. Most of Cairo could see the fireworks when the graphite rained down, shorting out the entire electric facility in a deafening and vivid explosion of arcing electrons, followed by quiet deep blackness – a blackness that enveloped even the GIS compound. Their yard lighting wouldn't return until the backup generator came on line.

Phase Two followed on the heels of the first. In the darkness above GIS Headquarters, two Shrike UAVs had been hovering unnoticed for the past ten minutes. Now they landed silently on opposite corners of the GIS building. I looked skyward and listened carefully, but neither saw nor heard anything as the five pound, video monitoring VTOLs (Vertical Take Off and Landing) assumed their stations.

"Eyes in place." It was Red Dog. The Shrikes had landed and were transmitting audio/video signals of the GIS compound to Red Dog.

"All set, Bull?" I whispered.

Bull turned his head to give me a visual on his lips. I'm not much of a lip reader, but I think it was something like "Bite me." Bull was ready.

"This is Red Dog. Commence Phase Three on my mark.... Go!"

Immediately following the Captain's command, the far perimeter of the GIS compound lit up like a napalm attack from *Apocalypse Now*. The Seals had deployed flashbangs, incendiary torches, firecrackers, and probably a bunch of other stuff they didn't even have when I was on active duty. Everything had been timed to give the appearance of a sustained attack.

The diversion had the desired effect, drawing security guards away from our side of the compound and toward the action. Dressed in generic military camo, complete with helmets, kevlar vests, and armaments, Bull and I raced for the rear entrance to the GIS garage. As we ran I radioed our computer support.

"Tech Pot. Let me know when you've isolated our target system. Over."

No response. They were probably still looking for the programs that controlled building security. Many computer geniuses aren't good at multi-tasking – like maintaining communications while hacking. Bull and I kept low and kept moving forward in the darkness.

"We got it, Mesa Five. Woo hoo! We connected and our new friend let us in the back door. Ah . . . over?"

"Tech Pot, this is Mesa Five. Let me know when you are ready. But don't touch anything yet."

"Got it, Mesa Five."

Another minute passed.

"Mesa Five, we have isolated the controls. We're all set to go whenever."

"Tech Pot, sit tight. Don't worry about the noise. Do not . . . I repeat do not execute until I give you the signal. Over."

"Understood Mesa Five. We will wait for your okay."

Bull and I met no resistance until we reached the garage entrance, which had been locked down.

Bull placed a small chunk of C4 and a detonator on each side of the steel gate. We backed off a few feet and Bull hit the switch. The gate detached on both sides, allowing us to remove it from its hinges and clear the drive. We'd need this exit for our escape. It had to remain open.

As we ran through underground the garage, we could smell the effects of Phase Four of the attack – tear gas and smoke screen. Even when the perimeter guards realized the assault had been a diversionary tactic, and that there were no attackers along the fence line, the burning tear gas and choking smoke would hinder them in their efforts to return to the building to take up their defensive positions.

I radioed to our computer hackers.

"Tech Pot, this is Mesa Five. Open the building doors. Over"

"Roger that, Mesa Five. Electronic locks disengaged."

They were starting to sound like real soldiers.

When Bull hit the glass entry doors, they swung open and shattered against the interior walls. A guard on duty inside a plexiglass booth stood and tried to unholster his pistol.

Bull raised his M4 rifle, pointing it at the man's head. The guard's hands left the gun and rose in surrender. I smashed through the window, released the door from the inside, and injected the guard's neck with a healthy dose of barbiturates. He'd be sleeping through the rest of the action.

Ahead of us lay a seventy yards of concrete corridor lined by grey metal doors with wire reinforced glass windows. Bull raced forward, checking cells, while I contacted Tech Pot for more help.

"Tech Pot. This is Mesa Five. Open the cell doors."

"All of them?"

"Yes. All of them. Now!"

There was an audible buzz and a few of the cell doors swung slightly open.

"Beth," I yelled. "Let's go. We gotta get out of here!"

With that, a cell door far down the corridor opened slightly and Beth's face peeked out. She saw Bull first and ran for him. As she tried to latch onto him with a hug, he pushed her farther along the hallway, past him and in my direction.

Beth alternately stumbled and ran toward me down the long

corridor. As she drew nearer, a black-uniformed guard rounded the corner at the far end of the hallway, past Bull. The guard raised his M-16, but too late. Bull cut him down with a three-shot burst from the M4.

"Find a car," Bull yelled over his shoulder. "More comin'."

By this time, Beth had reached me. I pulled her behind the entryway wall just as a hail of bullets flashed by, striking the exit glass and a few of the cars parked nearest the doors. With more gun fire in the corridor, I checked around the corner to see if Bull was okay.

I didn't see Bull. But three uniformed guards, armed to the teeth, were searching doors on their way in my direction.

I chanced a burst from my own M4. I hit one of them. The other two ducked into a cell. The cell turned out to be the wrong choice. A second or two later, both men came flying out the door and across the hallway, slumping against the far wall.

Bull pointed at me purposefully.

"Get the damn car."

Four more guards appeared at the far end of the corridor. Bull skidded a grenade down the concrete to where the guards stood. They retreated behind the concrete corner just before the blast.

Bull made a break for a cell closer to our end of the hall. When the bullets started flying, I fired back, past Bull and toward the guards. Bull slipped inside a new cell and I retreated behind the wall once more.

When the guards began advancing again, they carried Kevlar shields, interlocked to protect them from my fire. An arm appeared from Bull's cell and rolled another grenade the guards' way. This time they back-tracked only a few steps and shielded themselves from the blast with the Kevlar.

Just as I was about to lay down more cover for Bull, a voice came from the garage behind me. I swung around to face the barrel of a .45 automatic pistol. A guard had noticed the blown gate and snuck up on me from that direction. Instinctively, I dropped my rifle and pulled Beth behind me.

"The prisoner has escaped," I yelled in Arabic, as though the man couldn't see my camo duds. But it confused him long enough. While my gun lay on the ground and my hands were held in the air, Beth slipped my Beretta from its holster and emptied the clip into the chest of the recoiling guard as he fairly flew out the garage door onto his back.

Before I could even retrieve my own weapon, Beth had pilfered a fresh ammo clip from my belt and slapped it into the butt of the Beretta.

I picked up my rifle. The car keys hung on a board inside the guard station. I motioned for Beth to crawl through the broken window and grab a key.

I needed to help Bull. I peeked around the corner again. The four guards were approaching Bull's cell with caution. They were still too far from me to toss a grenade into their midst. And the gun wasn't much use against their shields.

I didn't have many choices. But I had to do something before more security arrived through the garage.

With rifle in hand, I dove from behind the wall onto the floor of the corridor and aimed for the guards' boots. Their shots flew mostly over my head, although one ricocheted off my helmet. On the other hand, my shots were hitting their targets. One by one, the black-uniformed attackers fell to their knees.

Bull saw his opportunity. His hideout was a mere ten feet from the place where the security guards knelt behind their shields.

Flinging the cell door open, Bull charged the unsuspecting guards, bowling over their shield barricade and dropping a hand grenade underneath. Bull's momentum carried him past the guards who scrambled from their backs beneath the shields for a new defensive position . . . as the grenade exploded.

From my position on the floor, I could see the guards had been laid flat. But I couldn't see Bull. I jumped up and ran down the corridor in the direction of the action. As the grenade smoke cleared I saw one badly wounded guard reaching for his rifle. This was no time to take hostages. As the guard rolled toward me, raising his gun to shoot. I took careful aim and planted the M4's 5.56 mm projectile on the bridge of his nose.

Bull came charging through the haze, vaulting the remains of the four guards.

"Watch where the hell you shootin'. I was over there you know."

"You're welcome," I said, as we both raced for the garage.

By the time we reached the door, Beth was gone.

Dammit! I didn't come this far to lose her now!

I stuck my head into the guard booth, just in case she might have taken cover there.

Outside in the garage, tires squealed. I swung around, ready to fire. Beth was in the driver's seat of a black Mercedes with the window down.

"Need a lift?"

Bull was still facing down the corridor, covering our rear. As I hopped in the car, he switched his M4 to fully automatic and laid down a stream of bullets in our wake. I slid over. Bull barreled in beside me, and in the same motion flung a final grenade into the entryway.

"What're you waiting for?" he said.

Beth slammed the sedan's accelerator to the floor, squealing the tires toward the exit drive.

"One of you guys know which way we're going?"

"Through the gate and hang a right, and then a second right," I said. "We'll have cover once we're outta the compound."

As soon as we cleared the building basement, we were drawing attention from guards in the courtyard. Bull and I returned fire – he, through his window, and I, over the car roof. As we squealed around the second right turn onto the roadway, we had two hostile vehicles in pursuit.

But no sooner had we cleared the gate than both vehicles exploded, leaving one upended in the gateway and one rolling across the yard.

"What the hell was that?"

"Mesa Five. This is Red Dog. You like those Switchblades? Over."

The Switchblade was yet another Unmanned Aerial Vehicle in the military arsenal. Weighing in at less than six pounds,

Switchblade was designed as a remote control kamikaze drone. It's nose packed four ounces of whatever explosive its operator desired. Since navigation was via video feed and GPS, Switchblade seldom missed its target. They'd been overhead the whole time.

"Gotta get me one of them." It was Bull.

It took only a few seconds of Beth's expert driving to clear the immediate kill zone. Two blocks further on, we pulled into a parking lot and switched cars.

"I get you a Mercedes and you get me a Hyundai," Beth said. "Doesn't seem right."

She smiled.

I moved for the driver's seat. She cut me off.

"I think I've got it from here."

"Yes, Ma'am."

Knowing that, although we couldn't see them, the military drones still had our backs, we drove a law abiding and inconspicuous speed through downtown Cairo and onward to the U.S. Embassy. Bull and I wouldn't be returning to the hotel.

When we reached the Embassy gates, the guards had flung them wide open in anticipation of our return. Beth pulled up to the front door, bringing us to a screeching halt.

Standing on the Embassy's from steps were Rasha and the rest of Tech Pot. I was relieved to see they had also made it back safely.

CHAPTER 50

My first order of business when we reached the Embassy was to give my lovely wife a big hug and kiss. Rasha may have been embarrassed at our public show of affection. But she would have to get over it.

Next up for Beth was a flying hug for Bull. She leapt up onto his chest, wrapping arms and legs around him. Bull's face flushed – which isn't easy to discern on an Indian. His eyes certainly got big. He looked like a kid who'd just walked in on his mom getting dressed. Beth hung on until he had no choice but to participate in the hug. He reached one arm around Beth's torso and patted her back lightly.

"Thank you," Beth whispered in Bull's ear. I think his face may have flushed even a bit more. He continued his gentle, albeit mechanical, back patting. Finally, Beth released him.

Rasha was next. Beth approached Rasha, her arms outstretched, taking care not to offend with American exuberance. Rasha rushed to Beth and they held each other in an embrace that soon turned to tears on both sides.

When the hug ended. Beth held Rasha's hands in hers.

"Thank you, Rasha. Your bravery is beyond all measure."

Now it was Rasha's turn to blush. Her voice caught in her throat.

"I only tried to do what Elizabeth would do."

Then they were back to a full hug again, and more tears.

"Okay," I said, after allowing a reasonable period for hugging and crying. "Let's go inside, get cleaned up a bit and see if somebody'll cook us some real food."

Everyone agreed with my plan. It doesn't happen that often.

The Embassy staff treated Rasha as they would a foreign VIP, providing her a luxury suite with all the amenities, except alcohol, of course.

Beth and I shared her room. I paced the hallway outside as she showered. She took her time. I was glad she did.

Twenty minutes or so later, Beth's towel-wrapped head peeked out the door.

"Your turn, Babe."

She left the door ajar and moved to a large mirror, tossing the hair wrap onto a chair. There she stood in her Embassy-issue white robe, brushing her wet hair as I watched.

I sighed.

"It's good to see you safe and sound, Beth."

I flopped on the bed cover.

"Great to see you, too, Babe. It's been a long time. Now if you wouldn't mind cleaning up a bit, the bed would appreciate it."

She smiled in the mirror.

I sniffed my underarms.

"I reckon you've got a point little lady. Time to scrub up!" I bounced off the bed and headed straight for the shower.

While I was showering off the gun powder and grenade residue from tonight's activities, the Embassy sent my luggage from the Ritz Carlton up to Beth's room. I'd been wondering what I was going to use for fresh duds. Problem solved.

Before we headed down to meet with the rest of the group, I wanted to hear Beth's take on the failed operation. She gave me all the details – at least all I needed to know.

I also made a phone call to Langley to tell Director Holford that Beth was safe. It didn't seem I could rely on his underlings to relay that sort of news.

He was pleased to hear the good word and agreed to relay my gratitude to the Seal Team who had made the assault on GIS possible.

"There's one more thing you might be interested in, 'Mr. Weston.' The State Department has just sent the SCAF a memo. Our Ambassador is delivering it to the Chairman's Office as we speak."

"What's it say?"

"I'll send a copy to your phone. I think you'll enjoy it."

"Many thanks, Director, for reaching out and coordinating Beth's rescue . . . and for allowing Bull and me to participate."

He laughed.

"It didn't seem like I was going to be able to prevent you from getting involved. I just preferred a coordinated mission as opposed to a couple loose cannons tearing up Cairo."

Folks had used the term "loose cannon" to describe me before. "Loose smart-bomb" would have been more accurate – at least in my opinion. I wasn't sure whether either term described Bull, or whether it was possible to adequately describe him without employing telepathy.

I thanked the Director once more, then awaited his message.

CHAPTER 51

Before congregating with Mr. Hitchens and his staff, we'd each enjoyed a tasty and nutritious meal, cooked up especially for us by the Embassy's head chef. The food was necessary, though no one felt exactly rejuvenated.

Following the meal, our dog-tired operations team, and three fresh-as-a-daisy Embassy jockeys, convened for a debriefing in the main floor conference room. Mr. Hitchens fell into the latter category. It appeared as though he'd slept through Beth's rescue, probably trying to avoid any blame for its failure. Hitchens' security guy and his assistant were the other well-rested folks.

The table was one of those massive cherry jobs executives love to use to impress their guests. Hitchens had on another dark power suit, and shone as though he'd been detailed at the local body shop.

Once everyone was seated, Hitchens – who had assumed the head of the table – began.

"I must congratulate all of you on the fine job you did rescuing Elizabeth." He looked at Beth. "Elizabeth, you've had all of us here at the Embassy, and at Langley as well, very worried. We've been pulling out all the stops to find you and return you to U.S. soil. And now you're finally here."

Beth was hot.

"If you hadn't forced me to stay in the combat zone for hours after our mission had been completed, I wouldn't have been captured in the first place, you prick!"

I chimed in.

"I'd say she's right on. How about you, Hitch?" I spat out his nickname.

Hitchens sipped his water glass.

"I don't see any need for finger pointing. It was a collaborative operation. We're not even sure how the police found Beth in the first place." He eyed Rasha. She refused to respond, but locked her eyes on his.

"Yes, well," I said, "normally that would be the case. Except when the man in charge of the assignment changes the parameters in mid-operation and hangs the other team members out to dry – like you did to Beth."

My anger was obvious but, so far at least, controlled.

"And where do you get off implying Rasha was to blame for Beth's situation?" I said. "If it weren't for her help, there would've been a lot bloodier mess at GIS and more damage control for *you* to talk your way around. She's proven whose side she's on. But you . . . you're on your own side."

Hitchens didn't respond. I continued.

"Why did you insist that Beth go after the Aurora data when she'd already delivered solid evidence concerning the Senator's killer? I thought the Army told you to leave that alone."

Hitchens decided to try intimidation.

"Listen, Sonny. I've been leading covert operations since before you could wipe your own nose. Don't be questioning my loyalty."

Bull laughed.

"What's *he* laughing at?"

"You got a funny way of leading," Bull said, ". . . sittin' on your ass in the Taj Mahal while people who depend on you take the heat. Then somebody else has to come in and clean up your mess. Helluva leader."

Hitchens was about to say something when I jumped in again.

"You know those Aurora plans you just *had* to have . . . the ones the Army told you not to worry about? I just got a little note from the State Department about that. Signed by the actual Secretary of State of the United States of America." I thumbed my cell to bring up the message.

"I don't care what you say you've got there . . ." Hitchens' voice was approaching a yell.

Bull stood . . . all six-four, 240pounds of him.

"Well, we don't give a damn whether you care or not. So just shuddup and listen." Bull looked as though he might jump the length of the table. Hitchens showed the wisdom to remain silent.

"Here we go:

DATED: 10 November

FROM: Hillary Rodham Clinton
Secretary of State
United States of America.

TO: Commander-in-Chief
Supreme Council of the Armed Forces of Egypt.

Per face to face meetings earlier today between our Ambassador and your Deputy Chairman, there are three issues to which The United States requires Egypt's direct and immediate response:

Item first: Earlier today, your military conducted a missile test northeast of Cairo. Per numerous agreements and treaties between our countries, Egypt must notify the United States in advance whenever it plans a missile launch. The Guided Missile Cruiser, USS Vicksburg, attached to the United States Sixth Fleet in the eastern Mediterranean, came within seconds of destroying your missile in mid-flight. However, it appears that your missile self-destructed before our counterattack. As you know, clear communication between allies is crucial to avoiding such unintended encounters. We require your explanation regarding this missile launch in full.

Item second: In the wake of the assassination of United States Senator, Elbert Grossman, several days ago, the United States has conducted an investigation into his death. That investigation has led to conclusive proof that the Senator's assassination was ordered by the Director of Egypt's Intelligence Services Directorate, Murad Muwafi. We would like to believe that the Director acted strictly on his own behalf, as a rogue element in your government. However, we have no evidence to disprove that he acted under SCAF orders. We require that Egypt address the situation concerning Director Muwafi immediately and respond with evidence establishing that the SCAF was not complicit.

Item third: During our posthumous review of Senator Grossman's files and records, the Department of the Army of the United States has uncovered evidence that, several years ago, Senator Grossman, acting in a traitorous manner, improperly disclosed to Egyptian intelligence operatives, detailed plans for certain Top Secret military equipment belonging to the United States. The Army investigative service advises that, due to concerns about Senator Grossman's loyalty at the time, military engineers had subtly, but materially, sabotaged such plans before providing them to Senator Grossman. In accordance with our countries' mutual anti-espionage treaties, the United States requires the return of the stolen and altered plans, and warns that any attempt to use such plans to deploy the equipment described therein may result in extreme damage to property and loss of life.

I await your immediate response.

Sincerely,

Hillary Rodham Clinton
Secretary of State
United States of America

I looked up from my phone.

"Do you have something further to say, Mr. Hitchens?"

Hitchens stood and walked slowly long the table toward the opposite end where the rest of us sat.

"Ms. Weston," he said, extending his hand to Beth. "It appears I owe you a profound apology. I am truly sorry for the distress you have suffered over the past several days."

Beth stood. But instead of accepting his hand, she landed a roundhouse right fist on his jaw.

Hitchens staggered.

"I hope you understand my wife's sentiments, Mr. Hitchens. I share them."

Beth and I turned toward the door. Bull stood to follow us.

"Me, too."

Hitchens faced Rasha.

"I do want to thank you for your help in catching the rogue assassin and in freeing Ms. Weston." He offered Rasha his hand, accompanied by a smile I presumed was supposed to appear genuine.

Rasha extended her hand toward his, but only part way.

As he stepped closer, Rasha strode forward and kneed Hitchens in the groin. He doubled over.

Beth smiled.

The security guard moved to grab Rasha, but Bull stepped between them. When the guard tried to muscle Bull out of the way, Bull sent him wheezing to the floor with a right jab to the solar plexus.

Hitchens managed to straighten up and was about to slap Rasha on the face.

Again, Bull was there. He seized Hitchens' swinging arm in one of his extra-large hands, and wrenched it behind Hitchens' back, raising the arm higher along the man's spine until he ceased his squirming.

"That ain't no way to treat a lady," Bull said.

While holding Hitchens' hand pinned behind his back, Bull grasped Hitchens' belt buckle with his free hand and sent the alleged diplomat skidding across the floor.

The security guy got up on one knee, but a look from Bull sat him back down.

Hitchens' assistant cowered in a corner.

"Bull," I said, reaching for his near arm. "I think our work here is done. There's only so much cleaning up one trash man can do."

Bull surveyed the room once more. Hitchens lay writhing in pain against one wall. The Security Guard still sat woozy against the other.

"True dat!"

CHAPTER 52

Deversoir Air Base, northeast of Cairo.

The three scientists had been locked away at the Air Base ever since the disastrous Aurora launch. The Army was collecting others who had worked on the project, and their families, and bringing them all to Deversoir for similar incarceration.

Hamadi and his fellow scientists held out no hope of mercy. They had failed at an impossible task . . . failed to build Aurora. Now they would taste "justice.'

The morning after the test flight, with hundreds already under lock and key, Commander Saed entered the confinement center. All stood to hear the Commander pronounce their sentence.

"I have come to deliver a message to all of you from the Supreme Council of the Armed Forces of Egypt."

Hamadi felt his knees go weak.

"I have been asked to read their communication to you word for word, so there may be no misunderstanding."

The Commander produced a clipboard he had been holding behind his back.

Fellow Egyptians,

It is with great disappointment that we must officially relay to you that which you must already know . . . the Aurora Project has been a complete and utter failure. The aircraft exploded moments after engaging its main engines in yesterday's test flight. All further work on Aurora will be discontinued, effective immediately.

But you should not consider Aurora's failure to be your failure.

You have served diligently and capably for the past two years in an effort to make this project a reality.

This morning, it has come to our attention that the Aurora plans from which you have been working were not able to be successfully implemented. The Americans had intentionally designed faults into the plans . . . faults that none of you could have recognized as you carried out your duties. So we say again, this failure is not yours.

Rather, the fault lies with Intelligence Director Muwafi, who failed to perform due diligence in obtaining and delivering the defective plans to you.

We assure you that your services to our country are greatly appreciated. We further assert that the Director will no longer encumber you with ill-conceived assignments and impossible projects which waste the great talents of brave Egyptians such as yourselves.

We thank you again for your honorable contributions to this effort, and wish you and your families well.

Chairman
Supreme Council of the Armed Forces of Egypt

Hamadi couldn't believe his ears. Allah had saved them after all. Despite their inadequacies in building Aurora, the SCAF had somehow become convinced that the aircraft's original faulty design had led to its demise . . . not the insufficient skills of the Project's scientists.

This was exactly the sort of deliverance only Allah could provide.

*   *   *

The Commander watched as the assemblage hugged one another and sighed in relief. He knew their exact emotions at this moment. His fate rested with theirs. He could only be thankful that the Americans had adulterated the plans, and that the SCAF had chosen to lay blame for the oversight at the Director's feet.

Commander Saed knew that, for the first time in many months, he and these workers would sleep soundly tonight. Tomorrow's troubles would be sufficient for tomorrow. Today's burdens, at least, had been lifted.

CHAPTER 53

At the U.S. Embassy. Cairo.

The hard part was done. Beth was safe, and we'd made it back to the Embassy. We also learned that the Seal team had suffered no casualties. A win-win-win. We still needed to deal with Rasha's situation and to find a way home. By this point Bull and I were *personae non gratae* with Egyptian airport authorities. We wouldn't be flying EgyptAir on the way home.

The four of us met around a table in the Embassy cafeteria, three of us pounding coffee like it was the elixir of life and one drinking Egyptian tea.

"Rasha," Beth said. "What are you going to do? There's at least a good chance your bosses at GIS will suspect your involvement in our illegal activities there."

Rasha held her ceramic mug in both hands, once again worrying it with her thumbs.

"I have thought of this since I first contacted you, Elizabeth. I took a decision at that time to risk my position to deliver to you the information. I have a cousin in Saudi Arabia who may take me in, if I can reach there."

Her voice was sad.

"Or . . . if there is a way I could go to the United States, I should like to try to make a new life there. I have been a pariah in my own land for long enough. Even though I know for me to be happy and successful in the United States would not be an easy thing . . . do you think for me to travel there is possible?"

Beth looked at me, then back at Rasha.

"Rasha," Beth said. "My contacts are in the CIA. They are good contacts, and they may carry some influence with Immigration, but I don't know how far those connections will take us. Do you understand?"

Rasha lowered her head.

"I understand. And I knew there might not be a way."

I had a few contacts of my own. Military black-ops had resettled exiled foreign conspirators before. If they could do it for anyone, they could darn well do it for Rasha.

"Rasha," I said, "please let us see what we can do about getting you to the U.S. No guarantees. But before we leave Cairo, we'll have an answer for you."

"I am grateful for your assistance, Mr. Weston."

Beth gave me a worried look. She knew how long her branch of government took to get things done and probably assumed I was lending hope to a hopeless cause.

"I think the best thing for you to do right now, Rasha," I said, "is for you to take advantage of Embassy hospitality. Get some rest. Try to relax. One way or another, we'll at least get you out of Egypt."

Beth wore a doubting look, but I *knew* I could make good on that much.

Rasha brightened a bit and released the grip on her cup.

"Are you certain?"

"Positive."

"Thank you, Mr. Weston. This is a relief that will allow me to take some needed rest."

We all stood as Rasha departed, tea cup in hand, for her quarters.

"More coffee?" I asked.

Beth and Bull both held out their cups.

"I'll be back with a pot in two shakes."

When I returned with a carafe, Beth's arms lay crossed on the table with her head resting on top of them. She wasn't sleeping, but she'd just been freed from several days of hostile captivity. She needed to recharge.

"Beth. Why don't you go back to the room and crash for the rest of the day. Bull and I'll take care of extraction."

She raised her head.

"And Rasha?"

I've spoken with your Director a few times over the past days. I think I can swing his support . . . if necessary. You're no help to us half-dead anyway."

Beth managed to raise a sarcastic eyebrow above sleepy eyes.

"Don't get me wrong. You're still great eye candy."

I smiled.

"Good save," she said. "You're right, though. I'm done for. See you guys later."

Again we rose as Beth returned to her room.

I looked at Bull. He seemed . . . well . . . like Bull. Neither his face nor posture showed signs of fatigue.

"Whattya want to do, my Dakota friend?"

"They got beers in this joint?"

I laughed.

"Let's find out."

*   *   *

As it happened, we were able to locate an "officers lounge" of sorts that offered Budweiser and Heineken. I let Bull blow off some steam by watching him stare out the window and not asking him any questions. Silence is comfortable with Bull . . . sometimes, even preferable. Anyway, he enjoyed two Heinekens and a few plastic-wrapped sandwiches from the cooler. I nursed a Bud, more for the camaraderie than anything else.

"If you're going to be jabbering all the time," I said, "I wish you'd go to bed, too. There's work to be done, and I'm not doing it chatting here with you all day."

Bull took a final pull, emptying the green Heineken bottle, and got up to leave.

"True dat."

"Would you cut that out! 'True dat' is gangster lingo, not Indian."

"Hey, Indians can say 'True dat' if we wanna. After you took it all away, you white folks gave us back a free country. We can say whatever we want. First Amendment, yes?"

I couldn't think of a proper rebuttal.

"True dat," I said.

CHAPTER 54

That night, as Beth and I lay in bed, I was awakened by the rumble of a thunderstorm approaching. Soon I heard the comforting patter of raindrops on the Embassy's stone window ledge. I could imagine sheets of rain washing the grey film from Cairo's buildings, then gathering into shallow rivers, scouring the dust from Cairo's gritty streets.

Rain was rare for Cairo. To me, the downpour seemed oddly well-timed, cathartic, washing away the unsettling events of the previous days – Beth's incarceration, the firefight at GIS, the unpleasant encounter with Hitchens, Rasha's new dilemma.

But more than that, the rain reminded me of Egypt's recent revolution . . . a peaceful outpouring of rage that sought to wash clean the country's long-corrupt political system. Was there hope for that cleansing? Thus far, the revolution remained only a symbol of change. Would it take hold, bringing to the Egyptian people the freedoms they sought? Or would the well-entrenched military government continue pressing Egyptian society into decay, just as the dust and pollution would re-establish its hold on Cairo's busy streets and noble architecture?

These thoughts were too deep for tonight. I needed sleep. Tomorrow would have troubles sufficient for itself.

* * *

The next morning, I awoke to a pleasant surprise. My military connections had proven to be experts at back door maneuvering. In less than twenty-four hours, they'd arranged for Rasha's new U.S. Passport to be delivered to the Embassy.

And we were soon to be leaving Cairo. A Navy helicopter was on its way from the USS Forrestal – the lone carrier attached to TF-60 (the Mediterranean Amphibious Task Force) at present – to facilitate our departure for home.

Rasha, Bull, and I didn't have much luggage. Rasha hadn't deemed it safe to return home to gather her belongings, and Bull and I travel light. Beth . . . well, Beth had a full complement of various bags. All those Diane Sawyer outfits and power suits take up space . . . at least, so I was informed.

Before heading to the Embassy roof to meet the chopper, I allowed Beth to do the honors with Rasha, who still had no idea where she was going to end up.

Beth took Rasha aside and the two of them spoke quietly for a few minutes. Then Beth slipped Rasha's new Passport out of her pocket and opened it for Rasha to see.

There were lots of tears, hugs, salaams, and blessings going on in the women's sector. Bull and I were content to remain at a discreet distance.

My cell buzzed. Our chopper was about to land.

Embassy porters assisted with the luggage as we climbed the stairs to the roof, arriving just in time to feel the thumping blades of the Black Hawk reverberating overhead, and the rush of the rotor wash as the bird set down in the landing circle. Two Navy airmen directed us to our seats, issued us communication and sound control head gear, and stowed our bags. In a matter of minutes, we were ready to take off.

The pilot's voice rang in the headset.

"Everybody buckled in?"

Bull and I said, "Roger" and gave the co-pilot thumbs up.

Beth and Rasha followed our lead.

"Here we go."

The chopper lifted smoothly from the rooftop, angled into a slow arc, then swept us across the Cairo cityscape and toward the sea.

CHAPTER 55

At Red Wing, Minnesota.

The Task Force had dropped us off in Italy. From there, we'd flown all the way back to the States courtesy of the U.S. Air Force. It was quite an experience for Rasha, and for Beth, too, for that matter. For Bull and me, it was a trip down nostalgia lane. We parted company at Reagan National in D.C. Rasha would be staying in that area for now. And Bull liked his alone time. Beth and I flew Delta back home to Minnesota.

After stowing our clothes and cleaning up from our travels, we reclined on the red leather couch at 1011 Jefferson Avenue, our feet up on the wooden drum case and my arm around her shoulder.

"Do you think Rasha will be okay in D.C.?" Beth asked.

"Rasha? You can't seriously be worried about her. After all she overcame in Egypt – the rape, becoming an outcast in her own home, working her way up into an important technology job in Egypt's flagship intelligence ministry . . . if she can survive all that to become a hero, and save one, or maybe both, of our lives, how can you wonder whether she'll be okay?"

Beth patted my chest.

"But she's been cut off from any contact with us, Babe. She doesn't know anyone in Washington. She's all alone in a strange country."

"I know it was hard for her to say goodbye to you. But Holford found her a tech job with the CIA – maybe not working with Classified info, but a good job nevertheless. She'll meet new friends. Who wouldn't love Rasha!"

Beth sighed.

"You're right, of course."

"Plus, you left her the whole Diane Sawyer collection to get her started in western culture. That's gotta be a bonus."

I smiled.

Beth backhanded me in the gut.

"I do take some satisfaction in the fact that Director Holford canned Simon and Hitch," Beth said. "Unfortunately, those slippery bastards'll probably end up as hedge fund managers on Wall Street."

"I can arrange to have somebody tweak them every once in a while if you'd like."

Beth leaned forward and looked up at me.

"I don't even know what your definition of 'tweaking' is and I don't want to know. No tweaking! We can't make the whole world right, you know."

"Nope. Just our little corner."

Beth nestled her head on my chest.

"Did the FBI ever find out who killed the Egyptian President? Did the sniper admit to it or anything?"

"Oh yeah. Burton shot him, all right. But he didn't know who ordered the hit. According to Gunner, the FBI is still tracking satellite transmissions and analyzing Burton's computer. I'm glad it wasn't your job to solve that one."

"I guess you're right, Babe. I had my hands full with the business at hand. Speaking of which, what do you think the Army was shooting for when they told the CIA Aurora had *not* been compromised and we should leave it alone. I can't make sense of that one."

"Because the CIA is nosey?"

"Well, duh."

I chuckled.

"You want my guess?"

"Sure. Lemme have it."

"I think Senator Grossman stole the real Aurora plans and the Army figured it out too late to keep them out of foreign hands. And they couldn't get 'em back either. That digital stuff gets copied all over the place before you can erase it.

"If anybody found out the Army slipped up, somebody over there'd have egg all over his face. So the Army just kept it a secret, hoping nobody in Egypt could make Aurora work."

"Okay," Beth said. "But why tell the CIA to leave it alone? Why not just keep quiet about it?"

"I figure the Army had to give up some of the Aurora stuff to Holford when he demanded answers about that computer thingy Rasha gave you. So they couldn't keep it completely hushed up any more. Now what were they going to do? They had to tie Grossman to Aurora, but they couldn't very well admit Grossman stole the real Aurora plans and then the Army sat on its hands for two years."

"Keep going, Babe. I like the way your devious mind works."

I smiled.

"And I like telling stories.

"So anyway . . . the Army decided to tell the CIA not to investigate Aurora. 'It may look like it's been compromised, but it really hasn't.' Right?"

"Okay."

"Now, if the CIA obeys the Army demand and leaves Aurora alone, the Army's secret stays safe. On the other hand, if the CIA sticks its nose into Aurora and finds out somebody's actually building the darn thing, the CIA will tell the Army – to thumb their noses, if for no other reason – then the Army can take out the Aurora construction facility. It's a win for the Army either way. And the Army can always claim the stolen plans were fake, or 'altered,' all along."

"Not bad, Babe. Not bad at all."

"Sometimes I even amaze myself."

"Just don't get too big a head. I know somebody who saved your ass in that garage entry at GIS."

Beth pinched my thigh.

"And don't you think I don't appreciate it. You've saved my life, my dear. Now I must dedicate the rest of it to doing your bidding."

"Ha. Is that all you got? You already did that when we got married."

"Hmm. That's true. How about a foot massage?"

Beth bent one slim leg over the other and slipped off a white cotton footie.

"Now's a great time to start."

I gently raised Beth's chin until she was looking into my eyes and gave her a brief kiss on the lips. A million foot massages wouldn't begin to cover all I felt for her.

"True dat," I said.

EPILOGUE

After Egyptian turmoil in the wake of the assassination of its newly elected President had subsided, and plans were underway for another election, the Board of Directors of the Mediterranean Natural Gas Company convened in the Board Room at the company's Alexandria, Egypt headquarters to discuss the rapidly changing Egyptian political landscape.

Chairman: Do any of you have suggestions for our next move to increase the value of our contracts to provide gas to the Israelis?

President: We have made significant progress already, in my opinion. Removal of the Egyptian President cleared the way for a more educated and practical segment of the Egyptian population to consolidate behind a liberal candidate in the next election. The revolutionaries were not ready for democratic politics. They held no consensus on a plan to move forward. They could not agree on a leader who would be electable. As a result, the only political party who had survived the years of Military rule was the Muslim Brotherhood. And they are hardly supporters of our company's best interests.

Vice President: And the repeated bombings of the Arab pipeline in the Sinai have also served our cause. Egypt's inability to deliver a reliable supply of natural gas to Jordan and Syria has crippled Egypt's already fragile economy. Egypt needs to balance its trade deficit, and do so in years, not decades. The only way for them to accomplish this is to squelch the attacks on the pipeline and increase natural gas sales wherever they are able.

Chairman: It is true that Jordan, Syria, and, Turkey have grown increasingly frustrated with the interrupted gas supplies.

Gas flowed through the pipeline only 245 days last year, and was halted by sabotage on thirteen separate occasions.

President: Yes. The pipeline sabotage, particularly when it occurs in a location inside Egypt, works to our long term advantage. Of course there are short term costs to our company. But over time, I believe the attacks will prove to have been a good investment on our part.

Chairman: Do our analysts continue to believe that we can generate increased Israeli demand for Egyptian gas over the next year, and before the Egyptians can elect another president?

Treasurer: Yes, they do. In fact, we predict that, upon cessation of the disruptive pipeline bombings, we can depend on Israeli demand to approach the maximum of seven billion cubic meters within ten months.

Chairman: That sounds unduly optimistic. On what do they base this prediction?

Treasurer: Of course, there is always a margin for error. But our direct contacts within the hierarchy of Israeli electric and industrial consumers indicate they are fed up with the inability to obtain a steady flow of gas, whether from Egypt or from Israel's other sources. Once we convince them that Egyptian natural gas can be relied upon, the orders will come in quickly.

Chairman: And to convince them, the pipeline attacks will need to stop. On what timetable should we arrange for that to occur?

President: It will take the Egyptians at least another year to elect a new president. The SCAF is in no hurry to relinquish its grip on government. And as we have mentioned, disillusioned revolutionaries have learned a hard lesson about democracy. They will demand more time to organize. Given these political timetables, and the rapid decline of the Egyptian economy, I believe the attacks could be halted immediately. The SCAF will see the economic wisdom in boosting Israeli sales. They will not be swayed by popular opinion. They are already held in deep disdain by the citizenry. They have nothing more to lose to public opinion.

Chairman: And by the time the bombings have ceased, and the gas supply is flowing steadily to Israel via the Al 'Arish to

Ashkelon pipeline, the value of those sales will become so great that a subsequent president will not be able to afford to terminate them. Very good, gentlemen. I believe the situation is finally moving as we had planned. By this time next year, Egypt will be economically locked into its business relationship with Israel, and our company's stock price will soar. I, for one, would prefer to see my retirement fund increasing in value for a change.

Well done, my colleagues. Let us look forward to a profitable and peaceful fiscal year.

With the meeting adjourned, and the Directors enjoying cocktails and hors d'oeuvres in the top floor Board Room, one of them paused at a window to enjoy the view of the Mediterranean coast.

As he watched the ships loading and unloading cargo in the busy industrial harbor, and the European pleasure boaters anchored not far from shore, he noticed something odd on the blue horizon. At first he thought it was a speedboat. As it got closer to shore, he could see the object left no wake. It must be an aircraft of some type.

He continued to track the odd object's progress toward Alexandria with interest.

As the craft approached the city, its course changed abruptly, slicing upward, assuming a course hundreds of feet above the streets of the city. It was at this point that the Director realized the object was headed directly toward him at incredible speed.

What the hell?

Seconds later, the Board Room at the Mediterranean Natural Gas Company burst into flame, the conflagration consuming everything and everyone inside.

* * *

The FBI investigation into The Raptor's satellite communications and other electronic records eventually revealed the persons or entities who had ordered and paid for all of his kills

– including the assassination of the Egyptian President. In exchange for a promise of future good will, the Americans had provided the Egyptians with evidence concerning the men who had bankrolled their President's killing.

A few days after receiving the information from the Americans, the Deputy Chairman of the SCAF was on the telephone with United States Navy Admiral, Daniel Waverley.

The Admiral spoke.

"I can confirm, Mr. Deputy Chairman, that your requested target has been eliminated."

"You have Egypt's gratitude, Admiral, for disposing of the men behind our President's assassination. We could certainly have dealt with the traitorous capitalists ourselves, but we have our hands full with politics, demonstrations, and religious tensions. Further questioning of our actions regarding the President's assassin is a detraction we can do without."

"We trust, Mr. Deputy Chairman, that you will attribute the explosion to something other than a cruise missile, as per your agreement with our President."

"We have no reason to create tensions with NATO or with the United States. We have always valued our respectful relationship with the American military. We will keep this our secret on both sides. Yes?"

"Agreed."

"I trust you have other business to attend to, Admiral. I won't keep you longer. And Egypt thanks you again, first for identifying the guilty parties in our President's assassination, and then for assisting with their discreet elimination."

"We both serve when we are called, Mr. Deputy Chairman. Consider the missile part of your annual military aid package. Good day."

Made in the USA
Charleston, SC
16 April 2013